DOMINIC

Gareth Harris Part 2

A BRITISH SPORTS ROMANCE NOVEL

AMY DAWS

Published by: Stars Hollow Publishing
ISBN: 978-1-944565-19-0
ISBN 10: 1-944565-19-1

Editing: Stephanie Rose
Formatting: Champagne Formatting
Cover Design: Amy Daws
Cover Photography: Dan Thorson
Cover Model: Adam Spahn

Dedicated to my character, Vi Harris.
You started as co-worker Vilma in *London Bound*.
Then became a Vi with four brothers in *That One Moment*.
You've been featured in eight of my books, and I owe my career to
you. Thank you for inspiring me to give you these brothers.
You introduced me to the most wonderful, devoted, and patient
readers I've ever met.

AUTHOR'S NOTE

There will be some football dates, games, and mentions about tournaments that will not be factually accurate in this novel. For the purpose of this story and to make it a more pleasurable reading experience, I took some creative freedom and dribbled with it. I hope you enjoy!

A Phone Call is Never Simple

Vaughn Harris

A SIMPLE PHONE CALL CAN CHANGE YOUR ENTIRE LIFE. I remember calling the ambulance when my wife, Vilma, died.

I remember calling a funeral director to plan arrangements.

I remember calling Manchester United to tell them I wouldn't be coming back. Ever.

I remember all these calls, and every single one of them chipped away at the life I once loved.

I didn't want to be on the phone. I didn't want to call anyone. I wanted to die in that bed with my best friend who was leaving me to raise our five children alone. Four wild sons and one emotional daughter. All alone.

Before I had to make phone calls, I saw our children as a dream come true. Our family was everything I never knew could make life worth living. Watching Vilma give birth to them made everything around us a bright, bold, beautiful spray of colour.

I was certain the rest of the world had never loved anything as much as I loved my wife. My family. I planned to spend my life with her, watching our children grow.

I planned to hold her in bed until we were old and grey.

1

That's the thing about plans. They can have a mind of their own. Life can tell you, "Fuck your plans. This is how it's going to be."

Life took her from me.

My best friend.

And for that reason, I didn't want to make any more calls. I didn't want to make any more connections. I wanted to lock myself away and rue the day I ever fell in love. Rue the day I ever gave someone control of my heart.

A simple phone call can alter everything you thought you knew about yourself.

A shrill ring from my mobile on my desk has me glancing down to see my daughter, Vi's, face light up the screen. If you want to get over a phobia of answering telephone calls, become a football club manager or a parent to five adult children who have all left home. You'll figure out quite quickly how to get on with life.

It's dark in my office at Tower Park. I came in earlier to oversee some groundworkers fixing the scoreboard, which took much longer than it should have. While I waited, I started looking at our striker, Roan DeWalt's, ankle scans. My daughter-in-law Indie tells me he can make a full recovery from the injury he suffered last week, but I'm not sure. There's a transfer window opening up soon, and I think it might be time for him to find a new team.

I glance at the clock on my computer and note that it's just after eleven. Vi can't be back from Manchester already. I swipe the screen and clear my throat before answering. "Hello, my darling. Are you back in London? How was Gareth's award ceremony? Did he give a speech?"

"Dad."

With only one word, I'm on my feet. It's incredible how you

can know your child's voice after being a father to them for so many years. Even factoring in all my blank years after Vilma died, I still know Vi's emergency voice without question.

"What's happened?" I snap.

"It's Gareth…and possibly Sloan. I don't know for sure. We were about an hour outside of Manchester and I got a call from a policeman. Gareth is hurt, Dad. It's…bad."

"How is he hurt?" I bark. He didn't even have a game. It's a Friday night. He was receiving an award, not playing football. How could he have possibly been injured?

"There was an attack at his house."

"What?" I roar, fisting my hand around my grey hair and squeezing the short strands until it pulls. "What kind of attack? Who the bloody hell is Sloan? I don't know any teammates named Sloan."

"Sloan is…with Gareth."

"Vi, you're not making any sense!" I exclaim and press my palm to my chest as an ache erupts within. Gareth doesn't have a girlfriend. I would know. Gareth doesn't have anyone whom he shares anything with except for his brothers and sister. Christ only knows how much he actually shares with them. He's a locked door.

"Dad, calm down," Vi's voice blubbers into the line, shaking me out of my thoughts. "Sloan is Gareth's stylist. She's the one who dressed the boys for Tanner's wedding."

"Oh, his personal shopper," I confirm, things slowly clicking into place. "Why the bloody hell was she there at this time of night?"

"It's new. We just officially met her tonight."

"Officially? What on earth are you going on about, Vi? Just tell me what's happened."

"I don't know many details about what's happened!" she exclaims, her voice rising in pitch. "The officer just said to come to the hospital straight away, but we're stuck in horrible traffic. There's some accident up ahead and we aren't moving at all. This is a nightmare. I'm about to get out and run. The policeman wouldn't even

3

tell me the extent of Gareth's condition. Only that there was a break-in with multiple injuries on scene."

"Fuck," I growl, a knot lodging in my throat.

"Dad, I'm scared," Vi's voice cracks. "He wouldn't tell me if Gareth's okay and that must not be good. What if—"

"Vi," I bark, stopping her line of thinking. "Put one of your brothers on the phone."

"Dad," Vi blubbers. "It's Gareth…He's unbreakable, right?"

"Pass me to one of your brothers, darling," I grind through my teeth.

There's a muffled sound for a second before Camden's voice cuts through. "Dad?"

"Camden, someone needs to help your sister. She's breaking down."

"Booker's got her. He's holding her."

I sniff and squeeze my eyes shut. "Right. What hospital then?"

"Dad." Camden's tone sounds cautious. More than it was a second ago. "It's Royal Trafford Hospital."

My heart plummets to the floor.

Not that hospital.

Anywhere but there.

Camden adds, "It's fine Dad. We're on our way there. We'll call you with updates."

He knows my issues with hospitals. Camden suffered a knee injury over a year ago, and it took everything I had to walk through the doors of the London Royal Hospital where he had his surgery. But I managed because it is a hospital that doesn't hold any memories for me.

Royal Trafford Hospital holds the worst memories of my life.

In the background, I hear my daughter crying. Full-on sobbing. I imagine Booker holding her against his chest, and the entire image brings back horrid memories.

"I'm coming," I grind out, my hand already digging in my

pocket for my keys.

"You're what?"

"I'm coming," I repeat a bit firmer this time.

"Are you…going to be okay?" Camden asks, his voice tense and disbelieving.

I nod confidently even though I don't completely feel it. "I'll be fine. I'll call you when I land."

I end the call without another word and stride out the door, punching the number to my secretary, Lilly, into my phone. I already have a jet on standby for a prospect I was going to meet with early tomorrow morning. That won't be happening now.

It isn't until I hit the motorway to the airport that I realise my hands have gone numb from how hard I've been gripping the steering wheel. When I loosen my fingers, the tremor in them is frightening.

I haven't been back to Manchester in twenty-five years. Gareth was injured in a football game four years ago, and I still couldn't bring myself to return to the city that haunts me with the memory of Vilma—the complete love of my life.

And Royal Trafford Hospital is exactly where my nightmare began.

Surrender and Dominate

Gareth

8 Years Old

"**G**ARETH, I WANT TO TELL YOU ABOUT THE TIME I FELL IN love with your father."

Mum's blue eyes look up at the ceiling as she lays her head back on the chair and stops writing in her journal.

I take a deep breath and reply, "I don't want to hear a lovely story about Dad right now. I'm cross at him."

"You're not cross, Gareth." She drops her chin to look at me sitting on a stool beside her.

"I am too cross. He's so mean. He's been shouting at everybody all week."

"We've had a tough couple of days."

"I know. He keeps dragging you to the doctors. I told him you don't want to go, but he says you have to. Why do you have to, Mum?"

She smiles a sad smile and takes a deep breath. "Daddy is trying to help me feel better."

"But you always look worse after you get back from the hospital. They aren't helping. They're hurting."

"I know, my sweet, wonderful boy. But this is what your daddy has to do to make sure he's done everything he can to help."

"Doesn't mean he has to be such a meanie."

Her chin wobbles, and the sad expression on her face has my stomach doing somersaults. I don't want my mummy to feel worse. I want her to feel better. That's my job. To make her feel better. "Tell me about when you fell in love with Daddy."

She smiles. I can tell that made her feel better, which makes me feel better, too.

"Well, we had just met the night before at a pub in London, and he claimed to be in love with me."

"The first time you met him, he loved you?" I ask.

"Yes," she replies with a giggle. A small tear slides down her cheek, but it doesn't seem like a sad tear. "He was crazy. I thought he was just a naughty footballer trying to..." Her voice trails off and she clears her throat. "...have a laugh. Anyway, I didn't believe him. Then he started going on about how he wanted me to go to his game in Manchester the next day."

"Exciting!" I reply, enjoying this part of the story.

"Most would think so, but I'm not like most girls. I didn't want to go to Manchester. I was having fun in London with my friends. But he wouldn't take no for an answer. He even offered my girlfriends tickets to the match. Then he booked us a private plane. He was completely mental."

"What did you do?"

"Well, I went. He wanted me there no matter what, and I would have been a fool to not accept a trip of a lifetime. The whole way there, I thought he was just a silly footballer with no sense about him. But that was all forgotten when I saw him play."

"He was quite good, right?" I ask, remembering the games I'd been to with Mum before Dad quit playing and moved us all back here to London.

"He was like a dream, Gareth. His movements on the pitch were as if he was doing exactly what he was meant to do in life. He had this glow about him that I had never seen on a man before. And I *knew that a man living with joy like that would have appreciation for a great many things in life."*

"Do you think I could be good at football, Mum?" I ask, my mind having a think on how I could impress my mum like Dad did.

"I think you can be good at anything you want, my boy. It doesn't have to be football. It just has to ignite joy and passion. And you have to want to bleed for it because you believe in it so fully. Something that you refuse to surrender to until you dominate it in every possible way. Do you understand?"

I nod, my forehead wrinkled as I think on the words she's saying to me. They seem important. More important than I can understand. But I want Mummy to be happy, so I'll say whatever I can to make her feel better. "I understand, Mum."

She smiles and I feel happy. I think I'm helping. I think it would help even more if I play football like Dad. I think that would make her smile forever.

So I decide right then and there that I'm going to play football. And I'll be even better than my dad.

3

Protect and Defend

Sloan

THE BEEP OF THE HOSPITAL MONITOR IS LIKE A TICKING TIME bomb. With every chirp, it grows impossibly louder. With every moment that passes without a word, my anxiety grows more and more intense.

What the hell happened tonight? How did we even get here? One moment I'm in Gareth's arms, wrapping my brain around everything that's about to change between us. The next, I'm on the floor and he's right beside me, blood pouring out of the side of his head.

My face crumples as I stare at the red stain seeping through the bandage around Gareth's forehead. He looks so weak in the hospital bed. So broken. So frail. Nothing like the powerful man who promised to claim me in ways no man has ever claimed me before.

My phone vibrates in my hand, and I swallow the knot in my throat to answer. "Freya, hi," I croak, my voice raw and worn out.

"How are you?" she asks.

I wince as the phone nudges against the bulge on my cheekbone. "I'm fine I suppose. The right side of my face is purple, but I barely feel it. Maybe I'm still in shock."

"Well, thank goodness for small favours," she replies, her tone soft. "Any change in Gareth?"

"No. He still hasn't woken up." I bite my lip to hold back the sob that wants to rip from my throat every time I think of that fact. "They said it could be hours or days…Whatever the hell that means."

"It's going to be fine," she states pragmatically. Freya is always good in a crisis. "Can I get you a cup of tea?"

"No," I grumble, running a finger along Gareth's IV'd hand. "They won't let you back here, and I don't want to leave his side."

"I'll tell them I'm his sister or something."

I half smile at the thought. "I already told them I'm his wife. Let's keep the lies to a minimum so I don't get kicked out. Knowing you're in the waiting room is comfort enough."

She pauses for a moment before asking, "What if the press gets wind of you calling yourself Gareth's wife?"

I groan and close my eyes, pinching the bridge of my nose. "I hadn't thought about that, but I honestly don't care. He wasn't going to sit back here alone. Good God, Freya…It's…Gareth. We've barely gotten started. If he doesn't come back from this, I'm going to—"

Freya cuts off my voice just as it begins to tremble. "There's no need to worry about the what-ifs. They are pointless and not reality. Gareth is going to be just fine."

Suddenly, I hear what sounds like a group of people arguing down the hall. I catch sight of long blonde hair as it blasts past the door, then reappears in the small window that looks into the room.

It's Gareth's sister, Vi. She's still dressed in her red gown from earlier, but her top is covered in a suit jacket now. She opens the door and glances at Gareth with a gasp just as their brothers—Camden, Tanner, and Booker—appear behind her.

"I'll have to call you back, Freya," I state and hang up as my watery eyes take in Gareth's siblings shuffling into the room.

You could hear a pin drop as they all stare gravely at their oldest brother lying unconscious. They are clearly shaken over the sight. I can't say I blame them. He lost a ton of blood, so he's white as a ghost with a horrible bruise down one side of his face, not to mention he's hooked up to a monitor. It's a scary image.

Footsteps sound off behind them, and my gaze lands on an older man who's just entered the room. He pushes past everyone to stand on the opposite side of Gareth's bed. He's straight across from where I'm standing, but he's so focused on Gareth, he doesn't appear to notice me.

I take a moment to look him up and down. He's over six feet tall and has the body of an athlete, though a bit softer than it was in its prime, I'm sure. The shape of his eyes are exactly like Gareth's, and it takes me all of two seconds to realise I'm staring at Vaughn Harris—Gareth's father.

"How did you get here?" I ask, my voice surprising me. He wasn't at the awards ceremony, so how can he be here already? It's only been a few hours since the attack.

He blinks rapidly and looks at me through narrowed eyes. He briefly flicks his gaze down at the casual clothing that Freya brought for me earlier. It's the look of a drill sergeant inspecting a uniform. Not friendly.

If this is how he reacts to someone in clean clothes, I shudder to think what his reaction would be if I were still in my dress that was covered in blood.

"Who are you?" he asks, his tone clipped.

I swallow down the knot in my throat. "I'm Sloan."

His lip curls up. "Why are you here with my son?"

"What do you mean?"

"Dad," Vi warns, stepping forward to stand at the foot of the bed. "Sloan is with Gareth. I told you that on the phone, remember?"

"I don't care," he barks, his eyes focusing on the bruise on my face. "I don't know her, and the nurse just told me she's claiming to be my son's *wife*. I'm entitled to ask her some questions."

I wince. "I…had to tell them that, or they wouldn't let me come back here to be with him. He was all alone. Vi was stuck in traffic—"

"Very well then. You still haven't answered my question. Why are you here claiming to be married to my son? Who are you to him really?"

His question gives me a huge gut check I wasn't expecting. So much of what Gareth and I have had has been in private. In his home. In complete secret. We've kept so much from each other, but I feel like I know him. I'm more to him than a stylist or a casual fuck, but we never labelled what we are to each other. Maybe in the bedroom, yes. But right now, we're still in a grey zone.

I step away from the bed and murmur, "I'm…nobody."

"Right," Vaughn states, confirming what I fear might be true after all of this is over.

I know none of what happened tonight is my fault, but I am the reason Gareth was distracted when he walked into his house. If I hadn't sent him into an emotional tailspin, who knows where we'd be right now. I've clearly done more harm than good in his life as of late.

Vi's eyes find mine and she mouths a silent apology, then walks over to speak quietly with her father. Gareth's brothers still seem to be in shock as they move in closer to him.

I suddenly feel very out of place.

This is his family. People that he knows and trusts. I'm an outsider and unwelcome. I don't belong here.

As I consider leaving, the older, white-haired doctor whom I spoke to earlier strides into the room with an iPad clutched in his hands. He slides past Gareth's brothers and introduces himself to Vaughn.

"Mr. Harris, hello. I'm Dr. Howard."

"Tell me what's going on with my son."

Dr. Howard eyes me with a frown before replying, "As I told his wife, we're monitoring Gareth closely at this point. Severe concussions like this can lift in hours or days."

"A severe concussion?" Vaughn's granite features morph into shock.

The doctor looks even more puzzled by the fact that I hadn't relayed this information to Vaughn already. "Yes, but he's stable and there's no swelling in his brain, which is a very good sign. A trauma to the temple can be quite dangerous, though, so we're monitoring him to ensure no brain bleeds form overnight."

Vaughn narrows his eyes at Dr. Howard, then turns to Vi as he states, "Right. We're taking him home."

"What?" Vi and I both exclaim in unison.

"I have a private jet here. We're going to get him to a London hospital. We need to get out of here." Vaughn looks around the room, his hands balling into fists by his sides. I notice a sheen of sweat on his forehead that I hadn't seen before. He's nervous.

Dr. Howard holds a hand out. "Mr. Harris, I assure you he's getting the best medical care here."

Vaughn doesn't look convinced. "I don't care what he's getting. We're getting him out of Manchester tonight."

"Travel is not advised in his condition," the doctor replies warily.

"It's a quick trip. Just get me the forms to sign. We're taking him home."

"Dad," Vi says, stepping up to Vaughn and lifting her hands that are hidden in the long sleeves of Tanner's jacket. "This isn't necessary. I think we should listen to the doctor."

"Vilma!" Vaughn nearly roars. "My decision is final."

Vi cowers like a whipped puppy beneath her father's harsh command. Booker rubs his hand along her back as she turns her face away from Vaughn. I look over at Camden and Tanner to find they are also frozen in fear. Or maybe it's just shock? I can't tell. Regardless, they are all acting like PTSD victims who have been triggered. What is with this family?

"Well, what are you waiting for?" Vaughn snaps at Dr. Howard, who flinches. "We'll need to arrange an ambulance transport and a nurse to fly with us. Better yet, a doctor. Perhaps I know someone."

Vaughn pulls his phone out and softly mumbles to himself as he attempts to make arrangements for his unconscious son.

Booker's eyes find mine as he cradles his sister against his chest. They all suddenly look so much younger than they did earlier this evening at the gala. Booker is clearly petrified; Camden and Tanner are paralysed; and Vi is a sobbing mess. They remind me of my panicked little Sopapilla at the hospital right before the nurses would come in to start a line on her. Meanwhile, Vaughn is on his phone sounding like Hitler calling in his troops.

It's then that I see all the overwhelming moments I had leading up to Gareth. Getting pregnant. Getting married. Sophia's cancer diagnosis and having to hold her down for doctors to treat her. Being forced to move to England and pushed into a job I'm not passionate about. Being told how to dress my daughter by Callum's mother, Margaret. The cheating, the divorce, the joint custody. It all comes bearing down on me like the weight of a lifetime's worth of submission.

Then I picture Gareth. Alive and virile. Strong and masculine. Every physical attribute an alpha male might possess. But instead of over-powering me—instead of pushing me, and pursuing me, and asking me to submit to him—he drops to his knees. He gives himself to me because he is selfless. Protective. Giving. *A true dominant.*

"Just wait a damn minute," my voice states in the small hospital room filled with Harrises. Chewing my lip nervously, I move to stand by Gareth's side. I clutch the rail of his bed tightly while channelling all the strength I had for Sophia when she was sick—when she needed an advocate and someone to be strong for her. "You're not taking him anywhere."

"The hell we're not," Vaughn replies. "You have no say here."

"I am his wife!" I exclaim, shouting my lie as a flippant retaliation.

"Oh, bollocks," Vaughn retorts and pins the doctor with a moody glower. "She is not my son's wife. Did you check her identification? She's not even wearing a ring."

"She came in on an ambulance without identification, sir. We had no reason not to believe her." Dr. Howard flicks a glance at me like he knows better, but he's not going to say anything because I'm the only one in this room who's on his side.

"You wouldn't know if I am his wife or not," I snap back at Vaughn.

He cuts me a warning glance. "I would know if my son was married. This conversation is over. I have a jet on standby, and we're bringing him back to London. He can recover at home with me."

"No!" I bark, squeezing my hands on the railing as hard as I can. I feel so overwhelmingly protective of Gareth in this moment that I can hardly stand the determination searing through my veins. "You're not taking him. Who do you think you are?"

"I beg your pardon." Vaughn narrows his eyes at me, then looks over at Vi for support. Vi continues to wither under his stare, which completely confuses me because she had no problem stepping up to me in the bathroom at the gala.

But he can stare me down all he wants. I may not be Gareth's wife, or girlfriend, or even friend with benefits right now because we haven't had a chance to discuss our situation, but I know what's best for him. I've been here. I've been in his life. And Vaughn's not taking Gareth away from me before we've gotten started.

I pull my shoulders back and push my chest out, lifting my chin high to show all the confidence I'm barely holding onto right now. "You can't just march in here and take Gareth away to London. Manchester is his home. His house and his life are here. You couldn't even be there for his award tonight—a truly amazing achievement he has worked so hard for. You don't get to waltz in here now and play caring father. That's not how being a parent works!"

"Oh, and I suppose you know so much about being a parent," he snarls at me, his cold eyes severe on mine.

"I do!" I nearly roar, my body leaning over the bed to challenge

Vaughn. "I have a daughter who is my entire world. And if she was unconscious in a hospital, I would damn well hope someone like me would put her health as top priority and not your level of comfort because you're in a city you're terrified of for some unknown reason!"

Vaughn's eyes are lethal on mine as we have a stare-down over Gareth's hospital bed. It's dead silent and when a familiar voice cuts in, I think I might be dreaming.

"Did you just dom my dad, Treacle?" Gareth's voice croaks from below.

My eyes fall down on him as a rush of emotions shoot through my entire body. His stunning hazel eyes flutter open to look up at me, and I swear my heart could burst out of my chest. "Oh my God, Gareth!" I exclaim with a sob, dropping down over top of him and grasping his face in my hands. "You're awake."

"Of course I'm awake. Fuck, there's no way I could have slept through you two rowing like that."

I laugh awkwardly and run my fingers over his whiskered jaw, taking in the furrow of his brow and his pale complexion pinking up in front of me.

"Why the tears?" he murmurs, lifting his hand and swiping his thumb across the paths of liquid running down my face.

"I don't like you unconscious," I reply stupidly because it's all I can think to say.

"Well, I'll try not to do it again in the future." Gareth's eyes narrow as he takes in the welt on my cheekbone. "Fuuuck, Tre. Are you okay?"

"I'm fine," I croak, holding back a small sob. "I'm fine because you're fine."

"You don't look fine," he replies through clenched teeth and reaches out to touch my cheek again. "God, what the bloody hell happened? I remember walking up to my house, but everything is fuzzy after that. Who did this to you?"

"We were attacked, Gareth," I state quietly, the heaviness of what's happened to us barrelling in on me full force. "Someone broke into your house and we were both attacked, but I'm okay."

"Fuck me," he growls as he slowly sits up while the doctor presses his stethoscope to his chest. Gareth shakes his head slowly and looks over at his brothers, who suddenly seem a bit taller now that their brother is conscious again. "I'm going to murder whoever—"

I press my fingers over his dry lips and shush him as the doctor steps back and reaches for the chart at the bottom of the bed. "Calm down, Gareth. The police don't know who did it yet. We can talk about everything later. I'm just so glad you're awake and talking. And that you didn't get amnesia and forget who I am."

Gareth's angry eyes soften at my small attempt at a joke. He cups my face again, stroking his thumb over my cheek. "I could never forget my wife," he states with a tiny grin.

I drop my face onto his chest with mortification. "This is really awkward."

He runs his hand down the back of my head and his chest vibrates with his voice. "I must be concussed because I'm certain I would never forget marrying you."

I look back up at him and expect to see teasing in his eyes, but I don't see that at all. I see…determination. Stone-cold, determination.

Suddenly, Dr. Howard clears his throat behind me, and I straighten to see Gareth's entire family watching us. They're all sort of staring agog, as if what they've just witnessed between us was something they've never seen before.

Dr. Howard moves past me with his flashlight to check Gareth's eyes while his brothers step forward and touch his feet under the blanket.

"Glad to see you awake, Gareth," Booker says quietly with a shy smile.

"You've looked better," Camden adds with a lopsided smile.

Tanner chimes in, "Yeah, thanks for not getting dead on us, big bro."

"Pupils are good. I'm just going to check your pulse here." Dr. Howard grabs Gareth's wrist and stares down at his watch.

As soon as the doctor releases Gareth's hand, Vi is in Gareth's arms, crying and murmuring unintelligible words into his shoulder. He runs his hand down the back of her head, soothing her until she's composed enough to stand up again.

Once she steps away, Gareth's eyes find his father, who's nearly hugging the wall. He's so uncomfortable. It's as if Gareth waking up reminded Vaughn that he is in a hospital and now he's frozen in fear.

Gareth clears his throat and turns his focus from his dad back to Dr. Howard. "So, what did you tell my wife about my condition? How long am I out of football?"

I back up from Gareth's bedside, suddenly feeling self-conscious. It was easier being Gareth's advocate when he was unconscious. Now I don't know how to feel. Gareth's hand quickly reaches out and clasps mine so I can't move away from him. I look down at him with relief. How does he have the ability to help me feel strong when he's laid up in a hospital?

Dr. Howard's eyes narrow sympathetically. "Well, we need to evaluate some new scans and do some cognitive tests before we know anything conclusively. But I'd venture to guess a couple of weeks at the very least."

Gareth closes his eyes in pain. "That bad?"

"With this level of concussion, it's necessary. You need rest and relaxation after a blow to the head. You're very lucky. Injuries to the temple can be fatal."

I inhale sharply at that comment and Gareth squeezes my hand reassuringly. Looking at me, he replies to the doctor, "I can handle some rest."

Vaughn is still silent as Dr. Howard tells Gareth that he's going to go put in an order for another head scan and that he wants to keep him overnight for observation. He pins Gareth with a serious expression and adds that no travel is advised, then makes his way out of the room.

Gareth accepts gentle hugs from all of his brothers and yet another long, tearful hug from Vi. It's clear that his siblings aren't used to their big brother being down.

Finally, Gareth's eyes turn back to his father, who still hasn't moved off the wall. "Am I dreaming, or are you seriously in Manchester right now?"

Vaughn's Adam's apple bobs with a swallow. "I'm here," he replies stoically—much more mild sounding than he was a few moments ago.

"Why?" Gareth asks, confused.

Vaughn looks around the room, clearly uncomfortable that he has to think about where he is again. "Well, you're hurt. I...had to be here."

"I've been hurt before," Gareth retorts.

"Not like this," Vaughn states firmly, his brow furrowed. "Which is why I want you back in London. They have the best doctors there. You can recover at home with me. I can take care of you. Vi will help."

My throat tightens with a tiny growl that Gareth hears. He gazes over at me and offers a small, reassuring smile. "I think I'm good here, Dad."

Vaughn's brow furrows as he stares at our clasped hands.

Then Gareth adds, "But I'd like it if you stayed in town for a bit."

"Here?" Vaughn asks, his hand going to the back of his neck and squeezing nervously.

Gareth exhales, and his expression shifts from soft and open to hard and closed off. The wall that I've seen on his face before is coming back. He's preparing himself for rejection. He's preparing to have his father do what he expects: Leave. Avoid Manchester and his home and any memory of a life he once had here.

Then, four words are uttered from Vaughn that shock everyone in the room. "Very well. I'll stay."

Question and Answer 4

Gareth

T HE AWFUL TEXTURE OF THE HOSPITAL GOWN IS SPIKING MY blood pressure, but my heart is also racing over the fact that Sloan is so fiercely by my side. It's no wonder she went after my dad. She's in full-blown fearsome mother mode, and it's making it really hard for me to focus on anything but her.

But after my family steps out into the waiting room for the police to come in to take statements, I learn the full scope of everything that happened and my hospital gown is the last thing on my mind.

Sloan and I walked into my house in the middle of a burglary. It was likely the same burglars who hit Hobo's house, but we must have caught them early. As far as the police could tell, there was only some minor vandalising that was noted. They are working with my security company to recover the CCTV footage which will hopefully provide some clue as to how they got in without setting off the alarm.

Whoever it was, one of them must have had somewhat of a conscience because they used my mobile to call an ambulance before they fled the scene. When the first responders showed up, Sloan had just come to, but I remained unconscious all the way to the hospital.

Sloan's eyes are red and downcast as she describes what she recalls to the female officer sitting beside her. "I woke up on the floor in the entryway and was covered in blood. It took me a minute to realise it wasn't my blood but Gareth's. His phone was laying right next to him, and it started ringing so I answered it. It was the 999 dispatcher. She said someone had called from his phone and the ambulance was close."

My muscles tense as I imagine how horrific that must have been for her to see me like that. Luckily, her friend Freya brought her some clothes, so she's no longer covered in my blood. It's clear she is shaken to the core, and I hate that I put her through all of this. I wish I could remember exactly what the fuck happened. Everything is fuzzy.

Throughout the questioning, we learn that there was no sign of forced entry, so whoever got into the house either had the code or they were agile enough to scale the large security fence. Because of that, my staff members who have access to my home will need to be questioned.

"Did you see or hear anything unusual when you opened the door?" the male officer standing beside my bed asks.

I shake my head. "I don't remember anything after getting out of the limo."

"Ms. Montgomery?" The man looks at Sloan. "It seems your injuries were less severe. What do you recall?"

Sloan stares at me with nervous eyes. Eyes that I want to soothe and kiss and take all this ugly pain away from, but I can't.

She clears her throat and replies, "I heard men's voices, but I don't know what they said. It all happened so quickly."

"Have a think and try again," the officer says, crossing his arms over his chest like he's interrogating her. "You got out of the limo, walked up the steps, went inside, and…"

Sloan's face tightens with horror as she recalls the blow to her face. The blow that apparently knocked her unconscious.

"I don't know," she croaks, her eyes welling with tears.

"Come now, it's right there," the officer says and my blood pressure instantly spikes.

"She told you she doesn't know," I snap, my voice deep and gruff, pushing the dull headache I have in my skull to a full-on migraine. "I think it's time for you to leave."

The officer slides his beady eyes to me. "Mr. Harris, please understand, your memory will never be better than it is right now. The more we know now, the more we can do to catch whoever did this."

"I understand that, but we're not recalling anything. And I don't like how you're speaking to her."

"Gareth, it's fine," Sloan murmurs softly.

"It's not," I retort dismissively. "She's not the criminal here. She's the victim. Fucking treat her as such."

The female officer places a reassuring hand on Sloan's shoulder. "You're right. We have enough information for tonight. We have your mobile numbers and you have our cards. Just call us if anything else comes to mind."

The male officer doesn't look pleased but begins to follow the female out. He pauses in the doorway and turns back to add, "Your home is currently a crime scene, and it will take us a day to clear. You'll need to find other accommodations until then."

"Very well," I reply through a clenched jaw. This prat is an obnoxious sod on a fucking ego trip. I need him to disappear.

As soon as the officer is out of sight, I exhale and realise how tense my body was the entire time they were in the room.

"Gareth, your pulse is racing," Sloan says, rubbing my shoulder.

"Fucking wanker," I mumble and attempt to relax my jaw.

"He's just doing his job," Sloan states softly.

"Sloan, that guy was pushing you way too fucking hard. You've just been attacked for Christ's sake." I turn my eyes to her sitting in the chair beside my bed. She's wearing jeans and a T-shirt, her messy hair scraped back into a low ponytail. The circles under her eyes are shadowy alongside the faint bruise darkening above her cheekbone. Anyone can see that she's been through a trauma. "He should have directed everything at me. It's my bloody fault we're here."

"What are you talking about?" she gasps, her golden eyes red-rimmed and glossy.

I ball my hands up into fists and stare straight ahead. "I should have been paying attention. I should have noticed something was amiss. I was so up my own arse, I wasn't thinking straight. It's my fault we're here."

"Well, I think some of that distraction was my fault, too," she retorts with a huff.

"No, it wasn't," I state firmly, looking at her again. "Don't push me on this, Sloan. I'm fucking sick over what could have happened to you tonight. I can't imagine if—" My voice cuts off. I clear my throat and push through the last part of my sentence that is almost too difficult to utter. "You have a child."

Sloan's eyes fill with tears that quickly fall down her cheeks. "I know that."

"She *needs* her mother," I state to the universe just as much as to Sloan. Sophia is near the age I was when I lost my own mother, and that realisation isn't lost on me.

Sloan sniffs loudly, then licks her lips as she grabs hold of my fisted hand. She pulls it to her mouth and drops a kiss on my knuckles. "I know that, Gareth. And I'm fine. Look at me. I'm right here and I'm okay."

I shake my head in disgust. "Where is Sophia?"

Sloan swallows and her chin begins to wobble. "She's at Callum's. She has no clue what's happened, and I'm going to keep it that way if I can."

I nod woodenly, knowing that's for the best. "My agent will keep this under the radar," I reply, dropping my head back on my pillow. "This is a private hospital, so stuff doesn't get leaked like it does elsewhere. He'll take care of it, and I'll do everything I can to keep you out of the papers."

Sloan runs her hand down my arm in a soothing manner. "Stop worrying about me, Gareth. Whatever happens, happens. I'm just grateful we're both okay."

I take a big breath just as my dad walks back into the room with my brothers and Vi. They are deep in conversation when I interrupt them to say, "The police said I can't return home until they've cleared the crime scene, so can one of you book me a hotel room?"

Vi nods and pulls her mobile out of her handbag. "I'm on it."

"Then you guys should all go home. They are going to run some tests on me anyway. No sense in everyone sitting around here all night."

Vi's tired eyes look at me sharply. "Gareth, I'm not leaving you. I'll book a room for myself as well."

Sloan's voice interrupts Vi's dialing when she says, "Or you can stay at my house."

I turn my eyes to her and feel an intense pressure in my chest that has nothing to do with my injuries and everything to do with Sloan.

She blushes from everyone's attention on her and adds, "There's room for whomever wants to stay. Of course, I understand if you're more comfortable at a hotel."

My dad begins voicing excuses for why a hotel would be better, but I cut him off and reply to Sloan, "I'll stay with you."

The corners of her mouth lift into a wobbly smile as she avoids eye contact with me. She's nervous. The truth is, so am I. Sloan is opening up her home to me. Her life. Hell, maybe even her child? Am I ready for this? I bloody well better be. I told her I want more. No more boundaries. No more secrets. I may be injured, but my feelings for Sloan are still as strong as they've always been. Maybe even stronger after all of this.

If she's going to offer me this olive branch, I'm going to take it and more.

Slow and Steady

Gareth

W HEN IT COMES TO HARRIS SIBLINGS, IT'S HARD TO DO anything significant without each other. When one is honoured, we all celebrate with them. When one hurts, we all feel the pain alongside them. The support and the bond that we formed at a very young age is intense because of our upbringing. We were parentless, so it was necessary to band together or we all would have turned out as complete head cases.

Well, more than we already are I should say.

So it takes a lot of convincing to get my brothers to go back to London. I know they have football schedules that don't allow them to be away, and I don't want anyone missing matches just to watch me. I tried to push Vi to go back with them for Rocky because Christmas is only a few days away, but she seems adamant on staying. Probably to ensure Dad and I don't kill each other.

After the CT scan, Dr. Howard said I needed to stay overnight for observation, but Sloan was released since her injuries are less severe. I hated seeing her go, but she seemed to want to prepare her house for my arrival tomorrow, so I let the boys take her back to her house when they left. The urgency I have to protect her is strong and not something I've ever experienced with anyone outside of my family. It's an unnerving feeling, so I ended up having my agent organise a security officer to watch over her house. Sloan wasn't happy about it at first, but I think the fact that I'm lying in a hospital bed made her less inclined to argue with me.

After a fitful night's sleep with Vi and Dad sitting in chairs beside me all night, I'm finally released the next day. We file into the car Dad rented and head toward Sloan's address. Her neighbourhood is similar to my father's in Chigwell, which I notice seems to soothe him somehow. That aggravates me further. He was harsh on Sloan last night and I don't fucking know why. But my head isn't in the right place to deal with his belated, overprotective bullshit right now.

A few minutes later, we pull up behind the security car in front of Sloan's home. The last time I was here wasn't an overly positive experience, so my nerves are on edge.

Sloan rushes out her front door, obviously having been watching out the window for our arrival. I struggle a bit to get out of the car as nausea and dizziness overwhelm me. Dad has his arm around me in an instant, but I pull away from him in frustration.

"I'm fine. Just give me a minute," I state, refusing his offer of an arm while leaning on the open car door.

"The doctor said you'd be dizzy, Gareth," Dad's gruff voice retorts. "Stop being stubborn and let me help. You don't want to injure yourself further."

"I just need a minute," I snap harshly just as Sloan reaches us.

She offers a tight smile to my father, then holds her hand out to me. "Allow me?" she asks and tucks herself under my arm and wraps her arm around my waist. She feels good. Warm and soft, yet her touch is firm on me.

She whispers under her breath so only I can hear, "Don't backtalk me, Harris. You may be injured, but I'm not opposed to spanking some sense into you."

A surprising chuckle rolls through my body, and I can't help but relish in it for a moment. I've had so very little to feel good about in the last twenty-four hours, so Sloan speaking to me like normal is refreshing. I wrap my arm around her shoulders and lean on her as she walks me toward the front door. Dad and Vi come in behind me with a couple bags of clothes that Vi went out and bought for us all last night.

We step inside and the smell of food permeates my nose instantly. I do a quick survey of the space and note that Sloan's house is so very Sloan. It's bright and cheerful. It looks lived in.

Beside the front door is a clothing rack full of garment bags. To the left is a formal dining room with a table that's covered in fabric and a couple of official-looking sewing machines stationed on either side.

"You have a beautiful home, Sloan," Vi states excitedly, then points to the dining room table. "Is that where the magic happens?"

"My colleague, Freya, does most of the magic," Sloan replies and her cheeks flush with embarrassment. "I don't do a lot of designing. My business consists of personal shopping, merchandising, and tailoring, which Freya is amazing at."

Suddenly, the sound of a door slams down the hallway. All of our heads snap toward the noise as I instinctively push Sloan back behind me, my entire body stiffening with alert.

"Yoo-hoo!" a female voice echoes down the hall. "It's me!"

"That's just Freya," Sloan states as she places her hands on my arm and moves to stand beside me again. "We're in the foyer!"

Seconds later, Freya's form fills the hallway entry. She lifts her eyebrows at me with a smile. "Well, hiya, everyone!"

"Hi, Freya. You remember Gareth," Sloan states.

"Of course!" Freya beams, her eyes unusually wide. "Nice to see you again. So bloody sorry to hear about what happened at your home. I hope the coppers catch the bastards who did that to you. I can't imagine the state you all must be in."

I nod and exhale, realising I'm still a bit tense from everything.

The adrenaline rush hasn't really allowed me to fully process all that's happened yet. Clearing my throat, I reply, "Thanks, Freya. It's nice to see you again. This is my father, Vaughn, and my sister, Vi."

Freya turns her smile to both of them. "Oh yes, of course. I saw them in the waiting room at the hospital, but it's nice to meet you both officially. Welcome!"

"Freya lives in the guest house out back," Sloan explains and eyes me nervously. "We're colleagues but more like family."

"So you both work from here?" I ask as I glance into the dining room and realise that Freya is the flatmate Sloan has mentioned before.

Freya replies, "Indeedy, we do! I was just nipping in to get some work done, but I'll put the kettle on and make us all some tea before lunch is ready. Nothing settles nerves like a good cup of tea."

"Tea sounds lovely," Vi says with a smile. "Can I help?"

"Of course! Mr. Harris, would you like to join us? You're staying for lunch, right?"

My father looks to me in question, but Freya grabs his arm and pulls him down the hallway before he can argue. He's completely out of his element. Hell, even I'm a bit out of my element. When the three of them are out of sight, I exhale with relief.

"How are you feeling? Do you want to sit down?" Sloan turns to point toward the living area. "I can turn the telly on. Or maybe that will hurt your head? If you just want to sit, I'll go get you some tea."

She takes a step to help me walk again, but without hesitation, I shove her over to the wall and crush my lips to hers. She lets out a tiny yelp of surprise, then softens against me as I cradle her face in my hands and press my body to hers.

Slowly, her lips part, allowing my tongue to dip in and taste her. Really taste her. I'm smelly and in desperate need of a shower, but I don't give a toss. I need to feel her in my arms. Taste the sweetness of her lips. Inhale the familiar scent of her that used to remind me of memories I'd long wanted to forget but somehow crave more than ever now. I hold her tightly and let the realness of her sink completely into my groggy head.

In the past twenty-four hours, I've gone from feeling euphoric because she was by my side, to being turned on because she was going to give herself to me, to being terrified beyond belief because I thought I lost her. I need to feel her in my arms and against my tongue to reassure myself that we're still us. We still make sense, even under the most horrid of circumstances.

Sloan's hands wrap around my waist as our lips move against each other. It's a soft, warm kiss. It's familiar because she tastes the same, yet somehow it's unlike anything I've ever experienced.

My dick thumps in my lounge pants, and I press my groin against her stomach so she knows the effect she's having on me.

"Good God, Gareth," she croaks, separating our lips and sagging into me. "I thought you were supposed to be injured."

My lips drag up to her forehead as I tuck her head beneath my chin. "This is the best medicine I've received so far."

She gazes up at me, her golden eyes wary as I finger her hair and glance at the bruise on her cheekbone that's turned a dark shade of purple overnight. "That looks bloody painful."

She glances up to the stitches on my temple that are covered by a clear waterproof bandage. "Yours looks worse."

I shake my head. "Have I mentioned I'm going to kill those fuckers?"

She smiles. "No you won't, because a pretty boy like you won't last a day in prison."

"Pretty boy?" I bark out a laugh. "I've been called many things, but pretty is not one of them."

With a soft huff, she presses her head against my chest. "I'm glad you're here," she mumbles into my sweater.

"Me too." I tighten my hold around her and look up toward the stairs. "Want to show me around?"

Her brow furrows slightly. "Like a tour?"

I nod. "Yes. I seem to recall you demanding a shirtless tour of my place, so this only seems fair."

She flushes and pulls her lower lip between her teeth before replying, "Considering you're concussed and your family is here, I think I'll go ahead and keep my top on."

I chuckle as she gestures around the main level and describes the rooms to me. She points down the hallway where there are two bedrooms and the kitchen. "Do you want to join them for some tea?" she asks, chewing her lower lip.

I shake my head. "Where do you sleep?"

"Upstairs," she replies with a shy smile.

Oh, how I always love a shy Treacle. "Let's see that room."

She shakes her head with a knowing smirk and turns to walk up the stairs. An image of our first night together hits me as I stare at her curves under her artfully torn jeans and T-shirt. Such a casual look that I note is very similar to how she appeared the night she tied me up in my kitchen. Had she been with her daughter that day? Is this what she's like when she's being a mum? There's still so much we have to learn about each other.

She passes a door on the right and I pause. "What's in there?"

Her face flushes. "That's...Sophia's room."

My brows lift. "I'd like to see it if she wouldn't mind."

"You would?"

"Yes. She's not napping in there, is she?"

Sloan laughs softly. "No, she won't come home for two more days...Just in time for Christmas morning."

I briefly wonder what Sloan's plans are for me for Christmas as she moves to put her hand on the knob beside me and murmurs, "And just for your information, Sophia is too old for naps. If I try to make her nap, she looks at me like I've grown three heads."

"She sounds cheeky," I reply with a half-smile. "I'm afraid my experience with children is limited to an adorable one-year-old and the little sods who come to Kid Kickers camps."

Sloan shakes her head. "Well, prepare yourself for all things girlie."

Sloan opens the door and my eyes are assaulted with an array of colours. Pinks, purples, teals, yellows. Bright, bold, loud colours. Sophia's bed is covered in a multicoloured quilt with stuffed animals strewn all over it. It's a messy bedroom. One that's played in a lot and not kept neat and tidy at all times.

"I keep all her toys in her room when she's away," Sloan states as I walk around and inspect everything. "It's too hard to look at them when she's not here."

This makes me frown and I turn my eyes to her. "How often do you have her?"

"Callum and I alternate every other week."

I nod and toss a tiny football in the air that Sophia had on her dresser and catch it. "How do you like that arrangement?"

"I hate it," Sloan replies without hesitation, then looks down and begins fidgeting with her hands. "Sophia and I have an unusually close bond."

"Don't all mothers have that with their children?" I ask, picturing the attachment I felt to my own mother. I can still remember the feeling of her skin on my cheek if I think on it hard enough.

"Ours is…different." Sloan looks pensive and unsure.

I prod further. "How do you mean?"

She sucks in a big breath of air, then shakes her head. "We'll have time to talk about all that later. Do you want to lie down? You must be exhausted."

"I'm okay," I reply with a frown, wondering what she's hiding from me. Whatever it is, I hope it doesn't involve more secrets. I want to move past that part of our relationship.

My wandering eyes land on a photo sitting on the nightstand. It's Sophia with her dad—the same smug bastard I met when I rang his doorbell looking for Sloan over a week ago. He appears miserable in the photo. His smile forced. Sophia's embrace unreturned. I can't help but ask, "Is he a good dad?"

Sloan clears her throat. "He's good enough to get fifty percent custody I suppose. I was going through all of that legal hell when I didn't see you last year. I was shocked that he wanted Sophia so much. He's a workaholic and more interested in going out with his girlfriend, Callie, than staying in and having family time."

"I see," I reply, my jaw tight. "And that's why you would disappear on me for a week straight, isn't it? You wanted to give Sophia your full attention when you had her."

She nods, her eyes downcast.

"Don't feel bad about that." I move across the room to her and crook my finger under her chin to force her eyes up to mine. "Don't you dare feel bad about putting Sophia first. I hate that you hid such a big part of your life from me, but don't think for one second that I'm upset by the time you spend with her. If my father would have dedicated himself to us fifty percent of the time when we were kids, it would have been loads better than what we got."

Her head tilts as her eyes shine with tears. "But your dad is here now, Gareth. After the way I spoke to him at the hospital, that has to say something, right?"

I nod and glance out toward the door where I can hear Vi and Freya's voices wafting up the stairs. "I guess."

My eyes catch sight of a photo of Sloan and Sophia up on the bookshelf by the door and I smile. It is the kind of photo a happy parent has with their child. Sophia's arms are wrenched tightly around Sloan's neck, and Sloan's arms are hugging her daughter so close that their cheeks are pressed together as they smile into the camera. They look like a perfect mother-daughter pair. Probably how Vi and our mum would have looked at similar ages.

The pain that image evokes forces me to change my line of thought. "Show me your room." I move out the door, needing some space from thoughts about either of my parents.

Sloan closes the door and walks me down the hall, past a

bathroom, and into her large master suite. It has an attached loo with a big glass shower and wooden bench inside. Without a word, I pull my shirt off and stride toward where she stands in front of the bathroom door.

"What are you doing?" Sloan asks, her voice tight with surprise.

"I need a shower." I toss the shirt on the floor and point to the area behind her.

She looks around nervously and makes a move to leave. "Okay, I'll, um…give you some privacy."

I hook her by the arm again and murmur softly, "Will you shower with me?"

Her eyes lift up to me warily. "Gareth, you're concussed. I really don't think that's a good idea."

I exhale heavily and utter the only thing I can. The truth. "I don't want to be apart from you right now, Sloan."

We undress quietly in her bright white bathroom. I can't help but drink in the image of her naked form in front of me as she turns the water on and steam begins filling the room. She's so beautiful. Tall and curvy, natural and unblemished. She's how she's always been, but somehow different now.

A shocking image of her stomach swollen with a child pummels me out of nowhere. And just when I think it's going to totally freak me out and bring my guard up, it does the opposite.

Without pause, I step up behind her and wrap my hands around her waist, pulling her bare back against my bare front. I drop soft kisses on her shoulder and up to her neck. She shakes her head and turns in my arms, stepping backwards and pulling me under the hot rainfall showerhead. She clasps her hands around my neck, and I pull her hips to my body and close my eyes as her hard nipples brush against my chest.

Through the stream of water running down over us, I open my eyes and bring my fingertips up, lightly touching the bruise around her cheek. "How badly does it hurt?"

She shakes her head. "It doesn't."

"You're lying."

She nods.

My heart sinks. "Sloan."

"Don't, Gareth." She angles her face up to drop a soft kiss on my chin.

I pull away. "Don't apologise for putting you in danger? Don't apologise for how much worse this all could have been? I can't not think about it. Seeing Sophia's room. That picture of you with her, smiling and happy and completely innocent. It kills me that I almost took that away from her. How old is Sophia?"

"She's seven," Sloan answers, swallowing nervously.

"I was eight when my mum died. That shit sticks with you forever."

She grabs my face in her hands and pins me with a firm look. "I'm fine. Sophia's fine. You're fine. Please stop this."

She lets go of my face and turns to grab a bottle of shampoo. Squirting a huge amount in her hand, she brings it up to my hair and begins lathering my strands. "Just let me take care of you right now."

My grim expression softens.

"Let me," she pleads again and turns me so the backs of my legs press against the wooden bench. "Not because I'm in control, but because we both need this."

She presses her hands on my shoulders, so I sit down and allow her to finish lathering me. She scores her nails all over my scalp, careful to stay away from my bandage, and my entire body hums to life. At the hospital, I was groggy and cloudy feeling. It felt like every step I took was in thick mud, slowing me down, trying to pull me into darkness. But right now, I feel good. Having Sloan's hands on me is incredible and invigorating. It washes away my stress and anxiety so all that's left is desire.

"Sloan," I moan, my head tipping back as she rubs the soap

down my hard shoulders and arms. She works her hands over my chest, my abs, my sides, my thighs, massaging all my aching muscles with firm, pressured strokes. The right strokes. The kind of strokes that she knew I needed the day we first met.

Everything about Sloan is right. Honest and decent. Understanding and sincere. Beautiful.

"Sloan," I state her name again and she stops rubbing my back muscles and pulls away to look me in the eyes. I grab her foamy hands and move them to touch my groin.

She sucks in a sharp breath of air. "Gareth, you're concussed."

"Sloan, please," I croak, my eyes closing in pain. "I need this."

When I open my eyes again, I find her looking down at my erection. She's chewing her lip thoughtfully, and I swear I see heat blossom in her eyes. Desire, passion, yearning. All the things that made me want her the first time.

After a short pause, she moves her bubble-covered hands down between my legs. She runs her fingers slowly over my inner thighs, her thumbs digging in the underside until they come together at my cock. She twines her fingers around me and squeezes the length of me, stroking and fisting up and down.

"Fuck, Treacle," I groan and watch her lower herself to her knees between my legs, moving out of the way of the water so it runs down onto my dick. She points my tip up toward the stream, and I suck in a sharp breath as the droplets slap against my most sensitive appendage.

I stare at her through the stream, and she looks pleased at the pain she's causing me. Bloody hell, she's gorgeous.

Once the water rinses the last of the soap away, she licks her lips and dips her head down to wrap her mouth around my straining cock.

I think I've died a little.

My death is confirmed when she begins bobbing her head up and down my length, paying careful attention to lick and suck as she goes along. Her nails bite into my thighs, and I'm too transfixed to do anything but press my back against the cool white tile wall and watch the beautiful show in front of me.

"Are you all right?" she asks, out of breath and straightening to check on me. "Are you feeling dizzy?"

"Yes," I reply instantly. "But only because my dick is in your mouth."

She smiles. "Are you sure you're all right? I don't want to make things worse for you."

"I'm perfect."

My response elicits a smirk before she drops down and continues the marvellous work she's been doing. I gently lower a hand on the back of her head, and I can't help but thrust into her mouth. I want to fill her. I want to choke her, gag her, control her. Give her so much that she gets a little scared, but then watch her relax because she knows I'll take care of her. This is my small moment of claiming.

The tip of my cock meets the back of her throat and she fucking moans. She moans like I'm in her pussy, and I can feel my orgasm building quicker than I ever thought possible. She picks up speed on me, riding my dick with her mouth and taking my control away with her eagerness. It's fucking hot. Annoying. But bloody hot.

My dick tenses with impending need to release. Before I shoot it down her throat, I grab her by the arms and yank her up on her feet.

"What are you doing?" she asks, her face confused as I grab her by the waist and pull her toward me. "Gareth, I could have finished."

Her breasts are right in my face. I can't help but drop a kiss on the nipple of one as I force her to spread her legs and climb onto my lap. She straddles me and frowns as I move a hand between us to position my cock between her folds.

"I want to come inside of you," I croak, my chest aching with an overwhelming feeling that I can't give a voice to yet. It's not the claiming sensation I had a minute ago. It's desperation. I press my tip inside of her and command, "Sloan, let me come inside you."

She nods and lowers herself, holding onto me by the neck as I press my face against her chest. "Fuck yes, Sloan," I groan as her tightness wraps around me.

"Gareth." Her voice echoes off the shower walls as she repeats my name and begins moving slowly on top of me. Smooth, artful strokes of her pussy around my dick that feels like the fucking waltz.

"Sloan." I say her name again because it feels good. It feels real. It feels important. "Fuck. Sloan, Sloan, Sloooan."

"Oh my God, Gareth," she cries, her voice hitching as she tightens around me. A spasm between her thighs shoots up into her apex, and I feel the lightning bolt of her orgasm. Every fucking pulse of her pleasure seizing up through her core.

She goes quiet on me, biting her teeth down on my shoulder as her orgasm descends. The pain of her bite has me erupting inside of her, my hot come shooting into her as deep as I can get it.

But it doesn't feel deep enough.

I don't know if it'll ever feel deep enough when it comes to this woman.

Shepherd's Pie Confessions

Sloan

A VERY BRITISH LUNCH OF SHEPHERD'S PIE IS SERVED AS SOON as Gareth and I come downstairs. Freya, Vi, Vaughn, Gareth, and I gather around the kitchen table and dig into our food like it's not completely obvious that Gareth and I both have wet hair.

In my youth, I would have been much more embarrassed by the notion of Gareth's family knowing I was intimate with their son when we're not an established couple. I married Callum so young, I never had any opportunities to be an adult couple in front of someone's parents. But after everything we've been through in the last twenty-four hours, I couldn't care less. Gareth needed me upstairs, and I can already sense that his mood has lightened toward his father, which makes everyone a bit less tense.

"The food is delicious, Sloan. Are you the one I pay my respects to?" Vaughn asks, looking up from his plate and eyeing me with his steely gaze. He's been overly polite to me since he arrived, our battle at the hospital all but forgotten.

I dab the corners of my mouth with my napkin. "Both Freya and me I suppose. I wanted you guys to have something comforting. Since I'm not the best chef of classic British meals, I enlisted her guidance. In Chicago, I would have whipped you all up tater tot casserole, but England doesn't have the exact kind of tater tots I like, so I embraced the culture for once." I smile and Vi, Vaughn, and Gareth look at me with puzzled expressions.

"What's tater tot casserole?" Vi asks curiously.

I press my lips together to stop myself from laughing. "It's a hot-dish with beef and these round, fried potatoes on top. Kind of like a hash brown but bite-sized."

"I want that recipe!" Vi states happily.

I wince. "It's so basic…Like, it's really nothing special. But it has a comforting feel to it that I think the British would enjoy. You guys really nail comfort food."

"I can agree to that!" Freya states brightly and forks another bite of her pie.

Vi nods in agreement. "Nothing beats beans on toast, but I've got loads of really great Swedish recipes from our mum. She was a great chef."

I can feel Gareth tense beside me and look over to see him staring down at his food.

"Was your mum a full-blooded Swede?" Freya asks innocently.

Vi nods. "She was. Most of her recipes were written in Swedish. I had to have them translated."

"That's so brilliant! Did you guys ever learn any of the language growing up?"

The table grows quiet as Vi and Gareth both shake their heads softly. What's not being said is that they were too young to remember, even if they did.

It's Vaughn's deep voice that breaks the awkward silence. "I learned a bit." We all turn to look at him sitting at the opposite end of the table from me. His aged face turns a deep shade of pink as he says, "Tack så mycket för maten."

I smile back at Vaughn, who quickly drops his head.

"What does that mean?" Freya asks.

"Thank you very much for the food." Vaughn looks up and

stares back at me, his eyes pink around the edges as he holds my gaze captive for a moment. It feels like he's saying something else, but I can't be sure. The longer he stares at me with that sort of intense twinkle in his eyes, the more I find myself softening to him. He was horrid at the hospital, but he's clearly a man who's just sad at the core.

It's Freya who's brave enough to breach the unspoken subject. "Did you meet your late wife in Sweden then, Mr. Harris?"

I swear the entire table takes a deep breath and holds it. Vi's fork of potatoes freezes in the air as she watches for her father's reaction.

"Excuse me?" Vaughn asks, breaking his eye contact with me to look over at Freya's bright, freckled face. His eyes are tight around the edges with obvious discomfort.

Freya flushes and slouches down slightly in her seat. "I was curious how you met your wife. You had such a large family together, I imagine it was a bit of a whirlwind romance."

"Freya." I state her name softly and give her a tight shake of my head. "I'm sure Mr. Harris doesn't care to discuss—"

"No, no, it's quite all right." Vaughn cuts me off and I look over at Gareth, who's watching his father intently when he adds, "It was love at first sight, so I suppose you could call it a whirlwind."

Freya beams back at him with glee. "Really? I always thought that was something made-up in romance novels."

Vaughn smiles tightly, his eyes crinkling around the edges. "Not for Vilma and I. I saw her across the room at a pub in London and I knew I was in love."

Vi makes a strange noise in her throat. "I never knew that."

Vaughn wipes his mouth with his napkin and rests it on the table. "Well, your mother didn't know it either. It took some convincing."

"Do tell!" Freya tuts. As much as I want to kick her under the table and tell her to shut up, I can't help but love my friend for being so brave and innocent.

Vaughn looks off into the distance as he tells the story about all but forcing Vilma to attend one of his football matches in Manchester. He said he loved her the moment he saw her, but it wasn't until he saw her after his match that he knew he had to marry her.

"Vilma was the woman of my dreams' dreams. She had this light in her eyes that she could so easily turn off and on. And when it was on and directed at you, you couldn't help but feel like you had this incredible gift. This incredible immortal amongst humans staring you right in the face."

"Blimey," Freya croaks, her eyes welling with tears.

"But she was definitely human enough to get pregnant. Gareth was the result of our wild and overexcited passion."

"Too much information," Gareth murmurs, but Vaughn keeps on going like he's in another world.

"At first, I thought it would be hard to have a baby. My football schedule was hectic and we had only just met. I knew I wasn't ready to be a father, but she was never afraid. She accepted the surprise like it was her destiny that she knew was coming all along. Her confidence made me feel brave.

"With every baby she gave me, I grew more and more in love with her. She took everything so wonderfully in stride, too. It was miraculous. Even the twins didn't shake her. By the time Booker was born, I had only fallen more in love with her. But, by that point, *love* seemed like a word that wasn't enough to describe what we shared together. What we had between us was ten times bigger than a feeling. More massive than a sentiment. We had a family."

The entire table waits on bated breath for what Vaughn will say next. One glance at Gareth and Vi tells me this isn't a story they've heard countless times over the breakfast table. They both look stunned into silence.

I have to admit I'm feeling stunned as well. After everything Gareth told me about his father, this is nothing I would have expected from him. He's cracked open that hard outer shell from the hospital and exposed a part of himself that I don't think he shows very often. Maybe it's because he's back in Manchester for the first time in years. Maybe it's because no one's ever been brave enough to flat out ask him these questions. Whatever it is, I get the feeling it's having a major effect on Gareth.

"I remember a bit of when you two were happy like that," Gareth states out of nowhere, his voice low and brow pensive.

Vi turns her watery, surprised eyes to him. "You remember those times?" She whispers the question but we all hear it.

"In the Manchester flat, yeah." He nods woodenly, his eyes darkened like he's haunted by the happy memories.

She shakes her head sadly. "I can't remember the Manchester flat. My memories only include the London house. That was, of course, when Mum was sick."

Vaughn clears his throat and looks down at his plate, a shameful posture hunching his shoulders. "Things were different in London."

"Dad—" Vi begins to soothe, but Vaughn cuts her off.

"In Manchester, things were happy. Warm. I remember I couldn't wait to get back home after travelling for matches because I missed the madness of our Manchester flat. One of you was always crying, or fighting, or needing something. It was chaos all the time. Your mother and I had to divide and conquer because she refused to ever hire an au pair. I bloody well loved every minute of it."

Gareth pulls his lip into his mouth and seemingly selects a spot on the table to stare at while his thoughts most likely drift to memories he's long since forgotten.

"The hotels our team stayed at for away matches were lonely. I'd have a room all to myself when I was so used to having a kid tucked up between me and your mother at night. So quiet, too…A lot like those hospitals."

Vi sniffs softly but Vaughn keeps going, clearly needing to get these words out so much that he doesn't even notice the tears streaming down his daughter's face.

"The hospital you were in last night is where I found out your mother was truly sick and not just run down from chasing after five kids. They told us there was nothing they could do for her and that our best bet would be to make her last days comfortable."

Vaughn inhales deeply and begins shaking his head back and forth. "That light she had—that magic, that sparkle—was being sucked out of her body. Like taking a colourful photo and turning it black and white."

Vi's voice is garbled when she says, "How awful, Dad. I can't imagine how hard that must have been for the two of you." She reaches out to touch his hand, but Vaughn recoils away from her.

"Vilma made peace with her diagnosis, but I certainly didn't. I couldn't get over the fact that the happy life we created was mocking me everywhere I looked. I couldn't enjoy the sounds of you kids fighting. Hell, I couldn't even play football anymore. I hated the pitch. I'd see the place she always sat for my home games and picture it empty. The image killed me. She was the root of our family. She held us all up. She was our magic, and I did not want to do this life without her.

"So I started taking her to other hospitals. Different doctors. I think we saw every doctor here in Manchester three times before I quit playing for Manchester United and forced her to move to the London house. I forced her to try surgeries that never resulted in what we wanted. I forced her to take medication that made her feel horrible. I forced her to keep fighting when all she wanted to do was go to the bloody beach."

Vaughn's voice cracks and he brings his fist to his mouth to bite down on his knuckle. I look around the table through watery eyes and see everyone else is crying, too. I even see a tear slip down Gareth's cheek, and it takes everything in me to not go over and hold him. I can so easily picture him as a little boy living through that horror at about the same age Sophia is now. It's everything I went through with Sophia but reversed. How would all of that look through a child's eyes? When you're young, your parents are supposed to be strong and protective. Not sick and crumbling.

Vi's wobbly voice breaks the silence. "What do you mean a beach, Dad? What beach are you talking about?"

Vaughn looks up at her tear-stricken face and it cuts straight through him. He bows his head in shame. "Vilma wanted to go to a warm beach. She wanted to put her toes in the sand and watch you kids play so she could pass on with happy family memories. It was such a simple request, but I was selfish. I wasn't ready to lose the love of my life—my best friend. That's why I begged her to fight with everything she had left to give. In the end, we all lost.

"If only I'd taken her to the bloody beach," he mumbles and rubs his hand over his forehead. "Maybe that light would have come back in her eyes before she died, and I could have remembered how she always was in the beginning. Not what I turned her into at the end."

The table grows quiet again, the faint sounds of Vi's running nose narrating the heavy emotion in the room. I can hear Vaughn swallowing his pain down, burying a knot that probably lives in his stomach permanently. The same knot that Gareth has for completely different reasons. It's no wonder this family is so pained by the loss of their mother. The entire story was a nightmare that these five children had to live through.

"Her light was still there in the end, you know," Gareth husks, his voice raw with pain. He aggressively swipes at moisture under his nose and adds through clenched teeth, "That light was there for me. I saw it every time I was with her. I even saw it when she died. And despite everything, she loved you, even at the end, Dad. She still completely loved you."

Vaughn's red-rimmed eyes pin Gareth with a knowing look. "I didn't deserve it," he croaks.

Gareth nods woodenly. "But that light was there all the same."

Vaughn purses his lips, tears filling his eyes as he covers his face to conceal his reaction. He sniffs loudly and looks away, trying hard to compose himself. "Thank you for telling me that."

Gareth shakes off his father's thanks, seemingly uncomfortable with what's shifting between them.

Suddenly, Vi's voice bellows, "We're going to the beach."

"What?" Gareth turns a confused look at his sister.

"We're going to the beach to have a wake for Mum."

"Vi, I don't think…" Gareth begins.

Vi is undeterred. "Her funeral was horrible and we were all too young to grieve her properly. This is what Mum would have wanted."

She looks back at her brother hopefully with bright, blue, begging eyes, but it's her father's response that gives her the permission she's longing for.

"I think that sounds like an excellent idea," Vaughn states with a stoic nod. "You're right. It's exactly what Vilma would have wanted."

"Exactly," Vi replies, then adds in a rush, "And I'm going to marry Hayden while we're there."

Gareth's face goes white. "You want to do a wake and a wedding?"

She nods firmly, not at all fazed by his expression.

Freya's voice chimes in next. "I think it's a lovely idea! The end of one love story, the beginning of another!"

"Thank you, Freya!" Vi exclaims and turns her eyes back to Gareth. "Life is short, Gareth. I don't want to wait anymore. This can work, but you have to be there for me or I won't do it."

Gareth scoffs and shakes his head from side-to-side, then begins nodding just as quickly. "If you want me there, I'll be there, Vi. You know that."

A wobbly smile spreads across her face. "Brilliant. You boys all have winter break coming up and the doctor should clear you to travel by then, so this will work. This is important enough to make work."

Vaughn nods firmly and reaches out to hold Vi's hand.

"Whatever you need, Vi, I'm here to help."

Gareth stares at his father, still greatly confused. This is a very different man sitting in front of us than the guy who showed up at the hospital. But this entire day has been confusing. Never in my life would I have expected to have some of the Harris family sitting at my table, so maybe that's just what Manchester does to them.

And maybe this is all a good thing. Maybe this is the start of some Harris family healing that Gareth so desperately needs.

7

A Noisy House

Gareth

THE NEXT DAY PASSES RATHER STRANGELY. FOR OVER TEN YEARS, I lived a life of seclusion in Manchester. It was my own little world where I worked out, trained, ate my prepared meals, and travelled with my team. I took the train to London on Sundays for family dinners when I could. I fielded calls from my siblings on a daily basis. It was a simple life. One that I appreciated because it kept me in a routine that I had complete control over. But when Vi suggested everyone fly in for Christmas Eve at my home in Astbury because of my travel restrictions, I could tell it was the beginning of a shift in our family.

So, once the police cleared my home, I said goodbye to Sloan, who was prepping for Sophia's return. I respect her space and I'm glad I'm not going to infringe on their Christmas together. I realised when I left that I probably wouldn't be hearing from her for another week. But it doesn't bother me as much as it did before because I know the reasoning behind it now.

By this afternoon, my entire family had flown in to Manchester on a private jet. My brothers moaned about how they'd have to leave for training really early tomorrow, but being together no matter what is the Harris way. The silver lining is that they've kept me too busy to give Sloan and her daughter much thought. Everyone filed into my house with arms full of presents, though. My dad, Vi, Hayden, and Rocky. Camden, Indie, Tanner, and Belle. Even Booker and his pregnant girlfriend, Poppy. She's not due for another three months, but she looks like she could tip over with that football attached to her stomach.

Thankfully, the damage to my house from the attack was minimal. My house manager, Dorinda, was quickly cleared of any involvement, so she was able to help get everything back to normal before I returned home.

Walking back into my house after knowing someone was in there was an eerie feeling. It was an even eerier feeling to look at the front door knowing that's where Sloan and I were knocked out and I still can't remember a fucking thing. The doctor said that something might trigger my memory someday or it may never return. Regardless, the police are working diligently to catch whomever did this. For now, I'm just grateful to have my family here with me to distract my thoughts.

My brothers made themselves at home in the theatre room right away, flicking through old football games and wrestling on the floor like animals, even pulling Rocky into the madness. Vi took over my kitchen like she'd cooked in it a thousand times before. It was madness but kind of nice. After seeing Sloan's home and Sophia's bedroom and hearing my dad talk about how he enjoyed the chaos of a big family, it made me long for a bit more mess in my life.

"Gareth, where's Sloan the Stylist today?" Tanner asks in a bouncy tone as he plops down next to me on the sofa in the living room.

It's a proper relaxed holiday as the telly blares some old film while Rocky plays on the floor with Hayden and her new toys. Booker and Camden are on the other end of the couch while the girls are all huddled in the kitchen, sipping wine. Dad is upstairs napping like he's been here a million times before and this isn't the first time he's stepped foot inside my house.

"She's celebrating at home with her…daughter," I reply, feeling my three brothers' eyes on me along with my brother-in-law's.

Tanner strokes his beard slowly. "So you guys aren't 'Christmas official' yet? Is that because you're still celibate and she won't buy the bull until she can sample the…milk?" His face falls in disgust over his own euphemism gone horribly wrong.

"You can fuck off," I grumble and shove him in the arm.

Hayden hits me with a warning look for cursing in front of Rocky. Thankfully, she's completely lost in her toys and not in a repeating mood.

Tanner chuckles like a moron. "I'm only joking. It's clear you've shagged her considering how possessive she was over you at the hospital. Bloody hell, it was kind of hot."

My nostrils flare and with one look, Tanner holds his hands up in surrender.

"Christ, calm yourself, bro. If I didn't know any better, I'd say you two are in looove." He drags out the last word dramatically and redirects his attention back to the television.

His comment has my shoulders tensing. Before I left Sloan's house, there was a shift in our relationship. But I haven't had a chance to discuss it with her, and I'd rather not be concussed when we do talk about where we stand with each other.

I can feel Camden's eyes on me from the other end of the couch when he asks, "So, are you bringing her on this trip Vi is planning?"

My jaw tightens. "I'm not sure."

"Why not?"

"Because we haven't discussed it."

"Why not?"

"Because we've had a bit going on as of late, Camden. Jesus Christ. Back off!"

Cam recoils and thankfully has the decency to close his mouth for a minute. Perhaps a bit more of a mess around the house isn't all it's cracked up to be when you're getting a Harris Brother inquisition brought down upon you.

The wake-wedding trip hasn't been at the forefront of my mind at all. I've mostly been thinking about everything Dad said and the way he's been acting since he arrived here. Speaking more freely about Mum. Being talkative and helpful when he can be. He's almost acting *human*. I can't wrap my mind around it.

"So, are you planning to be a stepdaddy to Sloan's little girl?" Tanner asks, apparently not done tormenting me.

"What?" I snap, sliding narrowed eyes at him.

He shrugs innocently. "Or, what is it they call them in America? Sugar daddy?"

"Piss off, Tanner," I reply gruffly. "Sloan doesn't need my money."

Tanner tilts his head curiously. "Who is her husband? He was at the pitch that day of the Kid Kickers camp, right?"

"Ex-husband," I correct, uncomfortable that he's pressing for information that I don't even have a full grasp on yet. "His name is Callum, but it's really none of your business."

"Everything's our business. We're Harrises. It's our job to be nosey sods." He shoots me a cheeky wink and adds, "You went from having no life to finding a woman who looked like she'd fight tooth and nail for you, bro. This is something we don't want you to muck up!"

Camden interjects, "I don't even recall you having a girlfriend when we were kids. Now you've gotten serious with a single mum?" He shakes his head and puffs his chest out as he does his ridiculous impression of the Queen. "Is this woman of noble birth? Is the child legitimate? Perhaps we should have them over for high tea."

"Oh yes," Tanner practically peals his agreement, his voice bursting with his own over-the-top impression. "I've just had a new vat of clotted cream churned fresh by my servants. I'd be chuffed to bits to have your little friends over. Please do send them an invitation."

I roll my eyes, but my brooding mood can't help but lift by these two having a laugh. Leave it to these wankers to not only invade my home but invade my personal life and still manage to amuse me. When I travel to London, it's easier to keep my private life private. Here, there are no kilometres to stop them from going balls deep in my personal matters.

"I don't even know how serious we are yet," I murmur half-heartedly.

"Maybe you should figure that out," Camden replies, eyeing me with a meaningful look. "A great place to do that is at Vi's wedding."

"I'm not so sure about that," I state quietly, anxiety prickling the back of my neck.

"We'll all have someone with us. So should you. What's the big deal?" Camden deadpans.

"Need I remind you that Vi's also organising our deceased mum's wake?" I retort, leaning back in my seat and shaking my head. "I don't think Sloan needs to witness the hot Harris mess that will be. She's already witnessed more of our family drama than she can handle, I'm sure. Plus she's a mother. I highly doubt she can leave her child on a whim."

"Even mums need a holiday on occasion," Hayden adds from his spot on the floor as he fake walks a babydoll in front of Rocky. I glare at him for siding with my brothers, but he just shrugs. "I have to constantly remind Vi to take a break from Rocky for her sanity. If Sloan's a single parent, I venture to guess no one is giving her reminders."

"Plus, I'd like to get to know her better," Booker states softly, breaking his silence from his spot beside Camden. He leans forward and runs his hands down his thighs. "She was brilliant against Dad at the hospital. None of us could stand up to him the way she did, Gareth. I liked seeing someone by your side like that."

He blinks his dark eyes at me, suddenly looking very old and wise beyond his years. Our youngest brother has changed so much in the past year. Perhaps it's because he's about to become a father, but seeing him like this is a bit disarming.

Camden and Tanner both nod, losing all signs of teasing. They are pushing for a reason. They see in Sloan what I've always seen in her. She's special.

Perhaps a trip together is the perfect time for us to figure out what we are to each other. We can detach from work and our lives here in Manchester and see where we stand.

The next day, things are a lot calmer around my house since the boys left for training. I find a few minutes to myself and sprawl out on my bed to reread the text thread between Sloan and I earlier this morning.

Me: Happy Christmas.

Sloan: Merry Christmas to you! You're up early. Is your family still there? Driving you nuts?

Me: Yes, but my brothers are leaving soon. They have to get back for training, which is good because it smells like balls in my gym. Only Harris Brothers train on Christmas Eve.

Sloan: LOL. That sounds weirdly adorable.

Me: It's not. Was Sophia spoilt by Santa?

Sloan: Definitely. How about your niece?

Me: Rocky is going to need her own jet for all the presents she has to take home.

Sloan: I completely get that. Sophia gets two Christmases now, so she's thrilled to get double the presents.

Me: One silver lining to having divorced parents I guess.

Sloan: I guess.

Me: Well, enjoy your time with her. Just wanted to wish you a

happy Christmas.
Sloan: Thanks. Miss you. xx

Our conversation was light and casual, which is probably okay since she's been hit with a lot of heavy from me and my family as of late. But my brothers are right. The way Sloan behaved at the hospital was anything but light and casual. And while I respect the time she has with her daughter, part of me wonders if she'd answer if I tried to ring her right now.

In our previous arrangement, she almost never answered. She'd usually text or call back hours later. It annoyed me, but now I know it was probably because she was waiting for Sophia to go to bed. But things are different now, right?

Steeling myself, I press SEND on her number and hold my breath as the line trills in my ear.

"Hello," Sloan answers after two rings.

"Sloan, hiya," I reply in surprise.

"Hey, Gareth," she replies back casually like it's completely normal for her to take a call from me. "How are you? How are you feeling?"

"I'm feeling well actually. Am I catching you at a good time?" I ask, propping my arm under my head.

"Yeah, you definitely are." Sloan's voice is soft. I swear I can hear the smile on her face. "I'm being ignored in my own home because Freya and Sophia are obsessed with Fortnite."

I chuckle at the image. "I'm sure those two gaming together is quite a sight."

"It really is," she replies with a fondness to her tone. "It's kind of annoying, though, because I've prepared a beautiful dinner and they won't even stop to eat. How about your group? Calmer now that your brothers have left?"

"Definitely," I reply with a laugh. "Before six o'clock this morning, Vi was already yelling at Tanner because he snuck into their room to wake Rocky."

"You never wake a sleeping baby!" Sloan exclaims.

"He learned that the hard way I'm afraid." I shake my head as I recall his wide, panicked eyes when Rocky began crying like none of us had ever heard before. He looked so pathetic.

"Was it nice having everyone at your house? Did it feel kind of weird there after…everything?"

Her tone tells me she's referring to the attack, so my body instantly tenses. "It was unnerving at first, but having everyone here helped me forget. The security company is coming tomorrow to see what we can do to make my place more secure. I refuse to let a couple of thugs scare me out of my own home."

"That's good, Gareth. Really good."

The line goes quiet for a few seconds, and I exhale with relief over how easy this is for us. Discussing the details of each other's lives with no limits. No boundaries. It's nice. I've lived my life privately for so long, but having someone to talk to about menial things feels better than I ever imagined.

"So, can I talk to you about something? Or do you need to get back to Sophia?" I ask, steeling myself to man up and do what I intended to do with this call.

"I can talk," she replies, and I hear the background noise soften as she walks away for some privacy.

"Okay. Well, I know you got hit hard with the Harris crazy over lunch at your house the other day, and I'm sorry you were stuck in the middle of that. I'm also sure the stress of the hospital probably makes you want to stay as far away from my family as possible, so I understand if you want to say no. But it sounds like Vi is actually going to go through with her wake-wedding idea. She's even picked a resort in the Cape Verde islands already."

"That's awesome!" Sloan replies politely. "I think it will be really good for your family."

"I want you there, Sloan," I blurt out.

"What?"

"I want you to be my date at my sister's wedding." My chest feels tight. I'm more nervous now than I was the time I propositioned her to dominate me.

"Gareth—" She begins to argue but I cut her off.

"I've given this some thought, and this is the more I told you I want that night outside your house. I know you have Sophia and that being a mum takes up a large part of your life, but you need time for yourself as well. And in regard to us, nothing has changed for me. I still want more. A lot more."

Silence descends on the other end of the line, and I can feel my heart sinking from her lack of response.

"Has something changed for you?" I ask, holding my breath high in my chest.

Sloan clears her throat and replies softly, "No."

"Thank fuck," I exhale, relief blanketing my entire body. "So, will you come with me?"

"When are you going?" she asks timidly, like she is actually considering it.

"In a few weeks. I don't know if Sophia will be with her dad. Or perhaps you want to bring her along? I'm sure she'd love the beach, but I don't know how she'd feel attending a wake. We could figure something out."

Sloan laughs softly. "Sophia will be in school, Gareth."

"Right," I reply quickly and shake my head like a moron. "So then, if we can work out the timing so you don't miss your time with her, will you come?"

"I need to think about it," she replies slowly, then rushes out, "It sounds lovely. But there's one thing I should know before I contemplate this further…Where are the Cape Verde islands?"

I laugh and we continue talking lightly for another thirty minutes. It feels good. Even though she hasn't agreed to come along yet, she's not saying no. That's a step in the right direction.

No Regrets

Sloan

A COUPLE OF DAYS AFTER CHRISTMAS, REPORTS STARTED circulating about an attack at the Harris Estate in Astbury that included an assault on Gareth Harris and a "female companion." Suddenly, this typically private Manchester United defender was all over the news. There were photos of Gareth's home taken from helicopters, including images of him coming in and out of his house. For two weeks straight, sports reporters remarked on when Gareth would return from his injury as they showed shots of him standing on the sidelines at games and practice. I never paid attention to how much media coverage he receives. Now that I am, I'm not sure I like what I see.

As a result of the extra publicity, Gareth's agent advised us to stay apart for a few weeks to make sure the "female companion" doesn't get a name and face. I am more than okay with it, especially since I am still recovering from everything that happened. Although my bruise has faded, it weighs heavily on my mind that the police still haven't found who attacked us.

Gareth spent an insane amount of money on a high-level security system at his home and insisted on installing the same at mine. Normally, I'm all "independent woman, hear me roar," but I couldn't object after being attacked. Certainly not when I have Sophia to consider.

The entire situation got me thinking, *Is this really the kind of life I want to drag my daughter in to?* I was so close to having my name and my personal life splashed all over the press. Sophia's face could have ended up in the papers as well. How would Callum handle that? Would he accept it? Could it complicate our custody agreement? There is so much for me to consider because my life is not my own. The control I experienced in Gareth's home during our previous agreement was a ruse. An escape from reality. We were playing make-believe, and I realise that time is over now that so much has happened.

I've just settled Sophia into bed after picking her up from the Lake District when my phone rings on my nightstand.

Despite the anxiety I have over Gareth's newfound spotlight these days, I've grown quite accustomed to the evening phone calls we've been having since his manager told us to stay apart two and a half weeks ago. Our chats have been very surface level, but there's something nice about having someone to talk to as I get ready for bed.

"Hiya," Gareth's deep voice husks into the line.

"Hey," I reply, biting my lip and wincing at the breathy tone of my voice.

"Sophia in bed?" he asks.

I nod. "She is. She's always exhausted after being at Margaret's."

"Ah, the scary, immortal grandmother."

"The one and only." I huff out a small laugh and roll my eyes. I'm amazed by how easily Gareth takes everything pertaining to Sophia in stride. I know he's older, but it blows my mind that he cares about me after finding out what I hid from him for so long.

Gareth clears his throat and says, "So, I've been giving you time to think it over, but I need to know your answer."

"My answer to what?" I ask as I toss a pair of Sophia's socks into the hamper.

"Will you come with me to Cape Verde?" he asks, his voice taking a more formal tone.

My heart drops. This is the conversation I've been avoiding because I know Gareth won't like my answer. With a deep breath, I reply, "I don't think it's a good idea."

"Why?" he asks through clenched teeth.

"Because you've been all over the media these last couple of weeks. I know you play professional soccer and you've always been a bit famous, but the attack changed things. To see your house splashed all over TV is really scary, Gareth."

"So I'll move!" he replies flippantly, like it's the solution to our problem. But it's not.

"That doesn't change anything."

"Sloan, the press have already backed off a lot. I'll be old news in a couple more days."

"Until something else happens."

"Nothing else is going to happen."

"You can't guarantee that," I argue as I drop down on my bed, holding my face in my hand and hating that I have to do this already. I've loved our nightly talks and having someone checking in on me. Even if it has been all surface level conversation, it's nice having someone care. But I'm living in a fantasy and I have to stop. "I have Sophia to think about. I don't want her life to be turned upside down because her mom is dating a famous athlete."

"You think I haven't thought about Sophia?" he exclaims. I can just see him gripping the back of his neck as he growls his frustration into the phone line. "Sloan, I haven't stopped thinking about Sophia since I met her on the football pitch and noticed that she has your eyes. I know Sophia is your top priority and I'm fine with that. Hell, I love that about you."

Wait, did he say love?

"I need you to give me a chance to show you."

"Show me what?" I ask, my heart pounding in my chest over the pain of losing him so soon.

"That you matter, too. That *we* matter, too. That there can be room in our lives for all of it. I mean, bloody hell, I fucking miss you, Treacle. Don't you miss me?"

My insides squeeze in on themselves from his remark. I miss him more than I've let myself fully admit. Honestly, the thought of not seeing him ever again nearly gives me the same anxiety I have when Sophia is at Callum's every other week.

"Yes, I miss you," I answer.

"Good," he exhales with relief and adds, "Then don't take me out of the game before I've had a chance to play."

It's those knee-trembling words from Gareth that have me sitting in my closet one week later, packing for a trip to the Cape Verde islands with the entire Harris family. For a woman who had complete control over a man only weeks ago, I sure wasn't able to put up much of a fight. And when I mentioned taking a vacation to Callum, who couldn't have cared less, I knew I really didn't have any reason to say no.

Plus, I think part of me knew that I would live my entire life wondering what Gareth and I could have been if I didn't give him this trip or the chance to show me his dominant side at least once.

"Mummy, why can't I come with you on your holiday?" Sophia asks as she pulls down one of the evening gowns I used to wear when I attended events with Callum.

"Vacation, Sopapilla. Americans call it a vacation." I reach over top of her and pull down my giant suitcase from the shelf.

Sophia rolls her eyes at my correction, then steps into a long, sequined, silver gown that sparkles under the closet lights. "I really want to go on your vacation. You're going to a beach and I love beaches."

I drop down on my knees to open my empty suitcase. "You have school, sweetie. We can't take you out of school."

She pulls the thin straps of the dress onto her shoulders and shuffles over to my wall of shoes. "Callie says no one likes African beaches anyway."

I look up from my suitcase and blink. Sophia has been dropping Callum's girlfriend's name more and more lately. I can't say I'm a fan, especially when it's this kind of shit. "Callie says what exactly?"

"She says the beaches are dirty there." Sophia steps into a pair of black stilettos and teeters awkwardly for a moment.

I have to hold back my knee-jerk reaction of wanting to rush over to Callum's house and punch Callie in her overly Botox-injected face. What kind of bullshit is that woman filling my daughter's mind with? Instead, I reply through clenched teeth, "Well, don't believe everything Callie says, Soap. The beach I'm going to seems beautiful in the pictures."

"Then why can't I go?" Sophia stomps her foot, looking seven going on seventeen. The hem catches under the heel and she begins falling over, taking a row of shoes down with her.

I rush over and catch her under the arms just before she topples to the floor. Stray shoes collect around us. Once she's propped back up, Sophia's big brown eyes find mine. Her little bushy brows scrunch as she hits me with a sassy look. "I'm cross at you."

I can't help but smile and kiss her forehead. She's so cute, even when she's mad. "Sophia, sweetie, I would love for you to come, but it's your week with Daddy. He needs his time with you just like I do."

"Daddy is always working," she harrumphs as she reaches out and begins playing with the long necklace I'm wearing. "I have to sit with Callie after school and she's boring. She likes really stupid telly where people are always shouting at each other, and she's not even watching it most of the time because she's staring at her mobile."

My body grows tense from her words. Callum demands fifty percent custody but from what I can tell, Sophia sees Callie and her grandmother more than she sees Callum. It's enough to make me want to scream.

I pull Sophia down onto my lap and tuck her head under my chin, relishing in the weight of her against me. "I'm sorry Daddy is so busy, Soap. But I think just knowing you're at his home makes him happy, so try to keep that in mind."

"Why do you have to go, Mom?" she asks, clearly stating "mom" instead of "mum." I notice she says it the American way when she wants something that she knows I'll say no to. My little girl can be really damn clever when she wants to be.

"Well, Mommy hasn't been on a trip by herself in a very long time. Not since before you were born."

"Really?" she asks, snuggling into me. "How come?"

My heart grows heavy as I recall all the years we spent in and out of hospitals and staying home to ensure Sophia didn't come in contact with germs when her immune system was suppressed. Even our trips back to America after we moved to England were limited because I didn't want to put her health at risk.

"Do you remember your sickie days? When we had to go to the hospital a lot?" I ask.

Sophia grows quiet for a moment, but I can feel her head nodding. "A little bit."

My lips curve up into a small smile. "I'm glad you can't remember it all because those were hard times for us. We were very busy, and there wasn't a lot of time for extra things since we were so focused on making you better."

She exhales heavily. "Fine, you should have a holiday I guess. But that means you have to take me on a holiday next time I have no school."

"I said it's called a vacation!" I growl playfully. She falls back onto the floor as I tickle her sides mercilessly. She erupts into a fit of giggles, and it's the best freaking sound of my entire life.

Every day that I put Sophia first and didn't travel or take time for myself was well worth it because of this moment right here. The flush of her glorious, healthy cheeks as she squirms away from me is a beautiful sight. She'll be eight years old in a couple of months, and her five-year remission milestone comes soon after that. She's not the sick baby she was so many years ago.

Yes, I'm nervous to leave her, but I need to see this thing through with Gareth. This trip will be a good test to see if we can be great together like he thinks we can. Then I'll decide what part he'll play in my future and with Sophia.

My phone vibrates on the floor behind me, so I take a break from Sophia tickles to see that it's a text from Gareth.

Gareth: I can't wait to see you again.

Me: Me too. I'm just packing now.

Gareth: Good. The car will be at your house to pick you up at eight a.m. tomorrow.

Me: I'll be ready.

Gareth: You better be.

Me: Is that a threat? :)

Gareth: Treacle, I have plans for you these next few days. The doctor has cleared me of my injuries. I'm back at practice and nearly at 100% again. And I haven't seen you in three weeks. This isn't a threat. It's a promise.

Me: Yes, Master. ;)

Gareth: Fuck me, I think I like the sound of that.

Free Falling

Sloan

THE CAR PULLS ONTO A TARMAC WHERE A SMALL PRIVATE PLANE awaits. I'm so nervous, my hands are shaking. It's a combination of not having seen Gareth in weeks, the uncertainty of how this is going to go, and flying private for the first time in my entire life. Callum comes from money, but Margaret is always in his head about how he spends it. I never realised how much he kneeled to her commands until our divorce.

The driver opens the door and gestures toward the black carpet stretched out to meet the steps that lead up into the plane. "Go ahead and climb aboard, miss. I'll get your bags loaded."

On wobbly feet, I make my way to the plane, tightening my long pea coat around my body like it can somehow protect me from what's to come. When I grab hold of the railing, Gareth appears at the top of the stairs. With one smouldering glance from him, I realise there is no amount of clothing that can protect from the effect he has on me.

He stands there in all his brooding, tall, dark, and handsome glory, wearing simple jeans and a dress shirt. But his hazel eyes are anything but simple. They are filled with heat and excitement. He looks like he's preparing to run out onto a soccer field rather than welcome me onto a plane.

I feel his eyes on me as I nervously climb the steps closer to his heat, closer to his allure. I feel like a comet orbiting straight into the sun. It was easier to consider ending things with Gareth when we only had phone contact. I told myself he wasn't that handsome and our connection wasn't anything extraordinary. But when I breach the threshold and he pulls me out of the cold January air, I realise that I am completely full of shit.

He steals inside my jacket, the warmth of his firm arms cinching tightly around my waist. His breath is hot on my neck as our bodies crush into each other, chests rubbing against one another with each intake of breath. He slides his nose down my neck and inhales deeply, causing a riot of goosebumps to erupt all over my skin.

Good God, he feels good. I worried it might feel awkward between us after the stress of the attack died down, but nothing about his touch on me feels wrong. It feels oh-so right.

He pulls back much too soon, but his eyes hold me captive with a look of certainty in them that's harder to accept than his embrace. It's a purposeful expression, full of so much need that I feel lightheaded under the weight of it.

"Fuck, it's good to see you, Treacle." His deep voice vibrates against my chest, and I have to blink slowly to control my internal reaction.

"It's good to see you, too," I admit and force myself to take a deep breath. The wound on his temple is only a faint scar now, but it isn't difficult for me to recall the moment I woke up and saw him covered in blood.

A shudder runs over my shoulders as I stare at his lips and will him to kiss me. But he doesn't. His eyes drop to my body instead.

"You're shaking. Are you cold?" he asks, running his hands up and down my back.

I shake my head. "Just…anxious I suppose." *Anxious to feel your lips on mine again.*

The corners of his mouth curve down sympathetically. "Me too. Come on, let's get you more comfortable."

We settle into a couple of tan leather seats that face each other while the pilot goes over safety features. It's a small luxury plane with six seats and glossy walnut trim throughout. There's a bathroom in the far back, and I exhale with relief when I see that there is no bedroom. I may be ready to kiss him, but becoming a member of the Mile High Club seems like too much, too soon.

I haven't forgotten about Gareth's promise to claim me right after the gala. Our moment in the shower at my house was only a glimpse of what I imagine to come. And with all the anxiety coursing through me, I find myself craving that control he had over me. Anything to help me find my footing because being whisked away on a private plane is so not my speed.

I look around the plane for some form of distraction. "Are we changing planes in London to join your family?"

Gareth shakes his head. "They left a couple of days ago, so they're already there."

"They are?" I ask in surprise as I slide the seatbelt across my lap and click the buckle. "Did you not want to go with them?"

Gareth shakes his head and leans forward, bracing his elbows on his muscular thighs to glance out the window. "No, I wanted to wait for you."

His reply has my head jerking back. He chose to wait for me? "You what?"

He looks over at me like he doesn't understand my confusion. "You drop Sophia off at her grandmother's on Sundays, right?" he asks casually like it's common knowledge to the whole world.

"Yes," I reply, my face bent with shock. Over the past few weeks, we've done a lot of talking on the phone, but I never expected him to remember my schedule with Sophia. I've been quite limited in what I've shared about her because I'm not sure where we are going in this pseudo-relationship, and I want to protect her until I do.

"So you took it upon yourself to work around my schedule?" I ask, wrapping my fingers tightly around the armrests of my chair.

Gareth nods again and turns to look out the window as we begin to taxi toward the runway. I can't help but stare at him in wonder. He's acting like this is no big deal, but it is a very big freaking deal. Gareth Harris is a famous athlete with a demanding schedule and an equally demanding family. He just went through the ordeal of having his house broken into, being attacked, and having media swarm his every move. His life is full, yet he didn't even ask before putting my plans with Sophia first.

I didn't know men like him actually exist. I was married to Callum for years and his schedule always came first. Even when Sophia was sick.

Especially when Sophia was sick.

Overwhelming need unfurls in my lower belly. Before I know it, I'm unbuckling my seatbelt. Gareth looks at me curiously as I push myself to a standing position. I hesitate for only a second. Then, in one shaky breath, I'm on top of him, my legs spread over his lap and his face clutched firmly between my hands.

His hands wrap tightly around my waist as I stare hard into his eyes for a moment. His hazel, brownish-green eyes that hold so much intensity in their expression. So much promise, and passion, and pain, and just…acceptance. My eyes flick down to his lips. With a deep breath, I press my mouth to his.

Most kisses are meant to be savoured, appreciated, welcomed.

This isn't one of those kisses.

This kiss is a brutal, needful embrace. It's hard and fast. It's expressing years of pent-up frustration because, in the seven years I've known Callum, I've never felt true, selfless respect. What actual generosity tastes like. After what feels like a lifetime of loneliness being cured with one kind act, this moment is something I have to claim for myself.

Gareth groans into my mouth, his hands running firmly up and down my back. His grip squeezes my ass and neck as I violently shove my tongue into his mouth and press against him as close as I can. He accepts me—all of me—giving up the control and only taking what I offer, not a smidgeon more.

This man is too much. He's too different. Too unique. Too special. The overpowering emotions raking through my body should terrify me. They should have me leaping out of this plane and never looking back because I have so much to lose in this fight. Instead, I slow my assault on his mouth and wrap my arms around his neck, hugging him to me as our lips hold against each other. Then we slowly, painfully, regretfully break apart.

Our breaths are hot on each other's damp lips as we recover. Gareth moves a finger up between our mouths, running his digit along the flesh of my lower lip as our foreheads come together.

"That was a gift," he husks, his peppermint-scented breath mixing with mine.

"What do you mean?" I ask, out of breath and nowhere near satisfied.

"You took that like you've taken other things from me before," he replies slowly, my eyes fixating on his lips the entire time. "And I'm not complaining because, fuck, I love seeing that look in your eyes again. But things are going to be different this week, Treacle."

I close my eyes, relishing in his endearment for me and nodding my agreement. "They are already more different than you know."

With a soft, chaste kiss on my forehead, he helps me off of his lap. I move back to my rightful place and we both buckle up, ignoring the fact that one of the pilots had been telling us to fasten our seatbelts multiple times.

As the plane prepares for takeoff, my eyes drink in Gareth's large frame as he adjusts the tightness around his groin. He looks exactly like the man I poured hot wax on, and blindfolded, and tied up. But somehow, he looks different. Changed. Maybe it's because he made being a complete gentleman seem so casual and easy. I don't know. Something is definitely different about him, though, and it's something I really, really like.

As the plane begins to pick up speed for takeoff, I nervously run my hands up and down my thighs in an attempt to control my emotions so I don't spontaneously combust.

Gareth sits back, eyeing me through his thick, black lashes. "Are you a nervous flier?"

I ball my hands up on my lap and squeeze my legs together. "It's not the flying that makes me nervous."

He smiles and the noise of the engine grows louder as the plane begins to ascend. Unable to hold Gareth's heated gaze another moment longer, I turn to the window and watch Manchester shrink smaller and smaller behind us.

If I look hard enough, I can probably spot the giant Coleridge Estate—the home I lived in for several years with my husband and child before everything changed. I'm a completely different person than I was when I lived there. So much more opinionated and strong. Back then, I was a desperate housewife trying to keep my husband happy and give my daughter a chance at a normal life.

Now? I'm not sure what I am doing. There is nothing about a life with Gareth Harris that would be normal.

"Have you ever skydived before, Gareth?" I ask, turning my eyes back to him.

He shakes his head curiously. "No, I'm afraid I haven't."

"Would you ever skydive?"

He quirks a brow. "I could probably be convinced."

I lick my lips and narrow my eyes. "It's crazy, though, right? You go up as high as a plane can take you. Then you decide to bail out of the one thing that's keeping you afloat and place all your trust in a tiny slip of fabric attached to your back. Why do you think people do it?"

Gareth shrugs. "The rush I guess."

"And why do people care about getting a rush?"

His lips thin and he leans forward to prop his elbows on his knees. His knuckles brush my shins as he answers, "Probably because it's dangerous and they come out of it feeling like they can do anything."

I chew on my lip, pondering his answer as the plane levels out and the pilot announces that we've reached our cruising altitude. "What if someone's too scared to skydive? Do you think that person's life is less fulfilled as a result?"

His brows knit together. "No, not at all. But I think with great risk comes great reward."

I nod slowly and do my best to hold Gareth's watchful eyes on me. "What if they've had enough excitement for one lifetime?"

He continues to stare at me, trying to decipher the meaning behind my words. Honestly, I don't even know the meaning behind my words. I know that I feel strange being so far away from Sophia. I feel protective over her history and my bond with her as a result of everything we endured together. I know it's something important I should tell Gareth, but that conversation is a lot like jumping out of a plane when I don't trust my parachute.

Until I know what Gareth and I are to each other, I need to keep some of my Sopapilla safely tucked away in my heart. Otherwise, it will make all of this that much more difficult if it doesn't work out.

"Are you missing Sophia?" Gareth asks, seemingly reading my mind.

I nod woodenly. "Yes. But, believe it or not, I'm happy that I'm here. I don't think I could have done this six months ago."

"What do you mean?"

"Before we started our little arrangement, I was a mess when Sophia was away from me to be at Callum's. Freya called them my dark days because I was barely functional. Sharing custody fifty-fifty was a really hard change for me."

"A mother's bond with her child is intense," Gareth muses, looking out the window, his thoughts drifting somewhere I can only imagine.

"You said you were best friends with your mom, right?" I ask, wanting to take the spotlight off of me for a moment, but also more curious about his past than ever.

"I was." He blinks slowly and turns his gaze back to me. He has a tight, emotionless expression when he adds, "She even wrote a poem about our friendship. Would you like to read it?"

I nod instantly and Gareth reaches into his back pocket. He pulls out his wallet, along with a piece of laminated paper that's bent from the trifolds of his billfold. He looks at me nervously for a moment before handing it over to me.

Friendship has No Age
You drive toy cars, I drive real cars.
You like juice, I like coffee.
You read comics, I read novels.
You go to school while I take care of the house.
Friendship has no age.
Friendship has no limits.
No rules. No boundaries. No distance.
Friendship can be young or old.
Rich or poor.
Healthy
or sick.
Friendship can be in a mother's eyes,
or a young boy's heart.
Between man and wife.
Through laughter and strife.
Friendship has no age.
There are no limits to friendship.
No beginning.
No middle.
No end.
Even in death, friendship still gives us breath,
as it lives on in our hearts and souls.
Our tight little hugs and soft, cosy clothes.
In our weak, frail bones, and our aching, broken hearts.
Friendship...has no age.

I finish, turning my head into my shoulder to hide the tears that have welled up in my eyes. Clearly, this was written by his mother when she was ill. It's almost too heartbreaking to handle, but I steel myself to be strong. I look over at Gareth to see the pain I feel reflected back at me.

He clears his throat and reaches out to grab the poem out of my hand. "I'm so sorry. I didn't mean to make you upset."

"It's okay," I reply as he tucks the paper back into his wallet. "That poem is beautiful, Gareth. I can't imagine what it must have been like for you to lose her."

He nods stiffly, his jaw muscle ticking as he looks out the window. "I think I was too busy to ever have a chance to actually miss her. My siblings really needed me a lot back then, and I guess distractions are good for avoiding grief."

"I guess," I reply half-heartedly, hurting for the little boy who had to take on so much.

"How do you manage your days without Sophia? I'm sure you miss her a great deal when she's with your ex."

A sad smile lifts my face. "Surprisingly enough, nothing has worked as well as you."

My answer surprises him. He crosses his arms over his chest and stares thoughtfully back at me. "So I guess I was right."

"About what?" I ask, puzzling over the weird expression on his face.

He inhales deeply and replies, "With great risk comes great reward."

I drop my head back against the seat cushion and shake my head in surrender. "Where do we go from here?"

Our attention is diverted toward the ceiling when the seatbelt light clicks off in the cabin. Without pause, Gareth undoes his buckle and moves over to the seat next to me. He grabs my hand and holds it between his own, squeezing my fingers tightly as he looks straight into my eyes.

"I hope that in between the moments of craziness with my family these next few days, you and I get a chance to reconnect and see what we could be together without boundaries. Without restrictions. I want to pick up where we left off, and I want you to stop being nervous and stop seeing this as less than it is.

"You played it safe with your ex, but being with me requires you to be brave. And, for the first time in my life, I want someone by my side. Someone to share the stuff that I've kept bottled up for fucking years. *I want that with you.* I need you to know that I'm all in, Sloan. And I'm not the kind of man who jumps out of airplanes for a rush. I'm the kind of man who stands on the ground, waiting to catch you."

My breath whooshes out of my mouth from his last words. I feel myself nodding over and over, my eyes never leaving his, even for a second. Honestly, we could stay like this for the entire six-hour flight and I wouldn't notice. Space and time don't seem to exist when I'm staring into the eyes of Gareth Harris.

Six hours later, we arrive at the resort on the island of Sal. The landscape has a desert oasis feel to it, with palm trees sprouted up all over the place. The hotel we're staying at looks like the palace in *Aladdin* plopped right on the beach. Inside the hotel are domed ceilings and arched windows. Dark wood furnishings, sprawling Indian rugs, and employees wearing crisp, white uniforms and carrying platters full of drinks. If this is how famous soccer players live, I could definitely get used to it.

Before we reach the check-in counter, I see Gareth's sister out of the corner of my eye, walking up from the beach. On one side of her is a handsome, copper blonde-haired man whom I assume is her fiancé based on how he's holding her hand. On the other side is Vaughn, who's holding a stunning little girl on his hip. They're all decked out in swim gear with overflowing bags of water toys tucked under their arms. They look sun-kissed, wind-whipped, and like a family on the perfect vacation.

"You made it!" Vi peals, ditching her man and rushing through the entrance of the resort. Her flip-flops clap loudly on the marble floor as she hurries over to pull Gareth into a hug.

"Hiya, Vi," Gareth replies, clasping her back and watching over her shoulder as the two men approach.

As soon as Gareth's dad reaches us, Gareth breaks away from his sister and steals the little girl right out of Vaughn's hands. Vaughn doesn't seem fazed at all, only smiling at his son who's now doting over his granddaughter.

I'm thoroughly enjoying the hot guy with a baby show when Vaughn shocks me with a tight hug as well. "Sloan, it's so good of you to come," he says, pulling away and smiling.

The hug takes both Gareth and Vi by surprise as they stare at their father like he's committed a felony.

"Thanks for having me," I manage to reply, my tongue feeling stroppy in my mouth.

"This is my daughter, Adrienne," Vi interjects with an affectionate smile. "Everyone calls her Rocky, though."

Gareth turns a proud smile to me as he shows off his niece.

"Nice to meet you, Rocky." I shake her tiny hand. My heart squeezes when she drags her tiny sunglasses off her face and hits me straight on with the most stunning blue eyes I've ever seen on a child. "Good God, she's beautiful!"

"Thank you," Vi replies with a pleased smile. "I can't take all the credit, though. This is my fiancé, Hayden."

Hayden shakes my hand. "Nice to meet you."

Vaughn's voice breaks up our introductions. "We've had a brilliant day at the beach, haven't we, Rocky Doll?" He pokes his finger into her side and she squeals with delight. "Your grandma would have loved it."

I see Gareth stiffen beside me, but Rocky's voice suddenly chimes, "Garee, swim." She wraps her little arms around her uncle's neck and basically makes me want more babies with one adorable grin. "Papa, swim!'

Gareth looks surprised. "Is she calling you *Papa* now?"

Vaughn smiles smugly. "That she is. You're not the only one she fancies, Gareth."

Vaughn laughs good-heartedly, but Gareth doesn't seem amused. "How long has that been going on?"

"A couple of weeks," Vi replies, her face appearing a little tense. "She went from repeating words to calling everyone by their names in the blink of an eye. You'd have heard it yourself if you were able to come to Sunday dinners. No worries, though! We're just glad you're feeling better and we're all together now. The boys are off on a boat excursion with the girls, but they should be back soon. We have a packed three days ahead of us."

Vaughn speaks up next, staring at both me and Gareth with a meaningful expression on his face. "I hope you're both ready for all of this. It's going to be a lot of family time. Some that I hope will allow us all to really reconnect."

His eyes settle on Gareth for a moment, and I swear Gareth looks like he's going to burst out laughing. Instead, he replies, "We'll be fine, Dad."

Vaughn nods. "It's a shame you missed out on the beach day today. It was good fun."

Gareth shakes his head like he can't wrap his mind around the image in front of him. When he's about to say something, Vi quickly steps between them, her voice shrill when she says, "Would you look at the time? We all need to get back to our rooms so I can finish prepping the dinner I'm making for all of us at our bungalow." She smiles at Gareth with wide, over-eager eyes, clearly in planning mode already. "You'll see it all on the itinerary when you check in.

You and the boys are staying here at the resort. Dad, Hayden, Rocky, and I are at an adorable stone cottage just down the beach. There's a map in your gift bag. Tonight we're having a traditional family dinner. Then tomorrow morning is the wake. After that, it's wedding day!"

Vi smiles a bit too brightly. Then I see Hayden rub a calming hand over her tight shoulders as she grabs Rocky out of Gareth's arms. "Go check in and get changed. Dinner is in two hours, and I really don't want you to be late."

The three of them and Rocky turn and make their way back outside. It's then that I notice Gareth is ten times more anxious than when we first arrived.

"Are you all right?" I ask quietly and reach out to touch his arm.

He nods, his jaw muscle ticking once before he turns to look at me. "I'm fine. I just have no idea who that man is because he certainly isn't my father."

Breaking Point

Gareth

A S AN ATHLETE, I'VE TRAVELLED THE WORLD TWENTY TIMES over. I've stayed in the best hotels, ate at fine restaurants, been given VIP status at the most lavish clubs. But I've never been on a proper family holiday. And seeing my dad wearing bloody shorts and sandals for the first time in my entire life while he carried Rocky like a doting granddad shouldn't have put me on edge, but it did. Then he referred to our mum as grandma and hugged Sloan. Hugged her! My dad isn't a hugger. He's stiff and emotionless. British. And what the fuck did he say out there? *Family time?* What in the bloody hell does that even mean?

I was quiet when Sloan and I checked into our room. My dad fucked with my head properly, so I went for a quick run on the beach when Sloan hopped into the shower to get ready for dinner. I hoped it might clear my mind and help me not be a moody sod all evening.

When I return to the room, Sloan is out on the balcony, curled up in a bathrobe with her mobile in hand. She's laughing happily and I see her daughter's face illuminating the screen. It's a private moment, so I pop into the loo and set about getting myself ready for dinner.

Twenty minutes later, I'm dressed in a pair of soft navy shorts and a white T-shirt. I see that Sloan is off the phone now and is leaning over the railing of the balcony, watching the sun set.

I inhale slowly as I get a full view of her body. Her creamy back is almost entirely exposed in a long, black and white striped beach dress. There's a single horizontal strand of ribbon tied in a bow across her shoulder blades, holding the dress closed. Other than that, I can see every beauty mark on her flesh.

The outline of her legs shows through the fabric of her dress as it blows in the wind. Her chestnut hair is wavy over her shoulders. She's any man's fantasy come to life. If I wasn't so desperate to touch her, I'd stay where I am and continue watching her like a creepy voyeur because the sight is spectacular.

I stride out onto the balcony and move past the small plunge pool to stand behind her. She turns her head when she feels my presence, but freezes when my fingertips trace along the line of her dress that rests above the swells of her arse.

"If your back looks this good, I can only imagine how the front looks," I murmur into her ear, splaying my hand flat along the flesh of her lower back and snaking my fingers inside the dress. I squeeze her hip and pull her back against me. Her entire body shudders beneath my touch. "I have so many plans for you, Treacle."

She peeks over her shoulder, her eyes gazing up at my face. "When are you going to be putting those plans into action?" Her lips remain parted, her breaths coming out quicker than normal. "That six-hour plane ride was freaking torture."

I smile a wicked smile and pull my hand out from inside her dress. "Later. Vi will kill me if we're late."

I drop a kiss to her temple, then watch her deflate and shake her head with a cheeky smile. She turns to eye me up and down. "Well, I have to say, the casual vacation look really suits you."

I quirk a brow. "I have a really great stylist I can put you in touch with."

She giggles. "How was your run?"

"Great." I move to stand beside her and prop an arm on the railing while placing one hand on the small of her back. "How is Little Minnow?"

"Little Minnow?" she asks, her brows knit together in confusion.

"Sophia," I correct with a smirk. "There's a football game we played at camp called Sharks and Minnows. All the other kids were fighting to be sharks, but not Sophia."

"That doesn't surprise me in the least," Sloan laughs, a look of pride washing over her face in response to my anecdote. "And Little Minnow is good. She had just gotten home from school, so she had to tell me about her day."

"Does she call you every day after school?"

Sloan nods. "Yes. At least, I like her to. It's nice to know she's safe since I really have no control over what she does at Callum's every other week."

"Control." I repeat the artfully chosen word with a smirk. "It's a fleeting thing sometimes, isn't it?"

"That it is," she replies, exhaling heavily. "I've noticed that the more you try to control something, the more it controls you."

My brows lift. "Perhaps it's better to let things go down their own natural path?"

"I suppose we'll see." She pulls her lip into her mouth and chews nervously. "So, should I be afraid of this dinner with your family?"

I bark out a laugh. "Yes, Sloan. You should be very, very afraid."

We make our way down the beach and find Vi's bungalow nestled amongst an array of papaya and mango trees. It smells of citrus as we walk past a natural pond situated in front of the stonewall cottage. The entire property looks like it was plucked out of an ancient holiday catalogue. That is until we walk into the three-ring circus that is the Harris family all gathered together in one place.

Tanner has Booker in a headlock in the foyer while Camden is full-on making out with his wife, Indie, against a nearby wall. Around the corner, I see Vi in the kitchen, pulling a large roasting pan out of the oven while Hayden dips his finger into something that looks like a chocolate mousse. Through the living area, Booker's girlfriend, Poppy, is propped on the couch while Tanner's wife, Belle, holds something up to her protruding belly. It's a bloody disaster zone.

"Let go of me, Tanner. I'm going to miss it!" Booker cries, his entire body bent in half as Tanner tightens his grip around his neck.

"I'll let you go as soon as you tell me your boy will be a striker and not a keeper. It's that simple!" Tanner rolls his eyes like this is the most normal conversation he's ever had.

"You're bloody mental!" Booker howls as he tries and fails to slip out of Tanner's arm.

Tanner's man bun suddenly pops up as he realises he has an audience. "Oh, hiya, guys. Don't mind us."

"No!" Booker squeals, his voice sounding almost girlie as his face turns a deep shade of purple. "Mind us, Gareth! Please, mind us. Belle is about to find my baby's heart rate with some Doppler thing she brought, and Tanner is being an exceptional brand of arsehole."

I feel Sloan trembling next to me and look over to see that she's covering her mouth to hide her laugh. She looks as if she's staring at a couple of naughty children instead of two full-grown men.

"Don't encourage them," I murmur into her ear and slip a hand around her waist to give her a warning squeeze. "Tanner," I grumble, shaking my head. "Let Booker go. You're being stupid."

"No, Gareth! It's my wife's machine. I get to call the shots."

"God, you're an idiot!" Booker bellows. "That's not how basic human decency works. Bloody hell! What if I, erm, make you the godfather?"

Tanner's eyes alight and he instantly releases Booker, who shoots up straight and rubs the angry red skin around his neck. His face is a deep shade of red and the veins in his neck are protruding angrily. "Fucking hell, you prat. We have a match on Saturday. What if you buggered up my neck?"

"Oh, stop crying, you baby," Tanner muses, stroking his beard like a creep. "This worked out for the best because the first thing I'll do as your son's godfather is teach him how to fight like a man."

"Godfather?" Camden's voice exclaims now that he's wrenched himself off of his wife and joined the scene in front of me. He drags poor Indie along behind him, and she adjusts her glasses sheepishly as she spots me and Sloan. "You can't make him the godfather before the baby is born. Can he?" Camden looks at me like I have the answer to his absurd question.

Indie grabs Cam's arm and attempts to pull him away. "Don't throw a fit over this, all right? You're going to ruin this moment for Booker."

"Specs," Camden argues with a wounded expression on his face. "Vi at least had the decency to make us all godfathers. This is total bollocks!"

Booker ignores Camden's whining and turns to me and Sloan. "It's nice to see you again, Sloan, but I really need to get over there to Poppy." Without another word, he turns on his heel and jogs into the living room, leaving me with our idiot twin brothers and Indie.

Indie shakes her head and looks at Sloan. "Who would have thought one little foetal Doppler would create such a fuss? By the way, hi. I'm Indie."

"I'm Sloan," Sloan replies with a smile and they shake hands.

"What is going on exactly?" I ask, frowning over to where I see Booker kneeling down beside Poppy, who's on the sofa.

Indie rolls her eyes. "Belle brought a foetal Doppler to keep an eye on Booker and Poppy's baby this week. Poppy isn't due for another couple of months, but she was nervous to come on the trip.

This is helping to calm her down."

"Oh, how cool," Sloan replies with a smile. "You and Belle are both doctors, right? I think Gareth mentioned that once."

Indie nods. "We met in med school, and it was love at first tequila shot."

Sloan chuckles. "That's so cute that two friends married two brothers."

"Cute or mental?" I retort and Indie laughs.

"It's cute," Camden and Tanner both growl in unison, then smile stupid smiles at each other.

Indie scoffs, "I like to claim that I met Camden before Belle met Tanner and crazy follows crazy, so I guess we're both gluttons for punishment."

"I love my wife's crazy. It's her best feature." Tanner waggles his brows suggestively at Sloan, and I give him a shove.

"Let's not act like you two didn't plan to marry brothers all along," Camden says, wrapping his arms around Indie's waist and pulling her back to his front. "You told me all about your plans for us when we got married in Scotland, Specs."

She giggles and pushes him off of her. "Planning is pointless when it comes to you and Tanner. We'd have better luck trying to herd cats."

A loud, scratchy sound suddenly erupts from the living room, so we all file in to see what's going on. Hayden and Vi give me and Sloan a quick hello as they trail behind us. Dad walks in from the back garden with Rocky on his shoulders as we all huddle around Poppy and Belle.

Dad is about to say hello, but Sloan and I are both distracted when the sound goes off again. It reminds me of a galloping horse. Sloan inhales sharply beside me, so I look over and see a knowing expression on her face.

"That, Poppy darling, is what I call a perfect heart rate," Belle states proudly from where she's at on the floor, holding something that resembles a microphone to Poppy's exposed belly.

Poppy gasps, her fingers holding the swell of her stomach. "Oh my God. This is so awesome, Belle! The fact that we can hear this whenever we want is amazing."

Poppy stares up at Booker for confirmation, and he is equally as awestruck. He remains completely silent, but I can see in his eyes that he's doing everything he can to keep calm.

Booker clears his throat and croaks, "It's really nice you can do this for us, Belle. Thank you."

Belle shoots him an easy smile. "I am a foetal surgeon, guys. This is child's play. Literally!" She laughs at her own joke as she hands the Doppler to a stunned Booker and begins teaching him how to use it.

Dad's eyes find mine. "Magical, isn't it?"

I frown. "Sure, I guess."

Sloan elbows me in the side, so I look over at her. "What?"

"Be nice," she says quietly. "It is magical."

I clench my teeth and murmur, "I agree, but I don't think I've ever heard my father use the word magical. This man is freaking me out."

She shrugs her shoulders and replies, "Maybe he's your vacation dad."

"Vacation dad?"

"Yeah, like he's more relaxed because he's away from work."

I frown over at him as he brings Rocky closer to Poppy for a listen. "He's something all right," I whisper through clenched teeth.

Once the excitement of the Doppler dies down, I introduce Sloan to the girls, who all instantly take her under their wings and steal her away to the kitchen for a glass of wine.

I watch Sloan carefully to make sure she's handling everyone okay, and she seems to be genuinely having a laugh. My brothers shoot me lewd smirks the entire time, but I ignore them. I also do my best to ignore my father, who's acting more like a dad seen on the telly, not the one I grew up with.

When dinner is ready, we move to the barbeque area outside. A long outdoor table with a fire-pit down the middle is situated on a flagstone patio. Above, there are several lanterns hanging from dragon trees that cast the space in a golden light.

"Rocky is out cold," Hayden states as he joins all of us at the table. "She's knackered after today."

Dad smiles proudly from his seat at the head of the table opposite me. "You kids were the same way. Get you a little fresh air and exercise and you'd sleep like the dead."

I frown at his remark as Vi begins passing dishes around the table. Dinner is delicious as it always is when Vi cooks. She chatters on and on about the plans for the wedding that's to take place on the beach in two days. Hayden's family is due to arrive tomorrow afternoon. It's only Hayden's parents, his sister, Daphney, and his brother, Theo, with his wife, Leslie, and their toddler, Marisa, whom Hayden is very close to.

Vi seems perfectly at ease with everything for someone who, not very long ago, was terrified of taking Hayden's name. I haven't been able to ask her if she's sticking with Harris or taking the Clarke family name yet. I don't really want to disrupt too much because she seems to be in a great mood. My hope is she already has it figured out.

There hasn't been any talk about the wake that's to happen tomorrow morning at ten o'clock according to the itinerary. It feels like an elephant in the room that everyone is ignoring. Similar to how we all acted as kids when Dad was being, well, Dad.

"I think Vi needs a hen do tomorrow night," Belle proclaims from her spot in the middle of the table between Tanner and Poppy.

Tanner replies, "If Vi gets a hen do, then Hayden gets a stag night." He waggles his brows at Camden seated across from him.

Belle swerves her dark eyes to Indie. "Tequila Sunrise night, don't you think, Indie?"

"What are you guys talking about down there?" Vi chirps, too far away to hear the conversation.

"A hen party. Just the girls. Sloan, you have to come as well. We'll teach you all about Tequila Sunrise nights," Belle states confidently.

Sloan shifts in her seat. "That is like a bachelorette party?" Sloan asks and the girls nod back enthusiastically. "Sure, I'd love to go. I've never really been to one."

"Never?" Belle asks disbelievingly.

Sloan shakes her head. "No. I mean, I got married so young right before I had my daughter, Sophia, so there wasn't really a chance for me to go to one."

"That's what babysitters are for," Belle retorts.

Sloan looks down at her plate, a tightness to her posture that wasn't there a second ago. "Sophia was a particularly difficult baby, so I never used a sitter."

Hayden is the one to speak up next. "Did she have colic? My niece, Marisa, had colic horribly. I was living with my brother and sister-in-law at the time, so I was there for all of it. Really bloody hard, but we found tricks that helped."

Sloan's cheeks flush and she sets her fork and knife down on the table. "It wasn't colic."

"Reflux?" Indie asks, her voice taking on a medical tone with just one word.

Sloan inhales deeply and looks over at me nervously. "Um… no."

"What was it then?" Belle pries, ignoring the cues that Sloan doesn't want to discuss the problem. "Was she a bad sleeper? Or perhaps gastrointestinal issues?"

Sloan anxiously chews her lip, and I frown back at her just as she replies, "Sophia was diagnosed with a type of brain cancer when she was six months old."

The entire table goes completely quiet, everyone's forks frozen midair as the weight of Sloan's words sink in fully.

Sloan winces and looks away from my hard stare. She splays her hands out on top of the table, a trembling in them that is visible only to me. "She's healthy now. Cancer-free by the time she was three years old. She's almost eight now, so her five-year milestone is coming up, which is a very big deal."

"What kind of cancer was it?" Indie asks and Belle leans in with sharp eyes, laser focused on Sloan.

Sloan begins discussing the particulars of Sophia's diagnosis and how they didn't know her issues as a newborn were symptoms of a much greater problem. When she tells us about the first seizure Sophia had in her crib at only six months old, my hands begin to tingle around the napkin I'm gripping like a vise.

Part of me is frustrated that I'm finding this information out for the first time along with my entire family. I thought Sloan and I had moved past the secrets and the boundaries. Granted, I know that I haven't officially met Sophia in any formal capacity. Sloan has to be wary of introducing her daughter to the men in her life, so I understand that. But I'm aware of Sophia's existence now, and *this* is a huge part of Sloan's life that is significant enough to share. The fact that she didn't tell me makes me wonder how much has actually changed between us.

But the bigger, more mature part of my mind knows that it's very typical for the Harris family to flush out personal details of one's life before a person is ready to share them. Even my brothers' wives seem to be hardwired with that "no secrets" rule of thumb when it comes to people they are curious about. They were like that with me when I first told them about Sloan, and right now they are hitting her with a Harris Mental Shakedown that no one can protect themselves from.

"Sophia spent her infancy and toddler years in and out of hospitals and doctor appointments. I didn't work because I was taking care of her and advocating for her health. I always said I got a medical degree from Google, which I know doctors hate." She laughs a nervous laugh as everyone at the table listens intently. "But we've been good for a long time now. Honestly, all that knowledge I used to have feels like it's from another lifetime."

Vi shakes her head. "That had to be so difficult, Sloan. I'm so sorry you endured that pain. I can't imagine Rocky being that sick. It would kill me. Completely kill me." Vi's voice cracks at the end, and Hayden grabs her hand tightly in his.

Sloan nods sympathetically. "I know it sounds bad and impossible—and believe me, it was—but you don't know your own strength until you're forced to use it. I'm sure any of you in my position would have been just as strong. Now, Sophia is healthy, and girlie, and silly, and begging me to let her play soccer. It's a big battle between us right now because I'm still so protective over her health."

An image of Sloan rushing out on to the football pitch plays in my mind, and it makes so much more sense now. Her hysteria, her fierceness, her unforgiving attitude toward her ex. At the time, I was so focused on the fact she had a child, I didn't really take note of how concerned she was for her daughter's safety.

"I can only imagine," Vi agrees. "If Rocky was ever ill like that, I'd probably homeschool her because I'd never want her out of my sight."

"Oh, I wanted to," Sloan replies with a laugh. "But when my ex-husband moved us to Manchester a few years ago, he was insistent that Sophia attend the same schools he did."

My brothers nod politely, a sense of wariness over the mention of her ex.

"But Sophia is doing great in school, and she keeps reminding me she's not a baby anymore. I live in the past too much, so it's hard to see sometimes. It causes me some serious control issues." Sloan laughs and shakes her head.

Belle's voice is firm when she chimes in next. "You have control issues because you are the mother of a survivor. Don't feel bad about that. I operate on babies in the womb. I see parents lose their children, and that's not how life is supposed to be. Children should bury their parents, not the other way around. You wear your control issues with pride because you still have your Sophia. You're an inspiring mother, Sloan. Truly."

Out of the corner of my eye, I see a teardrop fall down Sloan's face before she wipes it away quickly. "I don't feel very inspiring. I feel neurotic most days," she utters through a garbled laugh.

"You're not," I state, my tone fierce and unrelenting as I finally feel compelled to break my silence. Sloan looks over at me with wide, tear-filled eyes. Eyes that reach out and grab my throat, making it ache with the need to soothe and take away the pain she has suffered alone. But I can't change the past. I can only control the present. "Don't feel bad for caring deeply about your child. We should all be so lucky."

Sloan's chest quakes and she husks out a quiet, "Thank you," so only I can hear it.

As if my family can tell we need a minute to collect ourselves, they break away from our conversation and begin talking to each other.

Sloan leans in close to me, her voice trembling when she croaks, "I was going to tell you all of this, I swear."

I shake my head to silence her. "It's fine, Sloan."

She reaches out and grips my fisted hand that's resting on top of the table. "It's not fine. I'm so sorry you had to find out like this, Gareth, and I need you to know that I was going to tell you everything. But after the attack, there was never a good time. I was still coming to grips with the fact that you care about me after everything I hid from you."

Her eyes cast down with shame and anguish. I hate it. It reminds me of the person she was after Callum. Not the person she turned into with me or the woman who ripped her daughter off a football pitch in front of a slew of people. The pain in her body language has me desperate to pull her onto my lap and kiss away all her worries.

Every last thought, until it's only me and her in this moment. But it's not about us right now.

I lift her hand up and press it to my cheek so I can kiss the inside of her palm. "Don't apologise for this, Sloan. This is bigger than both of us. I'm just glad Sophia is okay, and I'm sorry I pushed you to come here. Had I known—"

"Don't be sorry," she cuts me off and runs her thumb along the scruff of my jaw. "I needed to be reminded I have a parachute on and it's okay to take some risks now and again."

She smiles and, fuck me, now I really want to kiss her. Take her away from this dinner and thank her for trusting so much of herself with not only me, but my entire family. Instead, I lean across the table, press a gentle kiss on her forehead, and murmur, "Thank you for being here."

I pull back and she smiles a small smile meant only for me, and our eye contact says so much more than words ever could.

We return to the conversation at the table that's a great deal lighter now, but I see my father watching us intently. His eyes are narrowed and his mouth is tight, like he's holding something back.

"Are you okay, Dad?" Vi asks, eyeing him cautiously from her seat right beside him.

"I'm fine. Just fine." He forces a smile, then slides his gaze to Sloan again. "I'm just having a lot of flashbacks after hearing everything about Sloan's daughter. What did you say her name is again?"

Sloan clears her throat and replies timidly, "Sophia."

He smiles. "A beautiful name. I'm so glad she's doing well now. I'd really love to meet her someday."

My head pulls back from his comment. If anyone will be meeting Sophia in any capacity, it will be me. Not him.

"I remember when Vilma was sick," he continues, his eyes still thoughtful on Sloan. "It's very hard to watch a loved one suffer like that, isn't it?"

Sloan's eyes flash over to me, but she turns a polite smile back to my dad. "Yes, it really is."

"They can seem so helpless. So tortured. And you have to watch them hurt. It's dreadful, isn't it? Doesn't seem fair."

My entire body is stiff. My posture ramrod straight. What the fuck does my dad know about my mother's suffering?

"Well, I'm certainly one of the lucky ones," Sloan answers, shifting nervously in her seat. "So many other moms that I met in the hospital had a much more difficult journey."

Dad nods heavily. "Was your husband helpful through it all?"

Instantly, I place a reassuring hand on Sloan's back and whisper in her ear, "Don't fucking answer that."

"It's all right," she soothes, looking over at me with wide, haunted eyes before turning back to my dad. "My husband was a very busy man. My family helped when they could, but it was mostly just me taking care of Sophia. As hard as it was, I think we're even closer now as a result."

Dad has a proud sort of smile spread across his face that has my hands clenching into fists. "That's a wonderful silver lining then. Vilma was always such a strong advocate of our family being close. She used to say that if we didn't know the size of all our children's feet, we weren't paying enough attention to one another."

"She did?" Booker asks, his voice high and curious like he's latching onto this memory of Mum and keeping it all for himself.

I'm actually gutted by his reaction. I can tell him so many more memories about Mum if he really needs them. Real, tangible memories that are hidden deep within me. I just never realised he wanted them so much.

Dad nods his confirmation. "I saw a quote once that an individual doesn't get cancer, a family does. And I completely agree. It's best when family rallies around each other to overcome an obstacle like that. And even though our Vilma didn't live through her fight, she would be so happy we're all here together like this, celebrating her life on a holiday."

Vi smiles a wobbly, relieved smile and tears begin slipping from her eyes. Suddenly, Dad reaches over and pulls her into a side hug. I notice the twins also seem touched by our father's words. I feel as though I've entered some sort of dinner theatre that everyone forgot to tell me about.

Is our father forgetting the piles and piles of awful moments that happened leading up to her death? Has he blocked those out? Am I truly the only one who remembers the way he picked fights with our mother time and time again? About how he made her cry, then left the room in a huff? I still remember the time he left her on the floor in the shower because she said something he didn't like. He broke our mother's heart over and over. And now everyone is hanging on his every word? What the actual fuck?

Dad settles Vi back in her chair, then stands up. He makes his way down the table, directly toward Sloan. My brothers swerve their eyes to me, then to Vi, wondering what the hell is going on. I wish I fucking knew.

Without a word, he moves past me and reaches out for Sloan's hand. She takes it as he pulls her up out of the chair and…

…hugs her.

He presses her head to his shoulder and hugs her like a father would embrace his daughter.

What the ever-loving fuck is going on?

I hear him whisper into Sloan's ear, "If there is anything you ever need, we are here for you."

Sloan's trembling in his arms, obviously overwhelmed with emotions. It only aggravates me further, especially when I look around the table and see everyone's reaction. They are staring up at him like he is God and they are prepared to follow him blindly. Never mind that he flooded the earth or sent plagues to entire nations. Never mind that he made his son die on a cross. Right now, he's having a revelation and we should all bask in the glory that is his name.

He pulls away and holds Sloan's face in his hands. "Unfortunately, we are experienced in painful pasts, so we are well equipped to be there for you in any way you need."

"What the fuck?" I grind out between clenched teeth, unable to contain my silence a second longer.

Dad and Sloan both turn to look down at me. Sloan's eyes are wide and wary. Dad's are innocent and confused when he asks, "What did you say, Gareth?"

I narrow my gaze at him with a slow, menacing shake of my head. "If you're a bloody expert on painful pasts, then we're all fucked."

"What do you mean?" he asks, his hands releasing Sloan as she sits back down in her chair and removes herself from the line of fire.

I stand up, splaying my hands out on the table so I'm eye level with my father. "If you're going to treat Sloan during hard times the way you treated Mum—the supposed love of your life—then I think she's better off on her own."

Dad's brows lift in challenge, his warm, loving eyes from earlier replaced with a cold, calculating stare. "I assure you, your mother was the love of my life. There's no doubt about that."

I bark out an annoyed laugh and shake my head. "And now we're all supposed to let you talk about those days like they were completely normal? Let you recite uplifting phrases about cancer and life lessons like you've learned so much?"

"Gareth," Vi states my name in warning, looking at me with pleading eyes. She's begging me to stop, but I can't stand this anymore. I cannot.

Dad replies slowly, "I never said I'm an expert, but I think I know a thing or two about enduring hardship."

"You know sod all about enduring anything. You buried your head in the sand the entire time!" I push back from the table and begin pacing as I take in the faces of my siblings, who all look shocked and afraid. They're the same faces they had when they were little and Dad yelled at them because he didn't know what to do with his grief. The same faces I tried to hide from him so he couldn't hurt them the way he hurt me on a regular basis.

I point an accusing finger at all of them. "You're all hanging on his every word because you think what we lived through was normal. But that's only because none of you remember what it was like when Mum was alive. I remember those days all too well, and they were a million fucking times better than the life we had."

"Gareth," Booker says softly, shooting me those eyes of his that I can so easily picture on him as a toddler, asking me for a snack, or a toy, or a drink, or a nappy change. "It wasn't all bad."

"Do you know who changed your nappies after Mum died, Booker?" I ask, propping my hands on my hips as I await his answer.

He tugs on his earlobe and shakes his head.

"Vi did," I reply, then move my eyes to Camden and Tanner. "Ask Vi how old she was when she was changing her baby brother's nappies."

"Stop, Gareth," Camden begs softly, his eyes downcast as Indie reaches over and takes hold of his hand.

"She was four. Fucking four years old and barely strong enough to hold Booker in her arms let alone wipe his arse. And I was busy chasing you twins around the garden so you wouldn't get too close to Dad and get us all in trouble, because all we had to do was look at Dad to piss him off back then."

"Come now, Gareth," Dad retorts. "Surely you can see I needed time."

"Well, you got it! Years of it!" I exclaim, moving in toward him so we're eye-to-eye. He winces at the volume of my voice but holds his ground. "Your grief started before Mum was even fucking dead, and none of them have a problem with it because they don't remember how good it was before. Family *was* the most important thing as long as Mum was healthy."

Dad exhales heavily and pins me with a pained stare. "Gareth,

I'm sorry for my struggles with your mother's illness, but that's all in the past and I'd like to forget about it."

"I can't!" I cry out and jerk away from him like he's just struck me with his fist across my face.

Vi leans forward in her chair, her eyes hurt and full of tears, but she's frozen in place just like everyone else. I can feel my brothers reaching out to me with their minds, but they are unsure of what to do when solid, big brother Gareth has a fucking meltdown for a change.

I fork my hands through my hair, an ache radiating in my chest as I add, "Don't you think I want nothing more than to forget how horrible you were to her? I do my best to forget about it every Sunday night because I get to hop back on a train and keep my distance. But now you want to come on this holiday and play happy family, and talk about Mum, and pretend that neglect and abuse never happened. That's complete rubbish and you know it."

"Gareth, that's enough!" he roars, his eyes turning back into the harsh robot I'm far more familiar with.

"Dad, stop," Tanner states in a deep, warning tone as he stands up and splays his hands out on the table. Belle stares up at him, surprised by this very rare display of gravity from Tanner. "If Gareth has something to say, I think we owe it to him to listen."

Camden and Booker stand up in unison and Vi rises to her feet a few seconds later. All four of my siblings are now staring down our father with a united strength against him I've never truly seen before.

Pride.

Fucking magnanimous pride ripples through my entire body from their display of loyalty to me.

But it's tainted because, even as they attempt to unite against him for me, I can see that they still love him. My siblings whom I raised love Dad unconditionally. Will that ever not hurt?

"I've said all I need to say," I state and make a move to leave but stop myself to add one more very important thing. Perhaps the most important thing of all. "But, Dad, don't you worry about Sloan. She's strong as fuck and can do what she needs to do on her own. But you can guarantee that if she does need someone, I will drop everything and be there for her just like I was for Mum and just like I am for them."

I point to my siblings and feel their eyes watching me with fear over what I might do next. And for a brief second, I feel myself turning into my father. Overbearing, intimidating, unrelenting. The same angry, resentful, monster he was for so many years.

But I can't pretend this is all okay and normal. I refuse to watch him hold the woman I care about in his arms, as well as the family I've spent my entire life protecting, and act like he knows how to be there for them.

He doesn't.

I do.

I always have.

Crash Into Me

Sloan

"**G**ARETH!" I SHOUT DOWN THE BEACH, MY VOICE MUTED BY the waves crashing onto the shore.

A flash of lightning flickers off in the distance, lighting up the sky and Gareth's silhouette. He's standing a ways down the shore, waves lapping up toward his feet, his head bowed.

I pause to pull off my flip-flops and lift my dress to jog toward him. My heart thunders in my chest over everything that was said at dinner. All the pain from Gareth's past rearing its head was horrible enough, but what he said about me? That proclamation of protection—that promise to be there for me—is overwhelming. With only a few words, I went from wanting to see how this week goes to *needing* to be the person in Gareth's life. This isn't casual anymore. Never mind the media, and the fame, and the fear. Gareth is not the kind of man you run from. He's the kind you chase.

I yell his name again and the wind finally carries my voice to him. His head snaps in my direction. A storm brews in the distance, perfectly matching the storm in his eyes as he turns on his heel to face me.

"I'm sorry, Sloan," he states sadly, pursing his lips together as I stand in front of him and fight to catch my breath. "I had to get out of there before I ripped someone's fucking head off."

I drop my sandals and reach out to touch his hand that's stuffed inside his pocket, but he pulls away. "Gareth, it's okay. I'm just worried about you."

"I'm fucking worried about me, too." He inhales deeply and kicks at the wet sand beneath our feet, his hands remaining firm in his pockets. "I thought I'd be fine on this trip with him. I mean, hell, I've been biting my tongue for years. I should be used to the taste of blood by now. But after everything he said at your house, then at Christmas and dinner tonight, it became too much for me to handle."

"What do you want him to say?" I ask, releasing the bottom of my dress and letting the fabric whip around my legs in the wind. A chill runs up my spine from the cold front moving in, so I cross my arms to rub my shoulders. "It seems like he's being more open and trying to at least talk about the past. That's good, isn't it?"

"But he's not talking about the right parts," Gareth states, looking up at me with a shake of his head.

"What are the right parts?"

He chomps down on his lower lip and his eyes narrow as he stares up at the sky. "The parts that are burned into my brain for the rest of my fucking life."

His gaze finds mine again, the moonlight and water reflecting in his eyes.

"Gareth—"

"It's not bloody fair! He gets to walk Vi down the aisle and play happy grandpa with Rocky like a normal dad or grandfather, or whatever the fuck he is now. Great for him. But why now? Why after I have done all the work? Why, after I've sacrificed my entire fucking youth for our family, does he get to come in and take all the glory? We don't need him anymore! Everyone's happy. Everyone's married, or getting married, or having children. Everyone's settled. Well, except me. I'm too fucked-up to figure my own fucking life out."

"You're not fucked-up!" I exclaim, my hands balling into fists from the anger that courses through me over him speaking about himself this way.

"I told you I was there when my fucking mum died, Sloan," he states, taking a step closer to me as he pounds his chest. "The second she took her last breath, I felt it beneath my cheek like needles pricking all over my body. You don't think that's going to fuck a kid up for life? It has. I can't forget that sensation. That moment. That touch. I had to be so brave those last few months she was alive because my father couldn't be. I was only a bit older than Sophia, and I was the only one there to comfort her. Can you imagine that responsibility for your daughter?"

"No," I croak with a small cry, my voice trembling with complete fear over the thought of it.

"When my mother was in pain, I let her squeeze my hand," he states, holding his palm out to me for proof. "And it wasn't always just physical pain. It was emotional, too. My father broke her heart and she still loved him through it just like my siblings still love him unconditionally now. I can't wrap my head around it."

"Neither can I," I reply honestly, his face blurring from the tears in my eyes.

"That's why I can't stomach the fact that he's calling her the love of his life and speaking openly about her again. It's too much. She's mine now, you know? Not his. She was my best friend, and he lost the right to talk about her the second he chose to be angry at her for dying." He leans over and braces his hands on his knees, the pain overtaking his entire body.

"Gareth, I'm so sorry." I make a move to hold him, but he straightens quickly and backs away from me again.

"I used to try to shove him out the door when he was yelling at her, but he was too big and too strong. It was like pushing a wall." Gareth's hands shake in front of him as he demonstrates the act.

"Gareth," I croak, tears falling down my cheeks. I can hardly bear to hear any more.

"I have nightmares about that weak feeling. About screaming at him with no sound coming out. About pushing him but him never budging. He always made me feel so powerless. That's why I fucking craved control in everything else in my life. Until..." He shakes his head and swallows hard, not wanting to finish his last thought.

"Until what?" I urge because whatever it is must be important.

His hazel eyes find mine and pin me with a fierce, terrifying look. "Until you."

My breath catches in my throat, a knot forming that's so big, I don't know how I'm still upright and breathing. My voice is a whisper when I ask, "What do you mean?"

He stares back at me with so much intensity, so much certainty, so much passion. "It was you, Sloan. You changed my entire thought process. Surrendering to you gave me a freedom that I'd never felt before. I've never experienced trust like that with anyone. Not even my siblings. I haven't trusted them with memories of our mum. I haven't trusted that they could handle their own problems. I've always just *controlled* them. But there's something about you that fucking frees me, but the freedom terrifies me."

My mind reels from his declaration, the emotions in my body crashing on top of each other like the waves on the shore. "Why are you scared?"

"Because if I try to control you, you might bolt."

"Why do you say that?"

"You ran once, Sloan."

"I came back," I state firmly, grabbing his face in my hands and not caring that he's wincing under my touch.

"But for how long?" He looks down, shaking his head like he doesn't know how to accept what's right in front of him. Like he doesn't know how to accept me anymore. "You're strong on your own and you have Sophia. My brothers have their partners. Vi has Hayden and Rocky. I have no one."

He pulls back from my grasp and tips his face up toward the sky.

"You have me," I say softly, letting the feeling of his earlier words take life inside of me. Recalling the words he stated about being proud of me for protecting Sophia on the soccer field. Remembering all the times he helped me feel strong when I was crumbling on the inside. He has me, body and soul. I just need to prove it to him.

"Look at me, Gareth. Now," I demand. His eyes snap open in response to the firm tone that I've used on him countless times. "You have me."

With a deep breath, I take a slow step back from him and, without breaking eye contact, I lower to my knees and splay my hands out on my thighs.

"What are you doing, Sloan?" he croaks, a deep husk of need in his voice that causes my thighs to squeeze.

"You have me, Gareth." I pin him with a look that forces him to hear me.

"Treacle," he states, his tense posture dropping as he lowers to his knees and cups my face in his hands. With a pleading expression on his face, he continues, "This isn't what I need from you right now."

"Yes, it is."

"I just told you it was your control that gave my mind rest," he argues, gently stroking my face and apologising over and over with the look in his eyes.

I shake my head. "Trust works both ways, Gareth. You don't only get to feel free by surrendering. You can feel free by dominating. Let me help you feel strong the same way you helped me feel strong."

He sucks in a sharp, shaky breath, his eyes glossy with tears. "I don't know if I can anymore. My mind is so fucked right now."

I have to stifle a growl of frustration because I hate this so much. I hate that he thinks he's broken. I hate that he thinks he can lose his family. Doesn't he see the way they look to him for approval in all things? Doesn't he see how much they all care about him?

Doesn't he see how much I care?

Suddenly, a drop of water hits my cheek. I frown and gaze up at the sky for confirmation just as it begins pouring down over us. It's a cold, electrifying rain that zaps every one of my senses. It feels almost like a cleansing. Like a sign for a fresh start and a new beginning.

I look back at Gareth, whose smouldering gaze is boring straight through me. Squinting through the rain, I push a couple of wet strands off my face and plead with him one more time. "Jump out of the plane *with* me, Gareth. You don't need to catch me when we can fly together."

With a flash of lightning and a crack of thunder, we collide into each other. Both moving in at the same time, so it's a perfect, symmetrical give and take of contact as our mouths connect. Gareth's hands grab tightly under my legs as he spreads them and lifts me up onto his lap. He leans back, pulling his lips away as I wrap myself around him, my hands hooked behind his neck. Slowly, he brushes back the hair that's covering my eye as he takes in every inch of my face. A deep shiver runs up my spine that has nothing to do with the rain and everything to do with the look in Gareth's eyes.

His gaze drops to my lips and he covers my mouth with his, a groan rattling through his entire chest as he holds my face where he wants me. His tongue demands entry, so I part my lips and welcome him gladly. He tastes of rain, and sea, and pure man. I arch into him and rock myself on his lap, desperate to feel him inside of me.

It's been weeks since our shower together at my house. He was concussed then, so we couldn't do all that we desired. But feeling his firmness nudging at my opening, I can tell he has recovered one hundred percent. Maybe he's ready to claim me like he promised once before.

"Gareth," I sigh, scooping my hips up into him and relishing in the feeling of his rough palms on my bare back. "I want this."

"Me too, Sloan."

"Treacle," I correct, dragging my tongue down his neck.

Suddenly, he pulls back and grabs my face, pinning me with a harsh look in his eyes. "Sloan," he repeats. "I'm calling you Sloan. And I'm taking you inside before I fuck you here in the rain."

I pull my lip into my mouth and nod. "Whatever you say, boss."

A tiny flicker of a smile ripples over his face, but it's gone just as quickly as it came. Without another word, he stands up, tucks me under his arm, and hurries me back toward the resort.

It's quite a trek in the wet sand and rain. By the time we get back to our suite, we're completely soaked to the bone. When the door clicks shut, it's like an audible warning for what's to come. Gareth's heat moves in close behind me, his warmth radiating like a furnace all over my exposed skin.

Slowly, he walks around to face me, and I cast my eyes downward as a sign of respect. To show him I'm taking this moment seriously.

True BDSM is never really what Gareth and I had together. We were a simple power exchange. But tonight, I'm hoping to explore new territory with him because we are changed. We are more. And I want to go all in because the thrill coursing through my veins is unlike anything I've ever felt before.

Gareth lifts my chin so I'm forced to look at him. "You're so beautiful," he husks, his eyes raking up and down my body like every inch belongs to him.

I smirk and reply, "I probably look like a wet rat right now."

"You look beautiful." He leans in and drops a kiss on my shoulder. "Messy and perfect."

His hand slides around me to grab the ribbon tie on my dress. With a tug, he undoes the bow and the shoulders of my dress instantly fall down to my elbows, exposing my bare breasts.

Biting his lower lip, he slowly peruses my chest before bringing his hands up and testing the weight of them in his palms. "Still the most beautiful body I've ever seen," he murmurs, dipping his head down and wrapping his lips around my nipple.

"Gareth," I cry out as one hand slices through his hair and the other grasps his shoulder for balance as he sucks hard on my nub. I silently beg for him to slip his fingers lower, into my damp panties so I can feel him inside of me. Feel the pressure of his hands on me. I'm dying for the sensation.

He pauses his assault on my breast and moves to the other. But before he gives equal attention to that nipple, he states in a deep, guttural voice, "You know what's more beautiful than dominance and submission, Sloan?"

I'm two seconds away from shoving my nipple into his mouth because I'm aching for the symmetry, but I manage to husk out a garbled, "What?"

"No boundaries at all." He straightens to stare deep into my eyes. The wicked promise in his has my entire body trembling. He licks his lips and adds, "Someday, I will claim you and do things that will have you begging for mercy. But right now, Sloan Montgomery... Right now..." He leans in to brush his lips against the corner of my mouth and whispers, "I'm going to make love to you."

My legs instantly give out from under me as he sweeps me up into his arms and carries me over to the giant, white, fluffy bed. He pulls the covers back and lays me on the cool sheets. His eyes remain locked on mine as he proceeds to remove the rest of my clothing, along with his own so we're both completely naked.

Now, here we lie, flesh on flesh, hearts on hearts, souls on souls. It's the most intimate I've ever been with a man in my life. Even when Callum and I were together, it never felt anything like this. I didn't know it could feel like this. So…close.

Gareth kisses me as he holds himself over top of me to gently part my legs. He kisses me as he slides his fingers down my ribs. He kisses me as he caresses my entrance. He kisses me as he nudges his bare tip inside of me, inch by perfect inch. When he pushes into me as deep as my tense body will allow, my head lifts off the pillow. My hands clutch so tightly around his neck and my legs squeeze so fiercely along his hips that he knows I need more.

That's when he begins the thrusting. The slow, calculated, rhythmic, and oh-so wonderful thrusting.

But it's not the skilled movement of his cock inside of me that has me coming apart at the seams. It's what he says with each stroke.

"This isn't temporary, Sloan." *Thrust.* "This can be us." *Thrust.* "We can be more." *Thrust.* "We aren't just one thing." *Thrust.*

"You're my Treacle and my Sloan."

Thrust.

"You're mine."

Thrust.

"Mine, mine, mine."

Thrust, thrust, thrust.

Gareth Harris makes love to me like only a man who loves a woman could. I clutch his body to mine, stare into his eyes, and accept his gloriously perfect words. And I wonder to myself when the hell I started falling for him, because there is no way this emotion inside of me is new. This is something that's been with me for some time now. It's familiar and comfortable.

It's a sensation that feels like home…

…A place I haven't been in years.

Okay

Gareth

SLOAN'S ENTIRE BODY DRAPED NAKED OVER TOP OF ME IS A sensation I never imagined I'd enjoy so much. She's light but long, so it's an even distribution of weight. Comforting in many ways.

It's odd because, when I think back to a year ago, there were so many textures that bothered me. So many things I avoided because of my tactile defensiveness that Sloan aptly diagnosed the first time we ever met. But the closer I've grown to Sloan—the more she's around me—the less I notice those issues.

Life is funny like that.

The morning sunlight streams in through the windows of our suite. My fingertips trace the length of her spine as I drop a kiss in her hair. *God, she always smells so fucking good.* The sweet scent that I hated the first time I met her has become something I crave.

She is the only reason I'm not waking up with a sense of dread after everything that happened last night with my family. If it weren't for Sloan, I probably would have been on a flight back home, back to Manchester, and back to the reclusive life I lived for over a decade.

But she stabilised me last night. She held me together and made me strong, just as I did for her the first time we slept together.

Sloan begins to stir on top of me when a knock sounds off on the door. My father's muffled voice follows.

"Gareth, it's me. I need to speak to you."

Sloan's head shoots up, her sleepy eyes wide and surprised on mine that are aimed down at her. With a smile, I push her hair back from her face and run my finger along the sleep creases on her cheek. "It's just my dad. I'll go deal with him. You sleep."

She shakes her head and blinks rapidly, trying to wake all of her senses. "No, no. I'll get up and leave so you guys can talk in private," she croaks and moves to scramble off of me.

In one quick shot, I wrap my hand around her leg and roll us so she's beneath me. Her legs naturally wrap around my hips as I use one hand to pin her wrists together above her head. My other hand squeezes her leg, my fingertips venturing near the crease of her arse.

Her golden eyes dart up at me with a dazed look of confusion. "Gareth, what are you doing?"

I drop a kiss on her neck and slide my free hand up to squeeze her arse cheek. "I said stay, Treacle."

She bucks lightly beneath me as I blow warm air over the part of her neck I just kissed. Her voice is breathy when she replies, "Don't you need to talk to your dad?"

"Yes and I'm commanding you to stay in this bed while I do." I tighten my grip around her wrists and press myself deep into her centre. A low moan escapes my lips when I feel the dampness of her along my bare shaft. "Fucking hell, Sloan. You're wet already?"

I watch her bite her lip and shake her head. "God, this is embarrassing with your dad right outside. At least let me put some clothes on."

"No," I growl as my erection grows harder by the second from holding her beneath me like this. It's a heady feeling to have her completely at my mercy. And knowing she's wet and wanting makes it really hard to not just thrust into her right here and now.

I take a deep breath and lift my head to look up at her. "You will stay naked and waiting in this bed until I get back or I will spank you for not following instructions, Tre. Understood?"

A small smile spreads over her face, and she quickly bites her lip to try to hide it. "Understood."

I grin and move in to pull her lower lip out from between her teeth and suck it into my mouth. I release it with a satisfying *pop* and add, "Good girl. I'll be back as quick as I can."

I throw myself off the bed and yell toward the door, "I'll be out in five."

After an ice-cold shower and a few minutes of mental preparation, I open the door to find my father propped against the opposite wall. He's dressed in a pair of tan trousers and a white dress shirt, clearly ready for the wake that's happening in a couple hours.

His steely eyes look me up and down, taking in my athletic shorts and wet hair. "Did I wake you?"

I nod and run a hand through my hair. "It's fine."

"I'm sorry. I thought you would have been out running hours ago."

"I said it's fine," I reply, ignoring his dig about my workout regime that he can't stop himself from slipping in there. Always the manager first, father second.

"I wanted to talk before the ceremony."

He steps back as I close the door behind me. "Let's go outside. Sloan is still in bed."

I see a flicker of interest in his expression at the mention of Sloan. "You two seem to be getting on well."

"We are," I reply with no emotion so he can tell it isn't a subject I'm wanting to discuss.

We make our way outside to a table and chairs by the pool. It's early, so there's only one small family out in the water as we settle in a couple of plastic seats under a white tent. Both of us face the pool with our elbows braced on our knees.

After a long pause, my father finally says, "Gareth, last night was—"

"A fucking mess," I finish.

"Yes," he agrees, looking down and rubbing his hands together nervously. "A lot of things were said."

I nod stiffly, my jaw clenched. If he thinks I'm taking them back, he has another thing coming. "They were all true."

He grimaces and runs a nervous hand through his hair. "I know they were. But, to be honest, I've buried a lot of those memories. They feel like they were from another lifetime. Another person even."

"Not for me," I reply, cutting him a severe look.

"I know," he replies with a sigh. "And now I understand why you wouldn't talk to me about moving back to London. I never realised how much you truly hate me."

His words bring me up short. "I don't hate you."

He turns his weathered eyes to me, pain and confusion all over his face. "You don't?"

"No," I reply with a scoff. "I'm just angry at you."

His face softens. "But can't you see I'm trying to make up for the past?"

"Dad, you can host all the Sunday dinners in the world, change all of Rocky's nappies, and hug complete strangers if you'd like. But acting like the past never happened is a fucking slap in the face after everything Vi and I did."

"Gareth," Dad groans, his head bowed in shame. "I don't mean it to be. I'm just trying to survive."

"So am I!" I exclaim, my muscles tensing all over my body. "And I was just trying to survive when we were kids, too. Most nine-year-old boys are out playing footy with their friends, not potty-training their twin brothers. Most male teenagers I knew had loads of girl-friends. I never had one because I was too terrified to bring any-one around you, not to mention I never had time for dating because I was too busy taking care of everyone. You weren't even remote-ly normal again until you started working for Bethnal. Then it was suddenly business as usual! Do you have any idea how that felt to a young boy who had been trying to make you happy for years?"

Dad winces at my last comment and shakes his head as if he can't bring himself to reply, so I reply for him. "It felt like nothing I did was ever good enough. No matter how hard Vi and I tried, nothing pulled you out of that darkness. Only football. Then you went on and on last night about the importance of family. Where was that man when we were kids? The man we grew up with didn't give a toss about family. He only cared about football!"

"I've changed, Gareth," he pleads, turning to face me with an urgent expression on his face, all the veins in his neck protruding as he attempts to hold himself together. "Please tell me you can see that I've changed."

"Of course I can see. Bloody hell, you're wearing sandals for Christ's sake," I reply flippantly and sit back in my chair, crossing my arms over my chest.

He watches me carefully for a minute, unamused by my remark, but I don't care. He doesn't deserve much better.

Running a hand through his hair, he composes himself before replying, "Gareth, when you were attacked..." He pauses, his voice catching in his throat as he looks away. "When Vi called me crying so hard that she couldn't speak, I thought I lost you."

The pain in his expression unnerves me as I watch him shift in his chair, directing his focus at the family swimming instead of me.

"And I thought to myself, *It's happened again. I've hurt and lost the one person I owe my life to...*Just like when I lost your mother." His voice breaks and his face contorts as he fights back the feelings boiling up inside of him. "I swore a long time ago I'd never return to Manchester because it holds too many tender memories for me, but I didn't want to abandon you the way I did your mother. I was certain if I could get up there and just get you home, everything would be okay. It wasn't until Sloan shouted at me that I even truly realised what I was trying to do."

Emotion swells in my chest at his mention of how she stood up to him for me that day. "She's not an easy one to fight off," I reply.

"I can see that, and now I can say I'm grateful for it because Lord only knows what could have happened to you if I had gotten you down to London. I wasn't seeing things clearly, but I could see that she was there beside you the way I should have been beside your mother. And seeing you two together like that was a wake-up call, Gareth. That's why I'm trying so hard right now. I want to be the man your mother fell in love with. The man I was when you were little and she used to bring you to the football pitch to watch me practice...Do you remember any of the good times, Gareth? Or have I spoiled all your memories?"

I stiffen as images flood my mind that I've been trying to keep away for years. "I remember some."

His face brightens. "I remember the day you were born. I had no idea the best adventure of my life would be making a family with your mother, and for years it was only you, me, and her. You two travelled with me to all my matches. It was brilliant. I loved parading you in front of my teammates and bragging about how you were going to put all their stats to shame someday. Your mother and I had so many dreams for you, Gareth. So many hopes.

"But when she got sick, I lost all hope. I lost myself. My body didn't know how to function without her. We were always a partnership. Fifty-fifty. But the moment she became ill was the moment I felt half of myself disappear. I couldn't even look in the mirror because I didn't want to see what I was without her. I hated her for leaving me, and I hated myself for hating her. It was a sick cycle I couldn't escape."

My heart pounds hard and heavy in my chest over his words. Words that I can actually sympathise with, which is an odd feeling for someone who's dedicated his entire life to outdoing the person speaking.

My voice is hoarse when I reply, "I wish you would have talked to me, Dad. You've never acknowledged any of this. You just fucking disappeared. I was a kid and we needed you. We needed help."

His face twists in pain and he nods stiffly. "You're right. I know you're right. But your mother was so independent. She never wanted to live like we had a lot of money, and she wouldn't dream of hiring a nanny. Not even when the twins were born and you know how wild those two were.

"I thought I was doing the right thing by refusing help. The Harris family only needed each other, you know? We were like a self-sustaining island. That's why I was so upset when you signed with Man U and moved away. You abandoned the island and I hated it. It's also why I pushed the twins and Booker to continue living at home and let me manage their careers so tightly. And why I bought Vi a flat in East London. I could see her getting restless, and I didn't want her to move as far away as you did. I didn't want to lose any more of my family."

I shift uncomfortably as I think back to how angry my father was when I told him I signed with Man U without his consent. It was one of our worst fights to date. The only fight he ever put his hands on me. I thought it was because he didn't want to lose me on his team. I never imagined it was because he wanted to keep me close.

"I honestly don't know what to say," I admit with a heavy sigh. "For years now, I've been trying to do better than you. Be a better father figure, a better footballer, a better person."

Dad's eyes turn red around the edges. "Gareth, you don't have to try. You've already achieved those goals. The incredible family we have is all because of you. You and Vi. We wouldn't be here if it wasn't for you, son."

"I don't know if I believe that," I scoff disbelievingly.

Dad turns and reaches out to put a hand on my shoulder. My knee-jerk reaction is to wince at the tender touch, but I clench my teeth and accept it for what it is.

An olive branch.

"You must believe it, Gareth. This family is more yours than mine, and it always will be. I'm just hopeful you'll still let me be a part of it."

I nod somberly, my head dropping down as I rub my hands together. "I think it'd be nice for the boys and Vi to see the real you."

A small smile lifts his face. "I'm only sorry it took twenty-five years for him to come back."

My body grows a newfound sense of calmness that I've never felt before. This conversation has been more impactful than I could have ever imagined. I'm actually shocked by how much I understand my father better now. The man was dying from a broken heart and doing the best he could under the circumstances. Sloan and I aren't nearly as connected as my mum and dad were, but the thought of losing her after everything we've gone through together terrifies me. She is a part of me as much as anyone has ever been.

Perhaps she's the reason I understand my father's position a bit more now.

"You're the glue, Gareth. You always have been. You are exactly like your mother in that way."

His mention of Mum brings her face to the forefront of my mind. Her smile. Her eyes. Her hair. Her touch.

Mostly her touch.

She was always wonderful. And she loved my father, even in the end. If she could forgive him, so should I.

"She was a great mum," I croak, tears sliding freely down my face.

"The best," Dad replies, swiping at his own tears. "And you'll be a great dad because you're just like her."

His comment has my head turning to look at him. "I'm a ways off from being a dad, don't you think?"

He shakes his head. "I'm in no position to give you advice, Gareth. But I do wonder if during your pursuit of being better than me, you might be ignoring your own path."

My brows knit together as I try to make sense of his last statement. "What the bloody hell do you mean by that?"

He smiles knowingly and replies like what he's stating is one hundred percent factual and there's not a shred of doubt in his mind. "You love her, Gareth. You may not know it yet, but I do."

Forever in Our Hearts

Gareth

THE ENTIRE HARRIS FAMILY AND OUR PLUS-ONES STAND IN A semi-circle on the beach, all dressed in white per Vi's request. My brothers and sister are clutching pieces of paper with our eulogies that Vi asked each of us to prepare. Apparently, we're going to put the messages in a bottle and send them out to sea at the end. None of this is something I'm comfortable with in the slightest. The truth is, I've never even been comfortable enough to visit Mum's gravesite. But I will do pretty much anything for Vi, so here I stand with my bloody paper.

Hayden is crouched down in the sand helping Vi as she fusses over a wreath of white lilies that's laying over top of a small, wooden raft. Rocky is in Tanner's arms, tugging on his beard as we all wait patiently for Vi to begin.

Once she has the wreath arranged the way she wants it, she turns and nods at Camden and Booker, who bend over to pick up the raft. They walk it out into the water and push it far enough so the tide carries it away. Eventually, Cam and Booker return to the group, and we have a moment of silence as it floats farther and farther out to sea.

After the moment of silence, Vi turns on her heel and stands to face us with the ocean at her back. She fights her blonde hair whipping across her face in the wind as she reads from her sheet of paper.

"When I was researching the funeral traditions of West Africa, I learned that many of the cultures here feel that the concepts of life and death are not separate. They say that when you're healthy and well, you are living a lot. When you are ill or dying, you are living a little.

"I like that thought because, when it comes to the Harris family, no matter how hard things were for us without Mum around or how difficult life got, no one could look at us and say we weren't living a lot. We lived, and we laughed, and we loved through the pain. Through missing Mum. Through not knowing her well enough before she died. Through growing up together and looking out for each other, no matter what.

"Some look at me and think it's sad that I grew up without a mother. But that is because they don't know the four men standing in front of me. No girl in the world is as lucky as I was growing up. The years I've spent yelling at you four and scolding you for making bad choices or interfering in my personal life too much have been some of the best years of my life. It's like Mum knew I would need all of you."

Vi pauses as she covers her mouth to hide her quiet sobs while Hayden wraps a soothing arm around her. Right on cue, Rocky calls out from Tanner's arms, "Mummy okay?"

Vi laughs a tearful, contented laugh and nods. "Mummy's okay." She walks over to hold Rocky and brings her back to her spot in the sand, clutching her against her chest for comfort before continuing, "Those years with my brothers are second only to the day I became a mother myself." She turns her eyes to our father. "And Dad, watching you fall in love with my daughter has made me so grateful to have you here with all of us. I know you're hard on yourself about the past, but I have a feeling the best is yet to come for you."

Dad smiles a sad smile as tears fill his eyes.

"As for you, Mum"—Vi looks up at the sky—"I've decided that being sad about your passing would be living only a little, and I want to live a whole hell of a lot. So, thank you for sharing your name, your birthday, and your love of cooking with me. And thank you for these four brothers of mine. No one can say you didn't live a lot, Mummy. No one."

With a tearful smile, Vi walks over to Dad with her piece of paper and hands it to him. He carefully rolls the sheet up and bends to pick up a corked, green glass bottle from the sand. He pops out the cork and slides the sheet inside before wrapping Vi in a long, tight hug. We all watch the emotional display of Vi crying on Dad's shoulder, none of us able to hold back our own tears any longer.

Sloan's small hand in mine feels like a tugboat rescuing a giant ship from the sea. How she's able to comfort me with her gentle calmness at such a difficult time doesn't seem possible. She rests her head on my shoulder and gently runs her hand up and down my arm in smooth strokes. I'm glad she's here. Standing here alone would have been ten times harder as I look at my brothers comforting their partners.

Everyone has someone now. Even me.

Vi finally pulls back from Dad and swipes at the tears on her face. "Who wants to go next?"

Booker instantly steps forward, his hand leaving Poppy's as he moves to take Vi's place. Vi gives him an encouraging rub on his shoulder as he clears his throat and unfolds his paper.

"I didn't know Mum as well as most of you did. I was only one when she passed and, sadly, my memories don't go back that far. So I never knew her face or how she smelled. I don't recall anything other than what you guys have told me and what I've seen in photos. But the thing I do share with our mum is an understanding of how incredibly hard it would be to feel poorly when you have a baby to care for. My son is still tucked safely away, but I already feel a tremendous sense of responsibility for him. And I can't wait for the day I get to meet him. See him. Hold him. Smell him. Knowing that Mum had that time taken away from her is awful to think about. But I've seen the way Poppy's eyes light up when our son kicks inside her stomach, or when he gets the hiccups and does what babies do in the womb. She's so in love with him and she hasn't even laid eyes on him yet. So I guess what I'm trying to say is that I'm grateful Mum and I at least had those moments together because, from what I can tell, they are very special indeed."

Booker tugs on his earlobe awkwardly before handing his message off to Dad to deposit inside the bottle. He pauses and pulls a small black and white photo out of his back pocket and hands it over to Dad. "This is one of our first ultrasound photos. I'd like it in there as well."

Dad smiles a wobbly smile and wraps the photo inside Booker's note. He hugs Booker quickly and before Booker passes me by, I pull him in to a hug as well. His shoulders tremble beneath my embrace and he pulls back to look at me, his eyes red-rimmed and glossy. His voice is quiet enough for only me to hear when he says, "Truthfully, Gareth, the best memories of my childhood all include you. I hope you know that."

His dark eyes are round and wary, obviously still thinking about everything that was said last night and unaware that Dad and I have talked.

"I know that, Booker. I know." I pull him into another hug and clap his back a few more times. "Thank you for saying that, though."

He nods and looks down as he steps away from me to resume his position next to Poppy.

Camden and Tanner are up next. They look at each other awkwardly before walking up to speak together as Belle sidles up next to Indie to watch their husbands give their eulogies.

Tanner points to Camden for him to begin, so Cam unrolls his piece of paper and says, "I'm not sure if I started reading a lot because I'm like Mum or because I wanted to be like Mum. Either way,

I love that I share this hobby with her. She used to make notes in the margins of her books like I do now. I like to think that every time I write a thought in a novel, she can see it from wherever she may be, like I'm having my own personal conversation with her about my current read. So, cheers, Mum, to many more books we can enjoy together."

Camden hands his paper off to Dad, who makes quick work of slipping it into the bottle while Tanner prepares to speak next. Tan tucks some loose hairs behind his ears and says, "To be honest, I don't have a lot to say. I'm just grateful to Mum for giving us this family. I may be the obnoxious sod of the lot and I know that most of you want to thump me daily, but I hope none of you doubt how much this family means to me. How much I value seeing all of you most Sundays and being involved in each other's lives so much. We play football and we play it well, but there's nothing we do better than family. We always have and I hope we always will. So, cheers, Mum, for bringing us all together."

Tanner looks out at the ocean as he hands his paper off to Dad. Camden wraps an arm around his shoulder, comforting Tanner in another one of his rare moments of solemnness. Once Dad has both their notes inside, he wraps the two of them in a hug that Tanner manages not to make a lewd joke about. Then Vi looks at me with bright, blue eyes.

Sloan gives my hand a tight squeeze, and I look down at her for a minute before taking my spot in the middle. With a deep breath, I unravel my paper and stare down at the words I prepared before Dad and I spoke this morning; before I blew up on my entire family; and before Sloan opened me up in ways I never imagined I could open up. I return the paper to my pocket and look at all the faces of my family members.

"I don't want to be distant anymore. I want to…be here. I don't want to fight or be angry at you anymore, Dad. I don't want to hold back memories of Mum because I'm resentful of what happened in the past. Being angry doesn't make any of our lives better. I just want to love you for who you are and stop begrudging you for what you were not.

"I think what I've learned over the past few years is that we all did the best we could. I wasn't perfect. Hell, I know that. And I don't hate the life I lived with all of you. I hope you all know that. Hate wasn't what pushed me to sign with Man U. Being a part of raising all of you was never a burden. Not once. It was an honour. And even though it might seem like I'm a moody arsehole, I hope none of you ever doubt how much I cherish our family."

Vi breaks out into a sob and hands Rocky off to Hayden. She hustles straight toward me and yanks me down into a tight hug. Her voice is soft in my ear when she croaks, "I love you so much, Gareth."

"I love you, too, Vi," I reply through clenched teeth and pull back to look at her tear-stained face. The two of us have been through a lot together, and our bond is something that will never break. She turns and goes back to Hayden, hugging him firmly before turning to look back at me.

"And now, to our mum," I start and inhale a deep breath as a large knot forms in my throat. I look down at the sand, unable to look my siblings in the face as I speak my next words. "I remember the day you died, you told me that it would bring you great joy when my heart became louder than my head. Well, I hope you're smiling from wherever you are because I don't think my heart could get any louder than it is right now, in this moment."

I sniff loudly, my feelings overwhelming me as I wipe away the tear that's slipped down my face. "I love you, Mummy. Thank you for this family, and thank you for being the best friend I ever had."

A heavy breath blows out from between my lips and, in one quick shot, my dad has me wrapped in a hug. A tight, fierce, overpowering embrace that I accept whole-heartedly because it feels genuine and true and exactly what I need.

When Dad releases me, I dig out the eulogy I didn't read and hand it over to him. He tucks it inside the bottle as I move back to where Sloan is standing, tears flowing freely down her face and her golden eyes alight with wonder. I wipe at her cheeks as she wraps her arm around my waist. I drop a soft kiss on her forehead, then turn to look back at my father.

He rolls the bottle around in his hands over and over as he says, "Love isn't supposed to be cute and easy. It's supposed to be raw and break you down until you find your true self. It's supposed to be so potent and wonderful that you don't want to remember the person you were before you experienced its greatness. That's the kind of passion you search for your entire life. And that's the kind of passion I found with your mother.

"I loved Vilma so fiercely that I felt the loss of her before she even died. I suffered the stages of grief while she was still here because I couldn't stop myself from mourning the impending loss of her. And because of my choices, I missed most of your childhoods, and you all deserved better than that.

"But I am awake now and I refuse to miss any more. I am done grieving. This isn't a day to dredge up old pain. It's a day to release it out into the sea and say goodbye to it forever. I want things to be better from here on out. I'm going to be there for Rocky's first steps and the birth of Booker and Poppy's son. I'm going to visit Manchester as often as Gareth will have me. Whatever any of you need, I'll be there. Even if what you need from me is space, that's fine, too. I'm going to make our family my priority the way I should have when Vilma died.

"That's why I think this will be my final season with Bethnal Green Football Club."

A collective gasp from the entire group has Dad's face turning a deep shade of red, but he shakes his head and adds, "Football isn't my passion anymore. I see now that it just helped me forget. It helped me feel human. It helped me by giving me a way to connect with you kids. I don't need that anymore. I'm back and I'm here, and

I want to spend my twilight years enjoying the family your mother and I created together."

He pauses for a minute to look up at the sky, tears running out of the corners of his eyes as he says, "Vilma, my darling, that is my vow to you. From Heaven, you can watch me grow old with our grandchildren and tell them stories about how wonderful you are. Your spirit will be the life of our family, even in your death."

Dad looks back at all of us and adds, "The bad got me to the good. And when I look at all of you, I only see good. Thank you all for being the second greatest loves of my life." He takes a deep breath and turns to the ocean. "Now, let's set this bottle out to sea, shall we?"

As a group, we move out toward the water and watch Dad launch the bottle with all of our eulogies inside. The words for our mother, about our mother, and, above all, about our family.

…What this day is truly about.

Swiftie Love

Sloan

"**S**LOAN, YOU LOOK HOT!" VI PEALS AS I WALK UP THE STAIRCASE and enter the VIP section of the disco bar that's attached to our hotel. This is where the girls told me to meet them for our Tequila Sunrise bachelorette party, but I'm shocked to find the club is completely empty. The lights are swirling and the music is thumping loudly down below, but there's not a person in sight other than our group of girls who are all seated on several black leather sofas.

I smooth down my nude-coloured, knee-length dress that's decorated with a cool, metallic shimmer and a T-strap back. It's a fabulous dress I bought for a client who asked me to send it back because it wasn't a well-known designer. I was bummed because it was a unicorn of a find, so I had to keep it for myself.

"You are the one who looks hot," I reply, eyeing Vi's trumpet-shaped, floor-length, red dress. Wide straps crisscross on the back, revealing more than a smidge of her tanned skin. "Aren't brides supposed to wear virginal white?" I ask with a smile as she pulls me into a hug.

She waves me off. "Red is my colour! And it drives Hayden mad." She giggles and turns to face the group with me on her arm.

122

"Okay, so you know Poppy, Indie, and Belle, but you haven't met Hayden's sister, Daphney, yet. Daphney, this is my brother Gareth's girlfriend, Sloan."

A younger-looking blonde waves from her spot on the other side of the coffee table as I say, "Nice to meet you."

"And this is Hayden's brother's wife, Leslie!" Vi adds, turning me toward a girl with auburn hair who's wearing a fabulously flamboyant dress. "She was my co-worker at Nikon first, though!"

"And if it wasn't for me, you never would have ended up with Hayden!" Leslie exclaims, hopping up from the end of the couch and rushing over to shake my hand. "Hey there! You're Sloan the American, right?"

I chuckle at the label. "That I am. You sound a bit American, too. Am I right?"

"I'm a born, bred, and cattle-fed Missourian! Where are you from?"

"Chicago!" I exclaim, tickled to have met a fellow Midwesterner.

"How crazy that we are meeting in West Africa!" she exclaims with wide eyes as she sucks through the straw of her drink.

Belle suddenly holds a glass out in front of me and says, "Drink up. Tequila Sunrise cocktails are the recipe to all that is good in life. You'll thank me later."

I accept it with a shrug and take a fortifying sip of the refreshing drink. "So you guys just arrived today, right?" I ask Leslie as Vi gets pulled into another conversation.

Leslie nods. "Yes. My two-year-old daughter, Marisa, cried almost the entire flight. It was awful. Luckily, my husband's parents are on babysitting duty tonight, so Mama gets to party!" She swivels her hips and takes another drink.

"Oh, that's so nice!" I reply with a smile. "My daughter, Sophia, is seven now, but she was three when we moved to England. I'm pretty sure that flight is where these came from."

I point to the fine lines by the corners of my eyes, and Leslie bats my hand away with a scoff. "Please, I don't see lines at all! You're gorgeous."

"And you're sweet," I reply with a laugh. Her accent reminds me of Sophia a bit because sometimes her words don't sound fully American. She's clearly been living in England longer than I have. "What brought you to England? Was it Hayden's brother?"

"No. He was just a lucky bonus!" She smiles a Cheshire Cat sort of grin. "I work for Nikon with Vilma…Sorry, I know the rest of you call her Vi. We're both camera bag designers and their headquarters are in London, so that's kind of how I ended up over here."

"Oh, how cool!" I exclaim. "I haven't really had a chance to talk to Vi much about her job. I'm, well…I'm technically just a stylist, but I love designing and sewing when I have time."

"OMG, me too! What do you make?" Leslie asks, her green eyes wide and excited.

"I make a bit of everything, but I really love designing menswear surprisingly. Tailored suits mostly."

"Shut up! That is so cool. My favourite is dresses. I made this actually," she states and twirls in her yellow floral-print, fifties-style, flare dress.

"Shut up yourself!" I repeat her sentiment because it's fitting. "It's amazing! It's so fun and flirty."

We sit down on a nearby couch so I can take a closer look at the stitching on Leslie's dress. I'm pretty sure we lose over an hour of the night talking about fashion. She has dreams of opening her own boutique in East London, but the kind of capital and contacts she needs for such an endeavour is far more than she can handle.

I understand the struggle completely. The high fashion industry is a very niche market. If it weren't for Callum's connections with the affluent residents of Manchester, I never would have acquired the type of A-list clients I currently have.

Leslie also opens up to me about how she knows a startup business would be a huge commitment. Her husband, Theo, owns a successful custom furniture store even though he had a rough start. The difference is that he opened his business when he was single and unattached. The thought of missing out on time with Theo and Marisa weighs heavily on Leslie's mind.

The conversation opens the door for me to talk about the struggles I face being away from Sophia since the divorce. I don't know if it's the Tequila Sunrise talking or what, but I even open up about Sophia's cancer battle and how overly cautious I am about her health and schedule.

Leslie has an incredible way of just listening, too. She doesn't judge or offer any words of advice. Rather, she simply nods or agrees at all the right times. It's a moment of genuine connection between two mothers that I've not had with anyone since I moved to England. My mother and sisters came to visit before the divorce was finalised, but their advice was to do whatever I could to work things out with Callum. That definitely strained my relationship with them when my marriage still ended in divorce.

But something about Leslie listening and giving me the opportunity to express my feelings out loud is incredibly uplifting. I don't know if it's because we're both American or if it's because of our similar interests, but I connect with her on a very different level. It feels like we were best friends in another life or something. It makes me sad that she lives in London and I live in Manchester.

It's almost eleven when I hear Belle screech loudly from her spot on the couch. "You've got to be joking!" she exclaims to the female waitress, who shrugs her shoulders sheepishly and hands her a drink.

Belle turns her wide eyes to all of us, fresh cocktail in hand. "You guys, guess what she just told me?"

"What?" Vi asks, leaning in to take a sip through her straw, clearly feeling no pain.

"Tanner and Camden booked out this nightclub for the evening."

"What does that mean?" Indie asks, adjusting the gold-framed glasses on her face.

Belle's dark eyes turn menacing. "It means they booked it out for the entire night because those wankers didn't want any strangers dancing with us. They paid off the hotel to keep us away from other men all night long."

"No!" Vi exclaims with her jaw dropped. "Did Hayden have any part of that?"

"Oh my God, I'm sure they all chipped in like the insane freaks they are," Belle all but growls. "If I didn't find Tanner's jealousy kind of hot, I would be really angry right now instead of slightly turned on."

"Ew!" Vi cries, plugging her ears and rocking herself back and forth. "Please tell me it's 11:11 so I can make a wish to go back in time and make that comment disappear from my mind."

Belle and Indie laugh and high-five each other.

"Guys!" Leslie bellows, standing up and holding her hands out wide. "I think you're missing the best part of this situation!"

"What's that?" Vi asks, lowering her hands away from her ears.

"We have the entire dance floor to ourselves!" she exclaims and gestures down to the fully lit floor. "We can dance like morons and not give a shit about embarrassing ourselves, which I'm highly familiar with!" Her eyes fly really wide as she points to the DJ booth. "We can request 'Dancing Queen' to be played on repeat all night long!"

"Maybe not *all* night long," Daphney says quietly, wincing with embarrassment.

"Fine, Daph, you can request some young girl songs. Taylor Swift is your jam, right?"

"That's Gareth's jam!" Vi shouts and bursts out laughing.

My eyes land on hers. "I'm sorry, what did you just say?"

Vi hunches over and hides her face, her contorted posture at complete odds with the fancy dress she's wearing. "That's supposed to be a secret!"

"You have to tell us now!" Poppy sings, clearly as interested in Vi's comment as I am.

Vi sits up straight and exhales heavily. "Gareth warms up to Taylor Swift playing on his headphones, but he'd murder me if he knew I told you that!"

We all burst out laughing so hard that I'm certain Poppy is going to go into spontaneous labour. The ammunition this little factoid gives me will be most useful indeed.

Leslie suddenly pulls me in close and murmurs, "From one brooding man lover to another, be careful with that Taylor Swift card. If Gareth is anything like Theo, he will make you pay."

I laugh at her warning and shoot her a lascivious smirk. "Oh, believe me, I'm counting on it!"

The girls all whoop with cheers as we head out and begin twirling the night away. Between Belle revealing her neon green panties when her curvy hips drop down to the floor and Indie repeatedly doing the robot, it's actually one of the most fun nights I've had in years. These girls are the kind of fun-loving women I've needed in my life since moving to England. The only thing that would make this night complete is my fabulous Freya being here. But this group tonight gives me a sense of sisterhood I didn't realise I was missing.

Several hours and several more Tequila Sunrise drinks later, we stumble back to the leather sofas upstairs. Leslie crows loudly that she has a gift for Vi, then bends over behind the sofa and pulls out a giant, black gift bag.

She plops the bag in front of Vi, who's shaking her head adamantly. "I said no gifts, Lez!"

Leslie pushes the gift closer to Vi. "This is a grab bag sort of gift. You can share it with the girls because Ameerah went a little overboard I'm afraid."

"Oh my God, Leslie!" Vi exclaims, her face the picture of horror. "You got this from Ameerah? I can't open it here! No way!"

"Yes, you can!" Leslie bellows back. "This is a bachelorette party and we have this entire club to ourselves for the night! And, like I said, there's something in there for everyone. So just man up and do your bridal duty or you'll deprive all of us of some fun later this evening." Leslie winks at me and I frown, still not sure what the hell is in the black bag.

With red cheeks, Vi proceeds to open a Pandora's box of sex toys galore. A candy bra, penis suckers, various vibrators, floggers, feathers, nipple clamps, handcuffs, sensual oils, lubes, and lotions. You name it, it's in that freaking bag.

The girls laugh as they grab some items for a closer look. When Vi pulls out a giant pink dildo and clicks a button that makes it light up, the entire group erupts into hysterics.

At the same exact moment, destiny plays a great hand.

Out of the corner of my eye, I see a group of men standing at the entrance to our VIP section, jaws dropped, eyes wide.

Camden, Tanner, Booker, Hayden, and a man in glasses who I can only assume is Leslie's husband, Theo, are staring at Vi as she holds an enormous glowing, spinning dildo in her hand.

I burst out laughing again and point behind the girls, who all turn to see what has me so shocked. They squeal with delight when they see the men who are moving in closer now.

"Well, clearly you lot are having loads more fun than us!" Tanner bellows with a stunned look on his face as he eyes the sex toys strewn all around us. "Wife! What do you have to say for yourself?"

Belle's eyes fly wide as she stands up and turns to face her husband. "What do *you* have to say for *yourself*? We heard you guys rented out the entire club without our knowledge!"

Surprise flicks across Tanner's face as he takes in the empty club. "I don't know what you're talking about."

She growls and smacks him on the chest, but my eyes are distracted when Gareth's face appears at the top of the stairs.

Gareth doesn't look at the dildo, or the sex toys, or the spectacle Tanner and Belle are making of themselves. He's a tall, dark, and handsome storm with eyes only for me.

My thighs clench together as he moves through everyone to stand right in front of me. He leans over top of me, caging me in on the couch and whispers in my ear, "Dance with me, Treacle."

I pull my head back to gaze into his dark, heated eyes. "Is that a command?"

He looks down at my lips. "You're fucking right it is."

With a gleeful smile, I take his hand, allowing him to pull me up off my seat. We stride down to the dance floor just as the music shifts into an erotic, slower song that pumps a deep bass through the speakers. The lights fade to yellow starry sprays that dance all around us. Gareth moves my arms up to his neck and pulls me against his hard body.

He nuzzles my neck, his lips soft on my skin when he whispers, "I couldn't get here fast enough."

I have to inhale deeply to get my libido in check so I can form coherent sentences. "Where were you?"

"Some rubbish pub," he murmurs, pushing my hair off my shoulder and dragging his lips up to my ear. "And all I could think about was that I rented out this whole bloody club and I wasn't even going to get to enjoy it."

"It was you!" I exclaim, pushing away from him, my eyes wide.

He doesn't remotely attempt to conceal the proud smirk on his face.

I give his shoulders a shove. "Gareth! The girls are raging at Camden and Tanner because they think they did it."

He shrugs. "It was their idea. I just pulled the trigger and did it under their names."

His body shakes with laughter as we look over and see the girls still arguing with the boys.

"They're fighting because of you."

"They'll be fine in a minute." He licks his lips and eyes my mouth. "I'm not sorry. I just got you to myself, Sloan. I'm not ready to share you with anyone else."

"I wouldn't have done anything other than dance," I argue, surprised by how good it feels to have him so protective of me.

"Exactly," he replies, looking down at my body. "Have you seen yourself tonight? You look fucking fantastic. I wasn't about to let you out in a foreign country with a bunch of people I don't know."

"This is a five-star resort." I roll my eyes half-heartedly. "You're being ridiculous."

"I'm taking care of what's mine." He tightens his grip around my waist and pulls my pelvis to his.

Tummy flips. Loads and loads of tummy flips. So many freaking tummy flips, I can barely breathe.

I wrap myself around him again, laying my head on his shoulder and reviewing all that's happened in the last twenty-four hours. From the flight, to the dinner from Hell, to the wake, to tonight. It's a rollercoaster I don't know if I ever want to get off of.

"Have you been having a good time?" Gareth asks and drops a kiss on my bare shoulder as his fingers run up and down the exposed skin on my back.

I lift my head and nod. "Yes, really good actually. I mean, I already love Vi and the other girls, but I really connected with Leslie tonight."

"Theo's wife?" Gareth asks, his brow furrowing in surprise.

"Yes. She's American and a designer. We have loads in common."

"You're both mothers, too," he states knowingly.

"Yeah," I reply, chewing my lip thoughtfully. "I don't really have any mommy friends."

"Well, you have Vi. Soon you'll have Poppy."

His statement catches me off guard. "Already seeing our future together, Harris?"

"Of course," he replies quickly. "Aren't you?"

I nod slowly, looking at every serious, sombre feature on his face. "I'm starting to."

Without another word, Gareth takes my mouth in a long, languid kiss. It's sensual and deep. Soft and wonderful. It's so wonderful, it makes sacrificing time with Sophia seem worth it for this chance at my own happiness.

Suddenly, we're bumped into as the rest of the crew joins us on the dance floor, catcalling and whistling at our public display of affection. Gareth doesn't stop smiling the entire time, the smug asshole.

A couple of drinks and several songs later, I'm leaving the restroom after freshening up my lipstick when Vi and Leslie stumble around the corner.

"Sloan!" Leslie squeals excitedly, clutching the black gift bag from earlier and gesturing to Vi. "Quick, Vilma, pick something out for Sloan."

Vi hiccups and rifles through the bag. "It's so weird giving my brothers' partners sex toys."

"Well, Adrienne doesn't get cousins unless those boys procreate."

Vi's eyes fly wide. "Good point, Leslie. That is why they love you so much at the office. You're a big picture thinker."

Vi giggles as she digs down to the bottom of the bag. "I'm like a sex Santa, and I know you're fucking my brother and this is weird, but I'm drunk and I hopefully won't remember this in the morning. Here."

I look down as she hands me a set of crystal-encrusted hand-cuffs with a really long chain linking them together.

"Really?" I laugh and hold them out to examine. "Something about me screams, 'Lock her up?'"

Vi shakes her head from side-to-side. "No! My brother is the one who needs to be controlled. He's completely overpowering. He's wonderful, but he's a lot. I have a feeling you're going to need these at some point in your relationship."

Oh, Vi. Sweet, sweet little sister. If you only knew.

Without another word, she stumbles into the bathroom with an equally tipsy Leslie. Biting my lip, I slip her gift into my purse and ponder whether or not I want to show them to Gareth.

I'm just getting them tucked away when a large pair of warm arms wrap around me from behind. The manly musk of Gareth invades all of my senses as I turn around and look up at him. "Where did you come from?"

He gestures behind him. "The loo, but I'm more interested in where *we're* going."

My brows lift. "Are you ready to go?"

He nods seriously, moving me so my back is pressed up against the wall. "Are you ready to go?" he asks me in turn, hovering over my lips with a hungry, possessive look in his eyes.

"That depends," I husk, pulling my lower lip into my mouth teasingly.

"Depends on what?" he nearly growls in a warning tone as his gaze flicks back and forth between my mouth and my eyes.

My tone is deathly serious when I reply, "On whether or not you'll admit to listening to Taylor Swift on the soccer field."

His entire body goes stiff against mine and not in the delicious, "We're about to get it on" sort of way.

"Excuse me?" he asks, his tone far different than it was a moment ago.

I try to maintain my composure—really I do—but I can't help it. I burst into giggles and drop my head onto his chest. Mumbling into his shirt, I reply, "We all know the truth."

He pulls back from me, crooking his hand under my chin so I have to look at him. "What truth is that?"

I lose all humour in an instant. "That you're a nightmare dressed like a daydream."

"That's it," he growls and in one swift move, he throws me over his shoulder. "You're going to pay for this, Treacle."

"Gareth!" I shriek, my hands fumbling to not drop my purse as I grapple for purchase on his back. "Put me down!"

"No," he replies flatly and smacks me hard on the ass. "You've been a bad girl."

"Gareth!" I squeal with laughter, then smack him on the ass right back just as Vi and Leslie come out of the bathroom and stare down the hallway at us.

"Vi, talk some sense into your brother!" I beg, pushing my hair away from my face so I can see them more clearly.

Gareth pauses and turns to lay eyes on his sister. "Vi, I'll be dealing with you later. I don't care if it's your wedding day or not."

"What did I do?" she asks, her eyes wide and wondering.

"You told her I am a Swiftie!" he growls and swerves back to head toward the staircase that leads to the club exit.

"I never called you a Swiftie!" Vi laughs as she runs after us, yelling loud enough for their brothers to hear from their spots on the sofas.

"Gareth's secret is out," Tanner mumbles and stretches his arms over the back of the sofa like it's a normal Tuesday.

"It wasn't a well-kept secret, was it?" Camden asks, completely serious.

"I never told a soul!" Booker exclaims, clearly taking this way more seriously than the rest of us.

Vi rushes up to stop her brother at the steps. "I swear, Gareth. I only told her you warm up to Taylor Swift. What's the big deal?"

He pauses and suddenly decides to lower me to the floor, but I can't stop the smile from spreading across my face. He points a finger at his sister's face. "Who else have you told?"

"No one!" she retorts and her cheeks instantly flame red. *Holy shit, Vi is a bad liar.* "A few people."

"Who?"

"Just…like…everyone here, pretty much."

Gareth's face distorts in anger as he visibly grows taller in front of her. Vi winces and looks to her other brothers for help, but they're now on one sofa, playfully eating pretend popcorn and enjoying the show. Tanner actually passes an invisible bag to Booker and Booker refuses. It's quite a sight.

"Gareth," I state his name calmly and move to step in between him and Vi. "Don't get mad at your sister. I was probably going to find out eventually, right?"

He pins me with an unimpressed look. "I would have taken that to my grave."

He's full-on pouting as he leans against the railing and ignores his sister's pleading. How can a huge, beast of a man being Taylor Swift's number one fan be this freaking sexy?

I gesture with my head for Vi to go join the others. I have a feeling I know exactly what will calm Gareth down. I reach up and run my nails along his shoulders in hard, smooth strokes while leaning in and whispering in his ear, "What if I told you I have something in my bag that you can use on me tonight that will get you your man card back really quick?"

He frowns down at me as I carefully open my bag to show him what's inside. His brows lift. "I'd say you love this game even more than I do."

I frown back at him, then it dawns on me. "Those are Taylor Swift lyrics, aren't they?"

A smile splits across his face. "Now who's the Swiftie?" And in one swift move, my manly Swiftie grabs my hand and hauls me out of the club.

Twenty minutes later, Taylor Swift is the absolute last thing on my mind as I lie spread out on the bed, completely naked. My hands are cuffed to a metal headboard and my legs squirm against each other as I wait impatiently for Gareth to come out of the bathroom.

He stripped me down to nothing and handcuffed me to the centre railing at the head of the bed while he remained fully clothed. He was definitely punishing me and, damn, it felt exciting. But now he's taking so long in the bathroom, I wonder if he's getting cold feet.

When he walks out shirtless and barefoot but still in his jeans, I instantly notice his determined face from earlier has vanished.

"Gareth, what's wrong?" I ask, lifting my head off the pillow to look at him.

"I'm not sure I can do this, Sloan." He swallows slowly, his eyes drifting down my body with a forlorn look on his face.

I smile playfully. "Do what? We haven't done anything yet."

He drags his teeth over his lower lip and replies, "I don't want to hurt you."

"You won't."

"What if I do?"

I exhale and spread my legs. "Then I'll tell you to stop."

The dubious look on his face shows me that he's still not convinced, but the heat in his eyes as he stares at my centre is at odds with that expression.

An idea comes to mind that might help him feel more comfortable. "Look in my purse. There's a feather that I think Leslie shoved in there at the club."

"A feather?" he asks, his tone curious as he finds my bag and pulls out a black feather that's attached to a black rubber stick.

"Start with that," I urge. "Do something small, then you'll feel brave enough to try more. It's similar to what I did with you when I measured you for a suit."

"You were a fucking goddess that night," he replies as he walks toward me. He trails the feather over the top of my foot, and I instantly recoil with a sharp inhale.

His eyes flash up to mine. "Do you like that?"

I nod, goosebumps erupting all over my body as my legs close and rub together with need.

Feeling encouraged, he gradually moves the feather up over my knee and stops at my hip. "How about that?"

I groan softly, my eyes closing because watching him watch me is another form of torture, and I can only handle one thing right now.

"Eyes on me, Treacle," he husks, his voice deep and gravelly.

I open them and stare up at him. The light hair on his chest, the lines of his hips, the way his jeans hang low around them. Good God, he's sexy.

"I want to hear words from your lips," he adds, his tone stronger as he moves the feather over top of my belly and traces a circle around my navel.

I pin him with a determined look. "I like it."

He nods, his hazel eyes darkening on mine. "Where do you want me to touch you next?"

I bite my lip and reply, "My nipples."

He smiles an oh-so sexy smile and moves the feather around both of my breasts, his eyes fierce on my nubs as they harden beneath his touch. "Would you like my mouth on your nipples instead?"

"Yes, please," I moan, my voice breathy as my entire body trembles for a lot freaking more.

The bed dips as he kneels beside me and crouches over to pull my left nipple into his mouth. He releases it with an audible *pop*. "Do you like it when I bite your nipples, Tre?"

"Oh my God, yes," I moan, my ass grinding into the bed as I fight the restraint of the cuffs. I ache so damn bad to score my nails over his bare back, but watching him come alive like this is its own form of aphrodisiac.

He moves over to my other nipple and bites down gently. I cry out when his teeth pull back and scrape along my flesh.

"Are you okay?" he asks quietly, looking up at me.

"Yes, Gareth," I answer, a nearly painful need pooling between my legs.

He stares deep into my eyes as he moves the feather down between my legs. With a gentle stroke up my inner thigh, he hits my sensitive nerve bundles. I buck up off the bed so high, my belly touches his chest. He growls as he watches me writhe beneath him.

"Jesus Christ, I can smell how much you want me, Sloan." His voice is guttural, needy, and wanting. He's overwhelmed just as I was the first time I took control of him in his closet.

"I want you so badly," I moan.

"How do you want me?"

"I want you inside of me."

"What do you want me to do inside of you?" he asks, tickling my clit with the feather until I'm desperate to scream.

"I want you to make me come!" I exclaim.

He moves the feather faster over me and states in a commanding voice, "Say please."

"Please. God, Gareth, please make me come."

Within seconds, he's tossed the feather and is kneeling between my legs. He rolls me over onto my belly, crisscrossing my cuffed wrists above my head so that I can no longer bend my arms or raise my head.

"I'm going to spank you now, Sloan, because you were a bad girl earlier."

"Oh my God," I groan loudly into the pillow.

"Is that a yes?"

"Yes, please," I cry out.

"Good girl. Tell me if it gets too hard, understand?"

I nod.

He reaches around and pinches my clit without warning, causing fireworks to explode behind my closed eyelids. His voice is firm when he demands, "Words, Treacle. I need to hear you say it."

"Yes, Gareth, spank me," I reply, my voice taking on a new tenor

I've never heard before. "I'll tell you when I've had enough."

He releases my clit and rubs his hand up and down my spine, stopping to palm my ass cheek in his big, meaty hand. Then he crooks his hands under my hips and props me up on my knees.

"God, you have a beautiful arse," he growls before giving it a light smack.

My moan is soft as I breathe out, "More."

"More?" he asks, desire and amusement in his voice as he pulls his hand back and slaps me again.

"Yes," I cry out, feeling the sting this time and nearly coming apart at the seams when all the blood rushes to my centre. "More, Gareth, baby. Please."

I hear him undo his jeans, then his erection suddenly drags against my slit just as his hand collides with my backside again. This time, the burn is harsher, his touch swifter. I feel myself growing wetter and wetter.

"Do you want more?"

"I want you," I reply, pressing my backside against his shaft and desperately rubbing myself on him.

"My hands or my cock, Treacle?"

"Your cock," I cry, my voice ripped from my throat as he impales me with his erection, filling me completely.

He stills inside of me and squeezes both of my ass cheeks in a punishing hold. "You like that?"

"Yes," I moan, rocking my ass against him.

"You want me to move?"

"Yes!"

"Your command is my wish," he states, then grips my hips hard in his hands as he begins thrusting into me at incredible speed. Our skin claps together as the metal handcuffs clink above my head. The restraints bite into my wrists, but the pain only further stokes the pleasure. The thrill. The tremendous building between my legs.

Good God, if this is how he felt when I took control over him, then

I can definitely see the appeal.

This experience is similar to how we were the first time we slept together, but it was Gareth who needed encouragement to dominate this time instead of me. That's the beauty of what we have together. It's not a power struggle or a dominant and submissive. It's a fluid ebb and flow. A balance. A partnership. As Gareth said to me before, we are not all one thing. We are more. So much more.

In only minutes, my body convulses around him. He follows soon behind, both of us too keyed up to hold out on our orgasms for very long. The moment Gareth finishes coming inside of me, he pulls out, grabs the key to the handcuffs, undoes my wrists, and pulls me on top of him. My body covers his as his arms wrap tightly around me.

Once we catch our breaths, he strokes my hair off to the side and drops a soft kiss on my forehead. "That was…" he starts, but it's me who finishes.

"Perfection," I reply against his chest, unable to lift my head to look at him right now.

His body shakes with amusement. "I'd have to agree. But we're perfect in other ways, too."

I nuzzle up to him, my body soaking in the heat of him like a cat lying in the sun. "I'd have to agree as well."

He continues playing with my hair and eventually adds, "I think in sexual terms, they call this rolling."

I look up at him, propping my chin on his chest, and reply, "I think I call this Gareth and Sloan."

After a quick shower, Gareth and I are lying naked in bed together, clean, satiated, and spooning like a couple that's been doing this for years instead of months. He's completely wrapped around me, holding me and caring for me. This man—this crazy, incredible man—is actually *with* me. It's still hard for me to believe that a human being like Gareth Harris exists in the world, let alone is sleeping in bed beside me. We are so different from what I had with Callum. I was never myself in all my years with Cal. I was always what I needed to be. But Gareth lets me be who I *want* to be, which is something I didn't even realise I so desperately needed.

This realisation is a lot to take in at once. The overwhelming emotion I feel toward Gareth is like a volcano inside of me that's pushing to erupt.

"Sloan," Gareth's hoarse voice croaks into the dim moonlight illuminating our bright white bed. "Are you still awake?"

"Yes."

"Are you happy?" he asks, his voice tender.

I inhale quickly, my heart growing inside my chest in response to his simple question. "Very much."

"What are you happy about specifically?" he asks and we both tremble with silent laughter.

"Us," I eventually reply, unable to wipe the smile off my face.

"Anything more you want to share with the class?" he asks and tweaks my side playfully before nuzzling his face in my hair.

I choose my next words carefully. "I don't think I've been this happy without Sophia beside me in a long, long time. I didn't know what I was missing."

Gareth grows quiet for a moment before asking, "How do you mean?"

My eyes look upward when I think back to how dense I've been. "I didn't realise how much I truly settled with Callum. My mother terrified me about how difficult it is to raise a child alone. She was actually extremely vocal about wanting me to get an abortion. Made an appointment for me and everything without even asking."

"Jesus."

"I know," I reply with a sad huff. "An abortion was never something I'd consider for myself, but she didn't care about my feelings. And neither her nor my sisters wanted me to marry Callum initially. But I was so desperate to give Sophia a different life than I had, you know? I wanted a complete family for her. A mother and a father. Stability. Now I'm sure they're dying to say, 'I told you so.'"

"You don't know that, Sloan," Gareth coos in my ear, squeezing my hip affectionately.

I exhale and shake my head. "I just wonder what might have been if I'd never married Cal."

After a long pause, Gareth pulls me closer, his hand wrapping around my wrist as our arms entwine across my bare chest. His lips tickle my ear when he whispers, "But if you never married him, you wouldn't be here with me right now."

My chin quivers as his reply shoots through my body and causes tears to prick behind my eyes. I sniff softly and ask, "Does that mean you're happy, too?"

"Are you joking?" he retorts, dropping a kiss on the side of my neck. "I'm completely happy. I didn't know what I was missing either."

I blink and allow the silent tears to fall freely out of my eyes and onto the pillow, grateful for our position so he can't see how much his words mean to me.

He tightens his hold on me and adds, "I never knew I could be like this with a woman. Ever. I think that after seeing my mum die, I got it in my head that women are fragile. It's why I was so protective of Vi and her choices in men. It's also why I never found a woman I was comfortable enough to really let go with. I put up a wall because I was scared of hurting someone. I never trusted myself with anyone enough to do what I did with you."

He kisses my shoulder and pulls me in closer. So close our breaths synchronise with one another. So close I can feel the pulse of his veins against my skin.

His chest vibrates on my back as he continues. "Since the second my mum died, I've had this discomfort lodged in my chest. Like I was constantly holding my breath and couldn't let it out. I never knew how to get rid of it, so I just got used to it. I got used to the pain and forgot what it was like to feel good. To let that breath out.

"Then, when you came to my house that night and asked me to kneel, it felt like I fucking exhaled for the first time since I was eight years old. You gave me so much strength by simply letting me surrender. Strength I didn't realise I was missing.

"Now that I've completely fallen in love with you, I can inhale and exhale over and over, and there's all the air in the world for me because you're beside me."

My breath catches in my throat as his words sink in. I roll over to face him, desperate to see his face after he uttered the most beautiful thing I've ever heard. His arms tighten around me as I cup his face in my hands, our legs intermingling as moonlight reflects in his eyes.

"What did you just say?" I croak, my emotions completely taking over.

He stares back at me, his face deathly serious. "I said I'm in love with you, Sloan."

"You are?" I ask, still unable to believe it.

"Like crazy," he confirms, stroking the path of a tear that slid down over my nose.

I bite my lip and smile a true, genuine smile. "Well, that's good because I think I'm in love with you, too. I'm not quite sure when it happened. Maybe it was right after the attack. Maybe it was on this trip. Or maybe it was back when you first kissed me outside of my house. I don't know. But at some point, you burrowed inside of my heart and made me feel something I've never felt before. And I know I'm divorced, and I have a daughter, and I am way more than a handful, but I think we can—"

My words are cut off by Gareth's mouth as he presses his lips to mine and kisses away the doubt, and the fear, and the laundry list of things in our lives that make us a highly complicated couple.

Because, right now, in the paraphrased words of Taylor Swift, we're just a man and a woman in a love story, just saying yes.

It's 11:11...Let's Get Married

Gareth

"**I** HAVE TO HEAD OVER TO HAYDEN'S ROOM, SO I GUESS I'LL SEE you on the beach?" I ask, draping my garment bag over my shoulder and propping myself in the doorway of the loo in our suite.

Sloan is wrapped in a fluffy white towel, finishing her makeup at the vanity. Vi's itinerary says we should arrive at the bride and groom suites by ten a.m. today before the wedding begins at eleven.

This morning has been interesting to say the least. Sloan and I woke at different times, showered at different times, and have been doing an awkward sort of "don't touch each other" dance all over our suite. We're acting like two teenagers who just lost their virginity and don't know how to behave around each other the morning after.

I'm over it.

"Okay, I'll see you later then," Sloan replies as she stares at me in the mirror, her mascara wand frozen in the air.

I move in behind her and drop a kiss on her bare shoulder. "Love you," I add with a cheeky smile and turn to leave.

She makes a strange noise in her throat and replies, "You're just going to drop it on me all casual like that, then walk away?"

A broad smile spreads across my face as I turn to see her still watching me in the mirror. "Should I have dropped it another way?"

144

She swivels in her chair to face me, her tan legs exposed as she replies in a rush, "Well, I mean, if we're going to just say it any time, I'm wondering what your family will think or how they'll see this. Will they think it's happening too fast because they barely know me? What if they think I'm a gold digger? And what happens when we get back to Manchester? I have to figure out what I'm going to do with Sophia and when it's appropriate for you to officially meet her. This is a complicated process, Gareth. We should talk about it—"

"Sloan," I stop her midsentence and her eyes shoot up to me.

"What?"

I hit her with a crooked smile and reply, "I'll see you at the wedding."

She puffs a strand of hair out of her eyes and replies, "Okay."

"I love you," I add with a smirk.

She bites her lip hesitantly, then adds with a small smile, "I love you, too."

She turns back toward the mirror and, before I realise what I'm doing, I toss the garment bag on the bed and stride straight for her. She looks up in surprise as I turn her in her chair and hoist her up onto the vanity. Her bare legs wrap around my waist for balance as I kiss her and add, "I seriously love you."

The smile on her face could light up the whole world when she replies, "I seriously love you, too."

My brows lift. "See? We're getting better at this already."

"Gareth, I want you to walk me down the aisle."

"What?" I exclaim, stepping inside the bridal suite after Vi texted me a 999 urgent message. "Vi, everyone is waiting down at the beach. Where's Dad?" I ask, looking around the room.

"I sent him down to the beach." She shrugs with a shy smile.

I exhale heavily and shake my head, taking a minute to look down at the stunning lace wedding dress my sister is wearing. "Vi, you are beautiful."

"Thank you. Now will you please walk me down the aisle?"

"Vi, no. Dad would be crushed. I just stopped fighting with him. I don't want to start again."

"It was his idea."

"What?" I ask, my eyes wide and jaw dropped.

"He said he would love to walk Rocky down the aisle and it would make him extremely proud to see you walk me down the aisle."

"Vi, you're his only daughter."

"I'm aware."

"He won't have another chance at this."

"I know," she replies, her eyes firm on mine. "Gareth, a lot of what you said at dinner the other night is true, and I want you to know we haven't forgotten any of it. All of our best childhood memories are because of you. You've always been there for us. You're the one who started Sunday dinners after all."

"What are you talking about?" I scoff as I unbutton the suit jacket that Sloan made me and put my hands in my pockets. This is a conversation we should have had last night, not minutes before Vi is supposed to walk down the aisle.

"Don't you remember those picnics you made for us every Sunday? We ate them at the park behind our house."

I shake my head. "Of course I remember, but that wasn't—"

"Those were Sunday dinners, Gareth," she interrupts. "You've kept our family together all these years, and there is no one else I'd rather have give me away to Hayden."

Her eyes well with tears as the gravity of what's about to happen sets in on both of us. I pull her into a tight hug, my lips pressing to her hair as I murmur, "You were a mini mum the second you were born, Vi. Don't you dare sell yourself short."

"Fine, we're both amazing." She laughs and pulls back, adjusting her long veil that stretches the entire length of her dress. "Now, let's go get me married before I change my mind and pull a runner."

I shake my head at her joke. "And what name will you be getting married under today?"

She inhales deeply, a look of peace flitting across her face. "Vilma Harris-Clarke. The one and only."

I nod and take her arm in mine. "It sounds perfect."

The ocean air is warm as Vi and I make our way down to the beach where the ceremony is taking place. In front of a large set of rustic, double doors draped in pink and white flowers, we spot Dad holding Rocky beside Leslie and little Marisa. They are huddling close to the doors to conceal themselves from everyone else on the other side, waiting for Vi's big entrance.

Vi is already crying as she approaches, her face lighting up at the sight of our tiny Rock Star in a fluffy pink dress. She pulls her arm out of mine and hands me her pink bouquet to reach out for Rocky, who instantly reaches back.

Vi pulls her into a tight hug, but Rocky's more interested in marvelling over her mummy's pretty dress and hair. She tugs on the white veil laying over top of Vi's long blonde curls. "Mummy pretty," she says, her eyes full of wonder.

"Adrienne pretty," Vi croaks, sniffling back her tears. She leans down to two-year-old Marisa who has her chubby arms wrapped around her mummy's legs. "Marisa pretty, too," Vi adds with a smile and tugs on one of Marisa's red curls.

Dad and I make eye contact and exchange a meaningful look of respect. He gives me a silent nod of approval that would have grated on my nerves less than forty-eight hours ago.

Now, it brings me peace.

Dad looks at Vi as she stands up straight and fixes the strap on Rocky's dress. "Are you ready, Vi, my darling?" he asks, his voice deep and full of emotion.

Vi nods and turns to me. "Completely ready."

Leslie squats down next to her daughter, fussing over her dress as she says, "Okay, Marisa, you're first. Do it just like we practiced." Leslie hands Marisa a tiny basket of pink flower petals.

Dad nods at them and pushes the double doors open to reveal our family all standing in the sand, lining the entire aisle and staring at us with big smiles on their faces.

On the right is Hayden's brother, Theo, and their parents, Winifred and Richard. On the left are my three brothers, their partners, and Sloan, who's standing closest to the door and is dressed in a stunning long, black dress. She looks every bit as beautiful as she always does.

At the end of the aisle is a large wooden archway draped in a waterfall of pink flowers. Beneath it is the pastor, Hayden, and his sister, Daphney, who has an acoustic guitar strapped to her chest.

Leslie gives Daphney a nod and she begins playing the Sleeping At Last cover of "500 Miles." Hayden's head turns from the ocean, and his eyes instantly land on Vi, who still has Rocky in her arms.

His smile falls.

He doesn't look happy.

He doesn't look sad.

He doesn't look angry.

He's overcome.

Vi's shoulders shake with silent sobs as Daphney begins to sing. She squeezes Rocky to her chest and points down the aisle. "Look, Rocky Doll. There's your daddy."

"Daddy." Rocky opens and closes her fingers in a wave, and the look exchanged between their little family seems private and personal, but we're all here to witness it. To witness their connection. Their love.

Their moment in time.

"Go see your Unky Hayden, Marisa," Leslie coos quietly and urges her daughter down the aisle.

Everyone's eyes are diverted to the adorable little redhead in a fluffy pink tutu dress. Marisa's eyes are wide and wary on all the people looking down at her, but she smiles a big smile the second she spots Hayden. Now in a hurry, she tosses her basket of flowers and makes a mad dash down the sandy beach aisle, tripping once and getting a face full of sand. Several people step out to help her, but Marisa shakes them off, not the least bit bothered as she pauses to spit some sand out of her mouth. She resumes her toddler run all the way to her uncle who's squatting down with wide open arms.

Hayden scoops up a giggling Marisa who's still picking at sand on her tongue, and everyone laughs at the tender connection between Hayden and his niece. He pulls his pocket square out of his suit jacket and dabs at her lips as she croaks out a loud, "Yucky."

Theo reaches out to take Marisa from Hayden, and Hayden resumes his stoic stance, smiling big and staring back at Vi.

"Ready, Rocky Doll?" Dad asks, holding his arms out to her.

"Papa!" she sings happily and falls out of Vi's arms and into Dad's.

Vi wraps her hand around my arm and takes her flowers back. Then, she takes a deep breath, bracing herself to watch her daughter be carried down the aisle.

About midway, Dad stops walking and lowers Rocky until her little bare feet touch the sand. Her chubby fingers hold onto his hands as he walks her a few steps before pulling one hand away. We all take a collective breath when Rocky releases his other hand and walks stiltedly by herself for several steps.

Vi sobs beside me as she watches Hayden rush over and crouch down in front of Rocky, holding his hands out wide. Rocky nearly falls but manages to straighten herself and resumes her walk right into an openly crying Hayden's arms.

"Oh my God," Vi exclaims, looking at me with red, tear-soaked eyes. "She just walked!"

"Did you know she could do that?"

She shakes her head. "Dad must have been practicing with her!"

"Incredible," I croak, tearing up myself and finding Sloan's eyes watching me instead of Rocky. She's covering her mouth and staring at me with wide, red-rimmed eyes full of so much love, it takes everything I have to not let go of my sister and go to her.

Hayden kisses Rocky, then passes her off into my dad's arms and swipes at his face to prepare for his bride.

As soon as Daphney starts the chorus, I begin to usher Vi down the aisle to her groom. I look over at her with a wide smile, honoured more than I can explain to be the one giving her away today. We've been through so much together. Lots of hard times but far more happy.

This moment—Vi's moment of achieving her happily ever after—is momentous to all of us. She is our sister—the woman we would all do anything for—and all of her dreams are coming true today. It couldn't be happening to a better person.

When we reach Hayden, I release Vi's arm to pull Hayden into a tight hug. We clap each other on the back, then I look into his eyes and give him a nod of approval. Hayden has a dark past, but he's more than proven himself to be good enough for our sister. It's a relief because I don't think I could have given Vi away to anyone else. Before I walk away, Vi surprises me with a wrenching hug around my neck.

"Thank you, Gareth."

I half smile down at her. "Thank you, Vi."

We nod at each other and the pastor begins the ceremony. I step away and join Sloan in the back. My entire body aches for hers. My heart, my soul, my hands. Our fingers thread together as we listen to Hayden and Vi recite their vows to each other and make a collective wish as the time hits 11:11 on the nose—a time once only special to Hayden but now equally as special to Vi. They honour Hayden's deceased sister, Marisa, and our mum with a single white rose that they release out into the ocean while Daphney plays the Sleeping At

Last cover of "As Long as You Love Me."

By the end of the service, my emotions have been raked over the coals. The overwhelming joy is too much for one person to handle. Vi's wedding is like a happy ending the entire Harris family has waited long enough for.

Back to the Real World...Cup

Gareth

The next morning, Sloan and I leave Cape Verde bright and early so I can workout at home a couple times before training starts back up with the team. Winter break is over and I need to do everything I can to prep for our match against West Ham United next Saturday.

The flight is longer on the way home. Time ticks by slowly as Sloan lies stretched out across my lap, sound asleep and perfectly beautiful. An ominous feeling grows inside my gut the closer and closer we get to Manchester.

Being in love on holiday is easy. Being in love in the real world will take some effort. What will we look like back in the real world? Will Sloan go back to not seeing me when she has Sophia? Am I going to meet Sophia properly sometime soon? Does Sloan have a timeline in mind for when I get to become a part of both of their lives?

I'm trying hard to think with my heart like my mother wished for me, but my head is grappling for a goal right now and it's two-footed.

When it's finally time to land, Sloan sits up to slide her seatbelt back on and I can tell she feels it, too. The fear that things will be different.

"You have a couple of days before Sophia comes home. Do you want to stay at my house?" I ask, my voice low as we climb into the vehicle that's waiting for us on the tarmac.

Sloan shifts nervously. "Is your home...safe?"

My brow furrows as I open the door for her and watch her step into the vehicle. "Yes, it's safe. But if you're not comfortable there, we can stay at yours."

Her face is pensive when she asks, "What about the press?"

I shrug my shoulders dismissively, then slide in next to her, tossing my hand on the back of the bench so I can turn toward her. "My agent emailed while we were away and said things have died down. We should be okay as long as we're not walking around in public together."

"I still don't think I'm ready to go back to your house, so mine would be best," she replies, pulling her lip into her mouth and staring out the window, her legs angling away from me instead of toward me.

I'm a defensive player, so I'm good at reading body language. Whatever's happening right now isn't good. The driver starts the car and I direct him to Sloan's address.

Once we've ridden in silence for a few minutes, I ask, "What is it, Sloan? Is it the house or us?"

She inhales deeply and looks over at me. "I need to talk to Callum."

I stiffen at the mention of his name. "About what?"

"About us."

"Why is it any of his business?"

"Because I need to be proactive and control the message."

"What bloody message, Sloan? I love you and you love me. Why would he give a toss? He's the idiot who let you go."

"I know, but he and his mother are very controlling, Gareth. You don't know them like I do. Horrible as she might be, Margaret loves Sophia dearly. I have to be careful that they don't find out about us before I tell them. They'll turn this into something unseemly."

My brow furrows. "You mean because I'm a professional footballer?"

Sloan shrugs. "They will dig up everything they can on you, I'm sure."

"So let them!" I exclaim with a bark. "Sloan, I don't have a nasty past. Compared to my brothers, I'm the fucking pope."

"Didn't you assault your sister's ex-boyfriend?" she asks, her eyes not leaving mine.

My teeth could crack I'm clenching them so hard. "He deserved it."

"I'm not judging, Gareth, but they will," she replies, wringing her hands in her lap and turning to face the window again. "And they will see the press about the break-in and attack. It will all come out."

I huff out an annoyed laugh. "So what? This is over before it's begun?"

Sloan's head snaps to me. "No! Why would you say that?"

"Because you're acting as if I'm a burden to you."

"I am not! I'm just telling you I need to be in control of this situation. That's all. Just fucking be there for me and stop being so intense about everything!"

Her tone brings me up short. I sit back and take in a few deep breaths to calm my anger. She's right. I know she's right. But I hate that she has this whole other part to her life that I don't have a say in.

I slide across the bench and pull Sloan onto my lap, my hands wrapping around her jaw so she has to look at me. "I'm sorry," I murmur, pushing her hair back from her face and staring right into her eyes. "I'm not used to this."

"Used to what?" she asks quietly, staring back at me with sad eyes.

I shrug half-heartedly. "Not controlling conflicts I guess."

She looks at me with a "come on, be serious" expression, then rolls her eyes with a dramatic sigh. "One night with a little power and it goes straight to your head."

In one quick shot, I pull her down and assault her sides with my fingers. She squirms and giggles and begs me to stop. The whole feeling of her laughing beneath me is fantastic. She looks young and carefree, as she should.

Once I stop, she sits back up on my lap and I slowly rub my hands on her legs. "In my family, I am in control a lot. I solve problems, I run interference. I'm used to fixing things. This is going to take some getting used to for me."

Sloan chews her lip thoughtfully for a minute, then says, "I get it. And I'm not going to fight you forever, Gareth. I want to be in a partnership. An equal give and take. I want someone to share my struggles and joys with because I've never had that. But we're still so new and I have to handle this how I see fit. What if this doesn't work out?"

"It's going to work out," I reply, running my hands up and down her arms soothingly. "I'm in love with you, Sloan."

"You don't know everything about me. You might hate my quirks."

"I love your quirks."

She rolls her eyes and groans, "You don't even know my quirks."

My jaw tightens as I shoot her a moody glower. With a deep breath, I state, "I know that you hate tea but love teacups. I know that you snore if you've had a really good orgasm before bed. I know that you aren't fulfilled as a personal stylist, and I'll do everything in my power to help you see your potential for more because you're bloody brilliant at making suits. I know you miss the sense of family but not necessarily your family.

"And I know that you'll never love me more than you love Sophia, and I think it's incredible that you're always a mum first. The truth is, I think that's what drew me to you the second I met you. You have this selflessness about you that I find really fucking attractive.

"And I know why you're so protective of Sophia and why being in a relationship with me where you had all the control was so necessary. But I think as much as you crave that control, you crave someone who will push back as well. Someone to challenge you on things and teach you how to live a little again.

"But mostly, I know that if I can connect with Sophia someday in a meaningful way, then it will be the moment I know you're mine forever and I can marry you."

"What?" Sloan gasps. Her jaw drops and she covers her mouth with her hands. "Gareth, what did you just say?"

I raise my chin. "You heard me, Sloan. I've known you for years now, and these aren't new feelings. These are dormant feelings that I'm tired of holding back."

"You're crazy," she replies, her jaw still dropped.

"I'm crazy about you," I reply and bring her down to my face. "I'm not rushing you with this Sophia thing. Do what you think is best. But please know that I'm here, Sloan. And I'm all fucking in."

Suddenly, my mobile vibrates in my jeans pocket. Begrudgingly, I move to pull it out and see that it's a London area code that I don't recognise. I shoot Sloan an apologetic look, but she's still reeling from what I've just said, so I don't imagine she'll notice I've taken a call.

I swipe the green button and answer. "Hello?"

"Harris, this is Gary Austin, the England Football Team manager."

"Yes, hello, Coach," I reply quickly and help a mannequin version of Sloan back down onto the seat. "What can I do for you?"

"Look, I'm not going to dance around this because I'm sure it's no surprise to you considering the media won't shut up about it," he grumbles in an annoyed tone. "I'm interested in inviting you and your three brothers to play for England at the World Cup."

My chest instantly tightens. I've received calls like this before for various Euro cups and tournaments, and it's always an honour.

But I thought it was just a rumour that my brothers might all be invited as well. This is next level success for our entire family.

I clear my throat and do my best to sound calm when I reply, "Thank you for your consideration. It's truly an honour, sir."

"Right. I haven't completely made up my mind about who I'm recruiting, but I've chosen to announce some early squad members to try to get the press off my bleedin' back. So I'm inviting you and your brothers to a behind-closed-doors training camp I'm putting on next month at Cobham Training Centre. The National Football Centre grass is getting reworked, so this centre is the best I can do during my limited time slot."

"Oh, sure, sure, Chelsea's club training grounds. I can be there, sir," I reply, recalling the game I played against Chelsea a few months back. Shutting down Vince Sinclair this year was a career highlight for me, so hopefully I can take some of that energy and apply it to this camp.

"There will be a press conference at the end of the camp, announcing who I select for the team. You just recovered from a concussion, yes?"

"Yes, Coach, but I'm fine."

"Are you fine enough to play at top-level in a month? I'll be organising a secret friendly match during the camp, and I need everyone playing at the top of their game."

"Yes, sir. I'll be ready," I reply, my tone firm.

"Ghastly what happened to you and that woman you had with you, son. I'm very sorry to hear of it."

My jaw tightens. "Thank you."

"All right then, my assistant will send you the details. Talk soon."

"Bye," I reply, still in shock as the phone hangs up.

"Who was that?" Sloan asks, her eyes finally focusing again.

"That was the manager of the England team asking me and my brothers to train with him next month at a camp."

"Is that good?" Sloan asks, her brow furrowing curiously. "Is it like a try-out?"

"Of sorts. And, yeah, it's good."

"Huh," Sloan replies, then shakes her head. "What a day."

I chuckle softly and pull her under my arm to drop a kiss on the top of her head. "What a year."

Sloan remains quiet for several minutes before looking up at me and asking, "Does it bother you that I know nothing about soccer?"

I laugh and shake my head. "No, but it does bother me that you don't call it football. What the bloody hell do I have to do to get you to change that?"

She smiles a naughty, shy smile. "I can think of a few things."

17
Unexpected Teammate

Sloan

MY HANDS CLENCH TIGHTLY AROUND THE WHEEL AS I DRIVE out to the Lake District to pick up Sophia. Normally, the anticipation of Sophia running into my arms and being reunited is the best. But this Sunday, my belly is full of anxiety as I ponder what I'm going to say to Margaret and Callum about Gareth. And I have to say something.

After everything Gareth said on the car ride to my house, I can no longer fool myself into thinking what we have is casual.

Gareth Harris doesn't do casual.

Looking back, I'm not sure he ever did.

The rest of the week, Gareth and I spoke about how we will handle our relationship for the next few months. For now, we're going to keep it out of the public eye. At least until the World Cup is over. The attention the Harris family will get if all four brothers are selected to play on the team will be quite intense, so keeping us quiet is best for all involved.

I drive into the large Coleridge Estate, pulling around the fountain to park. Margaret's dog, Rex, comes bounding up from behind the house with my beautiful Sophia hot on his heels.

"Mummy!" she squeals and sprints straight to me, her brown

hair tied back into a neat low ponytail like it always is when she spends the weekend with Margaret.

"My Sopapilla!" I squeal back, slamming the car door and dropping down into a squat with my arms wide open.

Sophia barrels into me at full speed and knocks me off balance, toppling me backwards onto the rough gravel. Rex pounces over to us, nosing his wet snout in between our faces as Sophia giggles and tightens her grip around my neck.

"Ouch, Soph! When did you get so strong?" I ask, giggling back and struggling to sit up with her all over me.

"I'm almost eight, that's why!" she exclaims gleefully, then finally releases my neck enough so I can sit up.

"Look at us! We're a mess!" I retort, wiping off the dust that's all over my jeans.

She kneels in front of me and smiles.

"You look like you've grown!" I state excitedly and squeeze her black jacket around her neck a bit.

"I have. And I have another loose tooth. See?"

She wiggles one of her upper teeth and I nod with wide eyes. "Oh yeah, that's going to come out really soon."

"I've been trying not to touch it so it falls out at your house."

"Oh? Why is that?"

"Because Freya gives me ten quid for each tooth!" She giggles.

"She what?" I exclaim, my jaw dropped. "I didn't know that."

She nods eagerly. "She told me not to tell you."

"You two shouldn't be keeping secrets from me!" I jest and roll onto my knees to tickle Sophia's sides. "What else have you been hiding from me, huh?"

"Nothing, I swear!" She laughs happily, and I laugh right along with her. I don't know if it's because I was on a trip but, damn, I've missed this kid.

"Are you quite done?" Callum's curt tone cuts into our fun as he stares down at us from where he stands by the fountain.

My smile falls when I see Callie holding onto his arm. She's dressed in yet another miniskirt with metallic sheen tights and a pair of stiletto boots that look a hell of a lot more ridiculous than Sophia's pink outfits that Margaret insists she never wear to the country.

The crunch of gravel by the house has my gaze snapping over to where Margaret has just come out. She cinches her white cloak up around her neck and makes her way over to Callum.

"Sloan," she says crisply, tilting her head down at Sophia and I. "Sophia, those are new trousers."

"Sorry, Grandmama," Sophia chirps.

I move up into a standing position and dust Sophia's bottom and legs off before doing the same to my own.

"No matter, they'll wash," Margaret replies, her tone softer than I've ever heard. She looks me up and down next. "You look like you've gotten some sun, Sloan. Were you travelling for business?"

"Pleasure," I reply with a polite smile. "I was wondering if I could have a word with you and Callum for a moment before Sophia and I head out. Do you have a little time?"

Margaret nods and I feel Sophia staring up at me. I crouch down beside her and push a strand of hair back from her face. "Sweetie, why don't you go out to the stables and see if that black cat is still up in the hay mound?"

"He is, Mummy! Come see!" She moves to drag me away, but I still her motion with my free hand.

"I need to talk to your grandmother and daddy. You go and take some pictures for me, okay?"

Sophia's eyes light up when I hand her my phone. Without another word, she dashes off to the back of the estate with Rex nipping at her heels.

I stand back up and tighten my black jacket around my body. The February air is cold on my face, but not as cold as Margaret's calculating stare.

Before I have a chance to say a word, Callum's voice cuts into my thoughts. "Well, I may as well tell you before you hear it from Sophia. Callie and I are engaged."

Callum stands up straight, one hand grabbing the edge of his suit jacket, the other wrapped tightly around Callie's waist. I look down and see the enormous diamond glinting on Callie's ring finger.

"Wow," I reply, my voice hoarse in my throat. "So soon?"

Callum scoffs. "It's hardly soon, Sloan. We've been seeing each other for quite some time."

I shake my head stupidly. Of course they have. They were together before Callum and I separated. My voice is tight and flat when I reply, "Well, congratulations to you both."

Callie giggles and drops her head on Callum's shoulder, her foot kicking out playfully as Callum grabs her manicured hand and kisses the top of it. "It just happened Friday night."

"So, Sophia knows already?" I ask, wondering if she was there for the proposal since it was his week with her.

"We told her along with Mother this morning."

"I see," I reply, my mind putting together the fact that Callum and Callie were likely not with Sophia and Margaret this weekend.

I look over to gauge Margaret's reaction and find her staring off into the distance. Her arms are wrapped tightly around herself, appearing completely disinterested in the conversation.

I clear my throat to drop my little news on them which is certainly much less exciting. Maybe this engagement of Callum's will work out in my favour. "I wanted to let you all know that I've started seeing someone."

Callum's eyes narrow and I look away from him to Margaret. "It's not an engagement or anything, but we're serious. I felt like you guys needed to know because he's a soccer player for Manchester United and a bit of a high profile one at that."

Margaret's eyes snap to mine, her brows puzzled in amazement. "What is his name?"

I sniff once and force myself to maintain eye contact when I reply, "Gareth Harris."

"Oh, for God's sake," Callum jeers, his voice taking on a smug tone. "I knew it wouldn't take long for you to start screwing one of your clients."

"Callum!" Margaret retorts, her tone scathing, eyes sharp.

"Mother, this is completely improper," Callum argues, smoothing his hair back like the arrogant asshole that he is. "What kind of example will it be for Sophia to see her mum wrapped up around one of those barbarians?"

"Gareth is not a barbarian," I reply through clenched teeth.

"He's a Harris Brother!" Callum retorts. "Couldn't even manage to shag a player from a proper family at the very least? That Harris family is as common as they get."

I inhale and exhale slowly through my nose, my hands balling into fists at my sides. "His family are good people, Callum, and Gareth is quite possibly the best of them. He just received an award for that youth enrichment program he runs. He hasn't met Sophia yet, aside from at that camp you enrolled her in without my knowledge, but he'd be a great example for her."

Margaret's eyes swerve to Callum. "You didn't tell her about the camp?"

Callum baulks half-heartedly. "She would have said no. Sloan is always going on and on about Sophia's health."

"Callum Coleridge," Margaret seethes. "She is her mother and the one who was by her bedside when Sophia was ill. She is the one most knowledgeable about her health. What you have done is unconscionable."

"But, Mother," Callum whines.

Margaret rolls her eyes, her gaze looking off into the distance again. "Callum, leave us."

"Leave you?" Callum argues, his head darting back and forth between me and his mother.

Margaret cuts him a hard glower. "Go check on your daughter."

Callum's jaw moves up and down as he attempts to speak but can't figure out what to say. In a huff, he storms off to the stables, leaving a dazed Callie behind.

Callie stares at Margaret. "What should I do?"

Margaret's eyes fly wide. "Go with him!" She flicks her wrist at Callie, who quickly scampers off, nearly tripping as her heels get stuck in some gravel.

Turning back to me, Margaret eyes me for a moment, then states crisply, "Walk with me, Sloan."

She tosses the tail of her cloak up tightly around her neck, her lips puckering as she braces against the cool breeze. I follow her around the side of the house to a Victorian wall garden area that's full of neatly trimmed shrubs that are brown from the cold winter. She stops to pick up a dead branch and drops it into a rubbish pile alongside the house.

"The grounds crew was supposed to pick up this pile weeks ago," she tuts, shaking her head in disappointment. She resumes her walk with me keeping pace with her and finally looks over at me and states, "My cancer has spread, Sloan."

I nearly trip over myself from her drastic change of topic and have to compose myself to reply, "I'm sorry to hear that, Margaret."

She looks forward, her pointy chin jutted out with determination. "The doctor says I have weeks, maybe less."

My breath exhales from my body. As many times as I've wished death on this woman, it somehow doesn't seem nearly as appealing as it once did. "Sophia will be crushed."

"You won't," she muses, sliding her eyes to me.

"Margaret—" I begin to argue but she cuts me off.

"Let's not beat around the bush here, Sloan." She stops in her tracks and turns to look straight at me. "You don't like me and I have issues with you, but the fact of the matter is your issues pale drastically in comparison to that floozy my son has wrapped around him like a second skin. And your issues with me pale drastically in comparison to the ones you have with my son, who is as pompous of an arse as I've ever seen."

My hand flies to my mouth to cover the laugh that threatens to escape. I manage to purse my lips together and nod.

"But the only thing you should trust is my affection for Sophia. That has never faltered."

All good humour is drained from me as I nod again. "You have been very good to her."

She inhales deeply and gazes back in the direction of Sophia. "I'm convinced that Sophia is the only thing that has kept me alive these past few years." She coughs gently and I swear I see a tear form in her eye. "But even that brown-eyed angel can't stop what's going on in my body, which means we need to settle things before my time comes."

I eye Margaret with genuine sympathy. "What is it that you need from me, Margaret?"

She cuts her eyes to me again. "Are you serious about this Harris fellow?"

I'm surprised by her question because it's not where I thought her mind was going. I'm also not sure what my answer should be. Do I minimise what Gareth and I are to lighten the severity of her reaction? Or do I tell her the truth and speak from my heart?

I exhale heavily. "I'm very serious."

"And is he serious about you?" she retorts back.

I nod, looking down and thinking back to our conversation in the car and the promise he made to me. "He says the moment he can win over Sophia is the moment he will know he can marry me."

Margaret has no outward reaction to the emotional response I just gave her, but she gives me a crisp nod like we've concluded some sort of business transaction. "Very well. I need you to know that I don't trust that Callum will have Sophia's best interests at heart when it comes to her future. I never realised how disinterested he was in fatherhood until the divorce. The past several months have been very eye-opening."

"Okay," I reply curiously, unsure where she's going with this.

"I am the one who urged him to put Sophia in the Kid Kickers football camp. I wanted him to get involved with the charity we've participated in for years, and I thought it would be a good opportunity for him to see Sophia be a part of something she loves."

"You've been a charitable donor to Kid Kickers?" I ask, my jaw dropped in disbelief.

"Yes, we have," she replies firmly. "We've been involved ever since Gareth Harris started the program years ago. When they reached out for sponsors to grow the program outside of the city, I pushed Callum to get involved. However, he can't seem to get his hands off that bloody awful woman long enough to get anything accomplished. And I'm far too old and unwell to fight with him about it."

"I had no idea," I reply, marvelling over the woman in front of me right now. Maybe I never gave Margaret a chance to open up to me like this before. Maybe if I had, we wouldn't have been enemies for so long.

"We've had our differences, Sloan, but Callum's remarks about the Harris family are quite unfair. I want you to know that you won't be hearing any argument from me in regard to your relationship with Gareth Harris. Lord knows he is far and away more admirable than that tramp Callum has attached himself to."

"Why are you telling me all of this, Margaret?"

"Callum has become a tremendous disappointment to me, and I refuse to let Sophia go down the same path." She turns and begins walking again as I hustle to keep up. "That is why I'm going to tell Callum that the fifty-fifty custody agreement is no longer necessary and we will be amending the terms."

"What?" I exclaim, running up to look Margaret in the face. "What are you amending them to exactly?"

"Callum has no interest in seeing Sophia every other week. He hardly sees her when he does have her, and I don't want Sophia's brain rotting away on the sofa with that woman he's chosen to marry. I'm going to urge him to revise the custody to every other weekend. Would that be satisfactory to you?"

I can't breathe. I can't breathe. I'm sucking in air, but none of it is getting where it should be.

"A simple nod of the head will suffice, Sloan."

I nod. I nod so hard I think my head might fall off my neck. "Do you think he'll agree to it?"

"He will if I tell him to," she replies, raising her chin high in the air.

My body sags with relief. She's right. Callum is completely ruled by his mother. I suspect the only real reason he wanted to move back to England was to secure his inheritance before she passed away. Margaret's estate is worth a lot of money.

"I can't thank you enough, Margaret," I croak, my throat closing up with barely contained emotion. "This means the world to me."

Margaret's expression shows zero emotion when she turns to face me straight on. "I'm British, Sloan, so please take what I'm about to say as a one and only occurrence." She looks me in the eyes, and I swear I see a flicker of admiration on her face as she adds, "You're an excellent mother, and Sophia is very lucky to have you."

Tears. Tears, and smiles, and head-nodding are all I can feel outwardly as my heart reaches out to the woman whom I thought hated me for all these years. I manage to find my voice enough to reply, "Thank you, Margaret."

And without another word, she turns to walk away.

The Responsible Brother

Gareth

THE SMILE ON SLOAN'S FACE IS PERMANENT AS SHE SETS THE table in her kitchen, humming a tune and doing fancy twirls every few steps as she goes back and forth for more supplies.

I sit at the table watching her hips sway and her chestnut hair flip. It's been a week since I last saw her, and she mentioned on the phone that she has some news to share with me, but she wanted to wait until she saw me.

"Are you going to tell me why you're so happy?" I ask impatiently. "Don't get me wrong. I'm enjoying the show, but the suspense is killing me."

Sloan sets a plate down in front of me and smiles. "Yes, I'll tell you." She takes a deep breath and sits down on the chair beside me. Splaying her hands out on the table, she looks at me and says, "Margaret and Callum sent a new custody agreement to my lawyer today."

My body instantly stiffens. The truth is, any time Callum's name is mentioned, I tense. I hate that wanker. "What kind of new agreement?" I ask, my tone wary.

Sloan bites her lip and surprises me when a huge smile spreads across her face. "Callum wants to revise our agreement so he only has Sophia every other weekend now, instead of every other week."

My brow furrows in confusion. "Wait, are you saying he wants less time with her?"

"Yes," she replies with wide eyes. "It was Margaret's idea."

I sit back in my chair as I attempt to understand. "This doesn't make any sense. You said when he asked you for a divorce, he threatened to go for full custody."

"I know."

"So, what's changed?"

"Margaret's changed," Sloan answers and props her elbows on the table. She proceeds to tell me all about her talk with Margaret last Sunday. About Callum's new engagement and how disgusted Margaret is by the way her son has been behaving. She even tells me about the Coleridge connection to Kid Kickers and how disappointed Margaret is in Callum's lack of interest.

I shake my head as I digest all this information. The truth is, I already knew the Coleridge name was involved in my foundation, but I wasn't sure to what level. And Callum's name has never been attached to anything, so I assumed it wasn't him specifically. But the biggest matter at hand is the change he's requesting with Sophia.

"So you're saying Sophia is going to be around a lot more?" I ask, looking at Sloan, who's watching me with anticipation.

"Yes," she replies with a smile and stands up to continue setting the table. She opens a drawer and grabs some silverware while adding, "The new arrangement goes into effect when Margaret passes away. Kind of morbid, I know, but I signed the new papers two days ago, so it's really happening!"

With a genuine smile, I rush over to scoop Sloan up in a giant hug. Her giddiness is infectious as I spin her around, her hands full of cutlery. She squeals happily and begs for me to put her down.

When I lower her to the floor, my smile slightly falls. "Is Sophia okay with this? I mean, I'm sure she loves her dad. This can't be easy for her."

Sloan nods, a look of understanding on her face. "She is. We had a long talk before I signed the papers. I kind of fibbed a bit and told her it is because Callum's job is so demanding and he will have even less time once Margaret passes on. But I honestly think she knows the truth. Sophia is so damn smart."

My lips pull into a sad smile. "I hate that she can sense his disinterest even more than I hate his disinterest."

Sloan gives my shoulders a reassuring squeeze. "It's okay. Trust me, I'm going to make up for it. And maybe her time with Cal will be better quality now that it's less."

"We can certainly hope," I reply before another thought dawns on me. "Does this mean I'll be seeing a lot less of you?"

Sloan's brow furrows as she reaches up to cup my jaw. "Not necessarily. Freya is basically an on call babysitter whenever I need her. She loves Sophia almost as much as I do, so you and I will have our time together. And I know this is a lot, but if you're ready to officially meet Sophia, I'd love that. But if you think it's too soon, we can wait."

I move in to press my lips to hers, halting her doubts right where they are. I pull back and murmur, "It's not too soon."

Sloan smiles and kisses me again. "Good. I'm thinking maybe at a park. I can make us a picnic or something."

"I have an idea actually. One that I've been thinking about for a while now." I rub the back of my neck nervously as Sloan waits for me to elaborate. "What would you say if I told you I want to start training Sophia in football? One-on-one. Just the two of us. Very low chance of injury. We'd take it slow for starters and build her up as you feel more comfortable."

Sloan's eyes go wide. "You would do that?"

"Of course I would. I know you're worried about her health, so perhaps we can speak to her doctor about it first. I'd be happy to go along with you to be sure he's given the full scope of what I'd be doing with her."

"Gareth," Sloan says my name with a sigh. "Are you for real?"

I shrug my shoulders. "It's not that big of a deal."

"You're a professional athlete who's training for the World Cup. It's a very, very big deal."

I roll my eyes as she stares back at me with her jaw dropped. "I do have one condition, though."

Her brows lift. "Name it."

My brows lift right back. "You never say *soccer* again."

She laughs at my response and thumps my chest playfully. "And what if I slip?"

I lean down and playfully kiss her nose. "Then I get to use the handcuffs again."

"Deal!" she replies with a giggle, her face so beautiful and full of light. I can't help but pick her up and prop her on the counter so we're eye-to-eye and I can take it all in.

"This is going to be good, Treacle. I can feel it."

"It's already more than good, Gareth."

"Hello there, Sophia. It's nice to officially meet you."

The brown-eyed stunner eyes me carefully from her spot on the grass in the back garden of Sloan's home. I've set up a child-sized goalpost, along with several bright cones for some drills we'll play a little later.

After a minute, Sophia accepts my outstretched hand in hers. "You can call me Sopapilla if we become friends, but I'm not sure we are friends yet."

With a smile, I drop down on one knee so we're eye level. Sophia's chestnut hair is tied up into a high ponytail, and she's kitted out in bright pink and green footy gear all the way down to her multicoloured football socks covering her shin guards.

Her mother certainly dressed her for this occasion.

I begin digging out several balls from the sack I brought with me and ask, "Do you remember me from the Kid Kickers camp?"

"Maybe," she replies, pressing her pointer finger to her chin in thought. "But there were a lot of you big guys running around."

I nod knowingly. "Three of those guys were my brothers."

Her eyes widen. "That's a looot of brothers. Are they quite noisy?"

I frown and do my best to answer her question with a serious face. "Quite noisy. But they live in London now, so I don't hear them nearly as well as I used to when we were young."

"London is where the Queen lives!" Sophia peals excitedly.

"Do you like the Queen?"

"Oh yes, I love her a lot. Mum took me to see Buckingham Palace once, and the Queen actually drove by while we were there. It was fantastic. I think she waved right at me!"

I lift my brows in appreciation. "I'm sure she did."

Suddenly, her face falls. "I wasn't invited in for tea, though."

"Are you mates with the Queen?" I ask, trying my hardest not to smile but failing quite a bit I fear.

"No, but my class had a tea party in honour of her birthday. We sent her an invitation and everything, but she didn't come." She stares down at her feet with disappointment.

I nudge her on the shoulder. "I'm sure she had a full schedule that day."

She thinks on that logic for a minute, then says, "Or maybe the postman lost the invitation."

"I bet that's it," I reply with a wink. "So, Sophia, would you like to play some football today?" I ask, handing her the special pink ball I bought for her to keep.

Sophia clutches the ball in her hands and looks over her shoulder at Sloan, who's standing watch from the paved area by the house with Freya right beside her. The two women have their hands covering their mouths as they appear to be whispering back and forth to each other.

Sophia crooks her finger for me to come closer and cups her hand to whisper in my ear. "Don't let my mum hear you call it football. She's very American and gets kind of cross when I say football."

"Not anymore," I reply with another wink, then shout over to Sloan. "Sloan! What game are Sophia and I going to play today?"

Sloan's eyes narrow in silent warning, and Freya hits her with an elbow to the arm. "Fine...It's football!"

Sophia's eyes are wide on me. "You know football and magic if you got my mum to call it that!"

I laugh and stand up quickly, spreading my legs out wide. "Are you ready to play some football, Sophia?"

She beams up at me and answers, "Call me Sopapilla."

The first half hour, I work on teaching Sophia how to kick with the sides of her feet instead of the tips of her toes. Then we move onto some basic manoeuvres, which is hilarious in and of itself because she has an anecdote or story for almost every move I show her.

"That pullback thingy you just did is like when I offer candy to Cason, then say, 'Teased you!', and pull it back before he can grab it."

"Well, that's not very nice," I retort, holding the ball on my hip to listen. "Sounds as if you're toying with Cason's emotions."

"He's not very nice to me!" she exclaims with a stomp of her booted foot. "Yesterday, he stole my new markers that Mum just got me. I had to chase him all the way to the boys' bathroom and wait for him to come out."

I tilt my head at her. "You know, when I was a kid, if a boy picked on a girl like that, it usually meant that he wanted to be her boyfriend."

"Gross," Sophia squeals and covers her ears with her hands. "Cason eats food off the ground. He could never be my boyfriend."

I chuckle at the wrinkle in her nose that reminds me so much of Sloan, I can't help but adore the child straight away.

To get us back on task, I re-introduce the Sharks and Minnows game I played with her at the Kid Kickers camp.

"You can be a minnow the entire time if you'd like," I state and softly kick the ball over to her.

"Oh yes, I do like!" She kicks the ball away from me as fast as her little legs can take her. I attempt to steal it. She laughs. I laugh. Then she *really* laughs when I accidentally trip myself up and fall on the ground. When I realise how much pleasure my pain brings her, I decide to fake injuries every few minutes to keep the laughs coming.

Playing with Sophia reminds me a lot of Booker when he was little and we were just starting to learn how to play football. Dad would run tons of drills on all of us in the back garden of our house in Chigwell. Up until my talk with Dad in Cape Verde, I probably would have soured that memory in my mind, associating it with him being controlling. But when I really think back, there were some good moments.

Gareth

16 Years Old

"Okay, boys. Let's run that drill again, but do it at full speed this time!" Dad shouts as he cuts through the back garden and read-justs the five foot slalom poles that are lined up only three feet apart. "Anyone who bumps a pole has to run out to Booker and Poppy's fort and back."

I hear Booker fretting quietly to himself, so I squat down beside him. His wide eyes are grave on mine. "I bump the poles every time, Gareth. I don't want to run."

I give him a soft nudge. "I'll run with you, Book. Don't sweat it."

He nods, still nervous. But the minute Dad blows the whistle, Booker's expression morphs into fierce determination.

Camden and Tanner zigzag through the poles first, both moving in and out with ease and natural athleticism. We've only been playing football for about a year, but the twins have picked it up like they've been playing their whole lives.

I head nod for Booker to go ahead of me, voicing words of encouragement behind him the entire time.

"Brilliant, Booker! You have it now. Only a few more to go," I call out.

He huffs and puffs, his eyes cast straight down on the ball as I easily zig and zag while watching him. The twins have finished their drills and turn to offer their own form of support.

"For a keeper, his feet aren't half bad!" eleven-year-old Camden cajoles.

"It's all that dancing he does with Poppy in the woods," Tanner mocks, then adds in a sing-song voice, "His lover girl."

Booker's neck turns red-hot from Tanner's remark. Suddenly, he hits the very last pole with the tip of his toe.

"No!" he cries out, grabbing the back of his neck and dropping to his knees.

I finish my drill and run over to pat him on the back. "Relax, Booker. You're only nine and nearly as good as the twins. Don't get down on yourself over this. It's just a drill."

"Looks like you're running, Booker," Dad shouts as he straightens the pole and stares over at Booker. Dad's gaze is firm and unforgiving—all business when it comes to football. At least he's talking to us again.

Booker's chin quivers. "I don't want to run," he whines, still out of breath from the drill.

"Come on, Book. I'll run with you," I encourage and begin walking backwards toward the woods.

Dad watches me with a furrow to his brow, and I see a tiny flicker of his expression soften when he looks down at little Booker. With an awkward cough, he states, "Or perhaps I'll race you, Booker."

Booker's eyes light up and, without another word, Dad takes off toward the back of our property, jogging right past me. His pace is fast for an old bugger, that's for sure.

My youngest brother hoots with glee and chases after Dad, running as fast as his little nine-year-old legs can carry him. With a smile, I jog beside him, cheering him on. "Come on, Book! I know you have more speed in you than that!"

His face tightens with determination as he picks up speed. At the same time, the twins catch up to us, suddenly flanking either side of me and Booker.

"We'll slow that old geezer down!" Tanner yells, closing in on Dad.

Camden cups his mouth and shouts to his twin, "Tanner, show Dad your butt! It'll blind him with its pastiness, and he'll have to stop so he doesn't run into a tree."

Tanner looks over his shoulder with a frown as he puffs out, "You really think that would work?"

With a shrug, Tanner does exactly as he's told and Dad stops midstride, covering his eyes and rerouting his run. When Booker gets a full view of Tanner's arse, he begins laughing so hard that he has to stop and bend over to catch his breath. I encourage him to keep going and tell him this is his big chance to win. But instead of waiting for him to listen, I rush over and toss him up over my shoulder.

Booker's laughter is infectious as we run past Dad, who's walking now and shaking his head at all of us. In our moment of victory, I can't help but think to myself, Dad isn't so bad when he's like this.

Sloan

Golden beams of light slice through Gareth and Sophia's hair as the March sun begins to set behind the trees, silhouetting their soccer drills taking place in my backyard. Honestly, the entire view is cinematic. Frame-worthy. Life-changing.

Freya exhales heavily beside me and murmurs, "Good Lord, this is better than *Heartland* and porn combined. This is better than *Heartland* porn. This is better than a filmed sex scene between Ty and Amy Fleming, and you know how much I hate that, that show never gets dirty."

I whack her on the arm. "That's my child out there."

"That's Gareth Harris out there!" she retorts, her eyes wide on mine as she fans her face. "He's being so bloody sweet to your child that I think I've spontaneously ovulated."

"Freya!" I scold with a laugh, then look out to enjoy the show again. I mumble under my breath to her, "Although, I will admit that this has been the best two hours of my life in England thus far."

"Right!" she exclaims and resumes her Gareth watch.

The sight of Gareth playing with Sophia is so beautiful, I want to film it and gift it to crumbling nations to raise spirits.

Sophia's giggles echo off the house as she stumbles and Gareth scoops her up under the arms, preventing her from crashing to the ground. He kneels down to tie the lace on her cleat, and they appear to be having an entire conversation with each other that I sadly can't hear.

"What do you think she's saying to him?" I ask Freya.

"She's telling him that she wants a little sister or brother."

"Freya!" I shriek. "You're the worst."

"I am not, Sloan. I'm speaking the truth. A man who plays with your child like that is a man who needs to propagate the species."

I let out a happy sigh that's mixed with a swoon and topped with a groan. "Is this what happily married couples with children

177

have on a regular basis?"

Freya shakes her head. "Beats me. But I wish it for you, Sloan. God, I really do."

A few minutes later, Gareth and Sophia have finished playing and we all go inside for dinner. As soon as dinner is over, Freya excuses herself with a wink and heads out back to her guest house. I can tell Sophia is wiped out when she asks to watch a movie as soon as she finishes her meal.

After she changes into her pyjamas, I get her settled in the living room with a movie before rejoining Gareth in the kitchen. I walk in to see he has already cleaned up the entire dinner mess and has moved on to the soccer supplies that are strewn all over the attached mudroom.

"I can get those," I state, reaching out for Sophia's cleats.

"I got them," he says as he sets them on the rug and straightens the several pairs of shoes that belong to me, Sophia, and Freya. We're complete slobs, but the cute smile on Gareth's face indicates he doesn't mind our mess.

I can't help but shake my head at him. "You're nice to my child and you clean? I'm convinced you're not human."

He chuckles and turns to prop himself on the doorframe, his arm muscle flexing as he runs a hand through his dark hair. With a happy sigh, he points out toward the living room and says, "She is brilliant, Sloan."

My brows lift with pride. "It looked like you guys were getting along okay. There was a lot of talking going on out there, but I couldn't hear the majority of it."

"That girl doesn't stop talking," he replies with a pleased smile. "But I don't mind because she's extremely entertaining."

"Oh, God." I cover my face and peek through my fingers to mumble, "What did she say?"

"She said you walk around the house naked sometimes."

"No!"

"And she said that you and Freya drink wine out of coffee mugs, but you lie and tell her it's tea."

"She knows that trick?" My face heats with embarrassment.

"I'm afraid so. She also said you and Freya are obsessed with horses?"

"Well, I'm afraid that one is very true," I reply flippantly and ignore Gareth's confused expression. I smile wide and shake my head as I think about how much more Sophia must have said. "Good God, are none of my secrets safe anymore?"

"Doubtful," Gareth replies, a weird look morphing on his face like he's holding something back. He shakes his head and adds, "But truly, she's amazing. She seems wise beyond her years but still really fun and playful. It's quite brilliant because, after everything she has been through—fighting cancer, moving to a new country, her parents separating—she's taking it all in stride. It's a true testament to how wonderful of a mother you are."

My throat closes up in response to his words and the intensity of his eyes on mine. I look away and move to the sink, my hands splaying out on the counter for balance.

Once again, I am overwhelmed by Gareth's remarks about how I am as a mother. "How are you so good at this, Gareth?" I ask, my voice soft.

"Good at what?" I feel his eyes on my back like a warm blanket. His footsteps are light as he moves up behind me, mirroring my stance over the sink.

I turn around and look him straight in the eyes, allowing him to envelop me like a warm cocoon. "At saying all the right things and not freaking out over how messy my life is because of that wonderful little girl."

Gareth's brow furrows as he tilts his head and looks at me. "You are who you are because of her, Sloan." He slides his hands up my arms, soothing me with his touch. "The fact that you fought for her, bled for her, sacrificed for her makes me care about you even more.

Knowing everything I know now, there's no way I can walk away from you two. I want your mess in my life, Sloan."

With a deep breath, I press my forehead to his chest as my heart threatens to explode out of my body. He wraps his arms around me, cradling me, comforting me, squeezing me to him as I take in his scent, his manliness, his perfect embrace. He's so much more than I ever imagined a man could be.

And he's mine.

My body reacts to that last thought with a base drum kick to my libido. I have to physically pull myself off of him and push him away from my body. Licking my lips, I move toward the door. "I think we need to maintain a five foot distance between us until Sophia goes to bed."

His chest shakes with a laugh. "Why is that exactly?"

"Because when you say things like that, it makes it really hard for me to remember that I have a child who's awake in the next room." I run my fingers through my hair and smooth my shirt down nervously. "Speaking of which, let's go check on that child of mine."

"You're the boss," he replies and follows me into the living room.

As if destiny is playing a funny hand in my life, I find Sophia out cold on the sofa, her mouth hanging wide open as she breathes deeply in and out. I look over at Gareth, who's smiling so adorably, I think I spontaneously ovulate like Freya did earlier.

I clear my throat and whisper, "I better get her up to bed."

Walking around the couch, I gently shake Sophia's shoulder. "Come on, Sopapilla. It's time for bed."

"Mummy, nooo," she croaks, her eyes not even opening as she goes right back to breathing heavily.

I smile up at Gareth. "You wore her out."

"Let me," Gareth says, stretching his large frame over the back of the sofa. He hooks one arm under her neck and the other under her legs. With great ease, he picks her up like a baby without so much as a grunt. "Lead the way."

I purse my lips and feel my head doing a lot of nodding. I'm nodding to hide the swooning. I'm nodding to hide the smiling. I'm nodding to hide the insane butterflies and the overwhelming urge I have to grab my phone and snap a picture of this stunning athlete carrying my daughter up to bed.

On shaky legs, I climb the stairs ahead of him and push open Sophia's bedroom door. I quickly pull back the covers and stand to watch Gareth lay her in bed, tucking the quilt tightly around her body.

"Is that good?" he asks, looking over his shoulder at me.

My head is tilted as my gaze drifts from his backside to his face. "It's perfect."

He huffs out a soft laugh, then pauses to push a strand of hair out of Sophia's eyes before backing away from her.

I resume mommy mode by flicking on her nightlight and kissing her on the forehead. When I walk out into the hallway, Gareth is leaning on the opposite wall, legs crossed at the ankles and an oh-so sexy smile spread across his face.

"Today was fun."

I close Sophia's door and lean against the opposite wall. "More than fun."

"Really? Do you think she likes me?"

I nod slowly. "I think she loves you."

Like a dam breaking, we fly off the walls and collide into each other, his lips on mine, our tongues dancing as we fumble our way down the hall toward my bedroom. His hands grope my ass as my fingers tug on his locks. Our motions frantic, desperate, and brutal as we rip at our clothes, unable to stop the momentum of the day that's resulted in this feral display.

We burst into my bedroom and break apart as I turn to slam the door and click the lock in place. I press my back to the hard wood, my chest heaving with deep breaths.

Gareth's eyes are dark and ominous as he slowly stalks toward me. "Is this okay?" he asks with a pained breath, his lips red and swollen from my assault. He points to the door. "What if she wakes up?"

"She won't," I husk and pull my T-shirt up over my head. My nipples ache inside my bra as I undo the clasp and let the fabric drop to the floor. "She's a heavy sleeper."

Gareth's eyes drink in my breasts that feel swollen and heavy under his heated stare. "Thank fuck for that," he nearly growls as he tears his own shirt off as well.

In three big strides, he grabs me harshly by my waist and lifts me up so my legs wrap around him. Our lips connect again, dragging over each other's jaw and neck as we pant, and squeeze, and writhe against one another.

We end up on the bed, the rest of our clothes eliminated as our bodies unite deeper than ever before. It's a perfect equal power exchange as we roll and switch positions, him on top, then me on top.

When Gareth moves to his side and spoons me from behind, our frenzy turns to a slow, sweet motion. The kind that feels so good, you never want it to end. The kind that feels like you want to live in it forever and ever.

Gareth's hand wraps around my throat. Not in a tight, dangerous sort of way. It's a claiming cupping, a heart-melting embrace of trust. I trust him to hold me there, and to love me there, and to make me feel safe and cherished as our bodies gyrate into one another in perfect rhythm.

He releases my neck and slides his hand down between my legs, stoking my orgasm to a breaking point.

"Gareth," I cry out softly, my hand reaching back and pulling him deeper inside of me. "I'm going to come."

"Come for me, Sloan," he rumbles in my ear, his lips tracing a path down my neck and lighting my whole body on fire.

"I'm coming," I moan out, my voice low but the pressure inside me tensing like a vise.

"I feel you, Treacle. I feel every part of you," he murmurs into my ear, then releases himself to the sensations as well.

When Gareth comes inside of me, a flash of a baby shoots through my mind and my heart lurches in my chest. An image of Sophia holding a baby sister or brother brings tears to my eyes.

As our breaths slow and our bodies relax, I find myself asking, "Do you want children someday, Gareth?"

Gareth's arm tightens around me as he sits up and props his head in his hand. I roll onto my back so I can see the look of surprise on his face.

"Where is this coming from?" he asks, his eyes that shade of moody darkness that I love so much.

"I think I want more babies someday," I admit before I lose my nerve. What I'm feeling in this moment with Gareth is completely new, and I'm owning it because the man whose arms are wrapped around me has taught me to be fearless.

Gareth's eyes blink down at me for a long pause, and I feel anxiety building in my chest. "I'm sorry to drop that on you, but I want you to know. I've never even thought about a sibling for Sophia before now. After she got sick, I never wanted to put myself at risk like that again."

I reach up and run my fingertips over the scruff on Gareth's jaw as he continues watching me thoughtfully. "But now I think it was because I just didn't want another child with the person I was with. Even on our best days, it never felt anywhere close to this."

Gareth nods, his thoughts clearly drifting as he processes everything I've said. He slowly lies back down and stares up at the ceiling, his chest rising and falling with deep, smooth breaths.

As the silence grows, I begin to panic. Maybe I shouldn't have said anything yet. What if it's too soon? Am I willing to lose him over this? My voice is weak when I add, "It's not something you have to answer right now. Just…something to keep in mind, okay?"

He nods, his jaw tight. I roll back over and pull the blanket up over my face. My thoughts are screaming chastising words at me. Why did I bring this up now? Why didn't I keep my mouth shut? What if I've ruined everything?

But the fact is, I want more with him. I can't help myself. Seeing him with Sophia today changed things for me. It's not only a love feeling I have for him anymore. It's a sense of family. Like what Vaughn said he felt for Vilma. This feeling in my chest is bigger than love.

Gareth's deep voice suddenly breaks through my swirling thoughts. "Babies would be good."

I inhale sharply, holding the breath high and tight in my chest as his words sink in. "Really?" I ask, needing to hear the confirmation so I know I didn't imagine it.

Gareth shifts to wrap his arm around my waist, pulling me to his chest. "Yes, really. I'd love to have a family with you, Sloan."

Tears prick the backs of my eyes as I bite my lip and try to contain the emotion swelling in my chest. It's a rush that I could possibly compare to skydiving.

But better.

So, so much better.

And with that, I drift off to sleep, dreaming of babies, and futures, and...family.

What feels like only moments later, I am woken up by the sound of banging on my bedroom door.

"Mummy, why is your door locked?" Sophia's muffled voice calls out, ripping me out of my glorious dream.

I sit up with wide eyes and see Gareth slowly coming to right next to me. "Shit!" I exclaim, looking at the clock to see it's after eight the next morning. "Gareth! Wake up!" I whisper-scream and begin shaking him awake.

Gareth scowls as his eyes flutter open to the sunlight streaming into the room.

"Mummy, what did you say?" Sophia asks through the door.

I clear my throat loudly as Gareth finally realises what's happening and bolts out of the bed.

I scramble off as well and look everywhere for my clothes. "Nothing, Sopapilla!"

"Oh, then why is your door locked?" she asks again.

"It must be stuck!" I rush over to my closet to grab my robe.

"Oh wait! Freya taught me how to undo the locks with a pen," Sophia says excitedly. "I'll be right back to save you, Mummy!"

I hear her little footsteps take off down the hallway and look over at a naked Gareth standing in my bedroom with sleep-tousled hair and holding his T-shirt over his groin.

"Shit! What do you want me to do?" he asks, his eyes wide and adorably freaked-out.

"Get dressed for one!" I shriek, finally finding my purple, silk robe and wrapping it around me.

"Fuck me," he says, finding his shorts and jumping into them first. "I didn't plan to sleep here last night."

"I don't even remember closing my eyes," I reply, knotting the belt around my waist and somehow still marvelling over how hot Gareth is shirtless.

He grabs his T-shirt again and asks, "Should I sneak out now while she's gone?"

"No!" I snap, my eyes swerving to the door. "She's probably just in her bedroom. She'll totally catch you." I thrust my hand into my messy hair and look around for a solution. "You could hide in the bathroom, but the shower door is glass. She'll see you if she goes in there."

I turn around, chewing my lip. "Closet, maybe?"

Gareth shrugs. "If you think she won't look in there."

"She probably will. She's always in my freaking closet. Freaking hell. I was going to talk to her today about you not being just my friend, but my boyfriend."

Gareth's face contorts slightly at the last word. "Isn't there something better you can call me? I've always hated that word. It sounds childish," he grumbles, running a hand through his hair.

My eyes fly wide. "This is so not the time to discuss your feelings about a silly word, Gareth. We have to figure out what to do with you before she gets back!"

"Right," he retorts, then looks behind him. "Window?"

"You know what?" I rush past him and pull back the curtains. "This little trellis here is no different than a ladder really."

"Obviously the exact same thing," he deadpans.

"We're desperate!" I open the window and nearly die when the alarm begins blaring loudly. "Shit! Freaking shit, freak, shit!"

I run over to the panel by my door, quietly cursing Gareth out for having the ridiculous alarm installed in my house in the first place.

Finally, I type in the code. When all goes silent, I hear Sophia shouting from her bedroom in a bored tone. "Mummy, did you set off the alarm again?"

"Yes, Sopapilla! Silly me. It's off now!" I call back casually, then hurry over to Gareth as he throws his leg over the window frame.

"God, this is something Tanner would do," he mumbles under his breath as he positions his feet on the trellis. "I'm supposed to be the responsible brother."

"Yeah, yeah. Get going. I think I hear her coming," I say as he begins to lower himself.

"It's a good thing I love you," he whispers as he takes his first step down.

"Wait!" I stick my head out the window. "Go around to the front of the house and ring the doorbell like you just arrived to pick up your balls or something."

His brows lift as an amused smile spreads across his face. "Balls. Got it. Anything else, boss?"

I bite my lip and lean my head further out the window. "Kiss."

With a naughty smirk, he climbs back up one step and plants a chaste kiss on my lips.

"I love you," I rush out. "Now don't fall because I'm pretty sure you're worth a lot of money to that football team of yours."

I close the window on his chuckles. Then I manage to pull the curtains shut just as Sophia bursts through the door with her eyes wide. "I got it, I got it! I'm going to go wake Freya up to tell her I can do it by myself now!"

"Sophia, wait!" I cry out as she turns to run down the hallway. If she goes outside, she may run into Gareth. "I, um, need a little cuddle first."

Sophia sighs and shakes her head. "Oh, Mum, you're so needy sometimes."

Unfriendly Friendlies

Gareth

ENGLAND TEAM CAMP IS GRUELLING. GARY AUSTIN IS NOT A manager to keep it light in order to avoid injuries. He requires high-intensity participation throughout the entire camp. Since this isn't the first time I've trained with him, I'm not at all surprised. My brothers, on the other hand, are a different story.

"Christ, this is a sweet, sweet form of hell on earth," Tanner baulks after his mile-long cooldown run. He yanks down the sweatband around his forehead and groans, "It's your fault we're here, Gareth."

"My fault?" I ask with a laugh and tip my head back to squirt some water into my mouth. "I didn't pull any favours to get you guys here."

"Austin makes Dad look like an angel," Camden huffs as he joins us on the sideline. He bends over to grab his water bottle and takes a swig. "This reminds me of my first camp at Arsenal. It was killer."

Booker jogs over next, having just finished his goalkeeper session on the far side of the pitch. "Hiya, guys," he says happily, his voice smooth and completely at ease.

"Why aren't you puking?" Tanner asks, staring at Booker like he has two heads.

188

"Why would I be puking?" Booker asks, pulling off his keeper gloves and dabbing the sweat on his temple with his forearm.

"God," Tanner scoffs. "Keepers have it so easy. What did you guys do over there? Sit down in a circle and visualise stopping the ball?"

"No, we worked on punting," Booker defends and looks to me for explanation. "We did visualisation this morning."

I roll my eyes toward Tanner. "Ignore him, Book. Tanner is just dying because the prat spent the last six months eating pancakes like they were his last meal, and he's out of bloody shape."

"Fuck off," Tanner cajoles, dropping down on the ground. "And the joke's on you because they were completely worth it."

Hobo is next to join us. The tall, curly-haired German's smile is pretty much permanent since he got called to join the camp. His dual citizenship in England and Germany made his presence on the England team a possibility, but it was his stellar season with Man U that earned him the spot.

Hobo looks down at Tanner's crumpled up posture as he sits on the grass. "Tanner, why do you always appear like a corpse at the end of camp every day?"

"I don't!" Tanner retorts with a serious furrow to his brow.

"You do. You are out of shape, my friend. I think perhaps you have been too repetitive in your workout routines." Hobo sits down next to Tanner and uses his hands as he gesticulates what he's saying. "See, every club and manager is different. I've played for so many teams, I am used to drastic changes in workout regimens. This skill makes me a valuable player. Let me show you."

Hobo rolls into a push-up position and looks over his shoulder at Tanner. "Tell me this. When you make love to your wife, is this how you do it every single time?" Hobo begins pumping his hips into the grass in the missionary position but with comical, fast, jerky motions.

Booker, Camden, and I burst into laughter as Tanner's face

crumples in disgust. "Fuck right off, German!" he bellows, bolting at Hobo and shoving him onto his side. "I can't even understand a word you're saying. What language are you speaking?"

"English, but I know four other languages if you prefer I try those instead."

Tanner blinks stupidly at him. "Why don't you try the language of shut the hell up?"

Hobo laughs, not the least bit put-off. "I can stay late and do some conditioning with you if you'd like."

Tanner swerves his eyes to me. "Gareth, control your teammate. I think he's coming on to me."

I laugh and shake my head. "He's your teammate, too, right now. And he has a point. You wouldn't be hurting so much if you watched your diet," I state, eyeing him seriously.

Tanner stares up at me. "Gareth, why do you hate fun so much?"

Out of the corner of my eye, I see the Chelsea team making their way onto the pitch. We've been passing them the last few days as our camp ends and their daily training begins.

I spot Vince Sinclair amongst his teammates, his beady eyes darting away from mine as soon as he sees me. He's been giving me a wide berth since the trash talking that happened in the tunnel at our last match. It seems uncharacteristic for him, but I imagine it's because he's angry he wasn't invited to train.

"Is anyone else surprised that Sinclair wasn't invited to this camp?" I ask, looking down at my brothers and Hobo.

"I'm not. That guy's a fucking wanker," Camden growls. "You saw that highlight where he tackled me from the backfield a couple weeks ago, right?"

"Yes," I reply through clenched teeth. It was entirely fucked-up. The reporters remarked on how lucky Camden was to be able to walk off a hit like that.

"He was completely going for my bad knee. The prat should have been red-carded." Camden rips up some grass and tosses it out in front of himself.

"Well, at least we won't ever have to play on the same team as him," I console.

"Thank fuck for that," Camden grumbles.

I stare at Vince again and an odd feeling pricks the back of my neck. One that I can't quite put my finger on.

The rest of camp goes incredibly. Tanner—whiny as he may be—picks up the pace and comes alive the last few days, especially when he and Camden break off into offensive work. They immediately click like no time has passed since Cam left Bethnal Green. And Booker is one of three keepers here. What he lacks in experience, he more than makes up for with his passion.

Eventually, Austin splits the group off into two teams for a closed friendly match, and I'm thrilled to see that he's put my brothers, Hobo, and me all on the same side.

Playing alongside my family again is a thrill I never realised I was missing. It's been years since we've all played together, but I guess all those years of going over match films with Dad has finally paid off. I know exactly what my brothers are going to do before they even do it. It's instinctual. Blindfolded, we'd each probably know where the other is at out on the pitch.

It's especially exciting to play with Booker. I was never able to play on a team with him since I signed with Man U before he started for Bethnal. But knowing I'm not only defending to keep my keeper safe, but also my brother, brings a whole new level of intensity to my game. Not that Booker needs my help. He stops three goal attempts from the other side with the ease of a seasoned athlete.

The rest of the team feeds off of our energy. In the end, our friendly match becomes a bit of a walloping as Tanner and Camden bounce the ball back and forth, scoring goals and sending the opposing keeper into fits. It's a beautiful game of football. If we never make it to the World Cup tournament together, this day alone will be an experience I cherish for the rest of my life.

But when Austin calls us into his office and says he wants all four of us to be at the press conference room at Wembley Stadium tomorrow morning, we're practically buzzing with anticipation. He won't tell us what is going to be announced, but we have a good idea what to expect.

Camden, Tanner, Booker, and I are seated at a long table up on an elevated stage. There are microphones positioned between each of us, and Gary Austin stands at a podium beside me.

The room is filled to the brim with over one hundred reporters, cameramen, photographers, and various team staff members who are standing off to the sides. This is the first official announcement from England concerning their World Cup squad, and the people are excited for what's about to be shared.

Austin clears his throat, and the chatter in the room mutes instantly as he begins speaking.

"Thank you all for being here today. I won't be announcing the entire twenty-three-man squad for England today. That will be released at a future date so that those men get their quality time.

"What I'm about to tell you all is a bit unorthodox, and that is why I've called this special press conference.

"The Championship League clubs have been making insane headlines as of late. Games have been utter chaos in the best way possible. Honestly, football fans are losing their minds with highlights of this calibre.

"And when great things like this happen, it is a genuine fear that the World Cup tournament will be anticlimactic. I mean, historically, coaches keep their game plans very simple with national teams. You can't expect these athletes to get together for a couple of camps and some friendlies and have the kind of chemistry that they do with their own teams they play with every day.

"But, I'm shaking up England's team this year. I'm dipping into the Championship clubs for my squad because there is certainly the quality of playing that I'm seeking. And there's a set of brothers whom I think can bring the spirit of football to an all new level for England and the World Cup.

"When you have four boys and a father who've lived, slept, and dreamt about football their entire lives, it's something you notice.

"Are there Premier League players who are more qualified to be on my squad? Absolutely. Are there four people more dedicated to the sport of football who have cleaner records and higher statistics? I'm sure there are. Are there four brothers who have more heart, more passion, more love for their family and this game? No. There is not.

"That is why I'm calling up all four of the Harris Brothers for the World Cup team. After what I've seen this past week at a private camp I held, I'm convinced they will lead England in this tournament and bring home some new gold trophies for our country."

Austin backs away from the podium and the press explode with questions, one after another, after another. My brothers and I look at each other. Our faces are composed on the outside, but anyone looking close enough can see that fire, that spark. That game time moment of adrenaline that shoots through an athlete's entire body right before a big play.

With a small nod to my brothers, I turn my focus back to our manager.

"Coach Austin, what about Tanner Harris and his questionable judgement last season?"

Austin pins the reporter with a menacing glower. "I'm well

aware of Tanner's past, and I'm not concerned about it in the slightest."

"Coach, don't you think Booker Harris is a bit too young? A bit too inexperienced? He's only played for his father's team."

Austin scoffs and shakes his head. "The Cup has had seventeen-year-olds play before. And have you seen the size of Booker Harris these days? He towers over his oldest brother, whose position on the squad is being doubted by none of you, I'm sure. Booker is fit and he's a fine keeper. He'll do the job well."

"Coach, can you remark on the bad blood between Vaughn Harris and the Manchester United Football Club?"

"No, I cannot. Vaughn Harris has not been asked onto my team, so his history with Manchester United is of no relevance to me. The only thing I know about Harris is that he runs a top-notch club in Bethnal and he was a joy to watch in the 80s."

"Coach! Coach! Gareth Harris's home was burglarised three months ago. There are rumours that it was foul play within the league. Players angry at you for inviting four brothers over other more qualified players. What do you say to that?"

My brow furrows. I quickly slide forward to the mic, giving Austin a nod that I want to take this one. "I've been told the incident is still under investigation. Unfortunately, no one has been caught."

Austin's eyes are narrowed at the reporter as he adds, "And if there are rumours of foul play within the league, I hope they catch the bastards who committed that crime. Any athlete not man enough to see that this game is about a hell of a lot more than statistics isn't a player I want to coach on my team."

Austin sits down in the chair opposite the podium, his forehead covered in a sheen of sweat as he takes a drink from his glass. The team publicist comes out next, announcing that my brothers and I will take a few questions before concluding the conference.

A male reporter catches my attention in the front row. "Gareth, how was the secret camp you just completed with your brothers?"

I lean forward to the mic. "It was an experience that I will remember for the rest of my life. World Cup or not, I'm thankful that Austin gave me the opportunity to play alongside my brothers again."

"Tanner, how does it feel to be playing with your twin brother again? Were you angry at him for signing on with Arsenal?"

Tanner laughs and shakes his head. Tucking his long hair behind his ears, he leans into the mic and says, "You're bloody well right I was angry. He doesn't call, he doesn't write. I don't even remember the last time he sent me flowers."

The reporters erupt into laughter as Tanner winks at Camden, who just rolls his eyes.

Tanner returns to the mic and says, "No, I wasn't angry. I was proud as hell. I'm proud of all my brothers every single day."

"Booker Harris! When is the new baby arriving? Are there going to be wedding bells in your future?"

Booker smiles a shy smile and leans in. "The baby is arriving any day now, and we're holding off on wedding plans until then. For now, we're just excited to become parents."

"Camden, any chance your wife will be on the medical staff for England?"

Camden laughs and shakes his head. "I'm afraid that's not up to me, but I'm certain my wife would do the job well. My knee has never felt better."

"Gareth, what do you think your father will say when he hears the news?"

I inhale a deep breath and exhale slowly before replying, "I think he'll say that our mum would have loved to be here for this."

Harris Sunday Dinner

Sloan

AFTER THE WORLD CUP PRESS ANNOUNCEMENT, GARETH'S TEAM played against Camden's in London and lost. Talk about a whirlwind of emotions for the family. But they apparently don't hold a grudge because Gareth is heading to Sunday dinner at their dad's house like he does nearly every Sunday.

The difference this time is that I'm joining him.

It was just going to be me because this is Callum's week with Sophia, but Margaret called to say she isn't feeling well and asked if I can keep Sophia. I have a feeling she is in bad shape because when I asked if she wanted me to bring Sophia out for a quick visit, she ardently said no.

Margaret is never one to show weakness.

Now, Sophia and I are on a train heading to London to attend our first infamous Harris Sunday dinner.

Sophia sits across the train car table, her feet dangling off the ground as she stares out the window to watch the English countryside whiz by us. "So, Mummy, do I call the little girl Rocky or Adrienne?"

"You can call her whatever you'd like," I reply, taking a sip of the coffee I just bought off the snack cart.

Sophia nods, her bushy brows furrowing as she gives it some

seriously deep thought. "Maybe I'll come up with my own nickname for her."

I smile behind my cup. "That would be just fine."

Sophia's thoughts are clearly rolling on top of one another when she asks, "So all these men play football?"

I nod. "Yes, they do."

"And you said two of the ladies are doctors?"

My smile is growing. "That's right."

"And there's a teacher?" Sophia's eyes are wide as she smiles brightly. "This family sounds so cool. I'm glad you are in love with Gareth."

I nearly choke on my coffee. "Who said I am in love with Gareth?"

"Oh, please, Mummy. It's so obvious." She rolls her eyes in that "seven going on seventeen" way.

I hold back a laugh. "How is it obvious?"

She pins me with a look before staring up at the ceiling and listing all the ways. "Like, how you check yourself in the mirror before he comes over. And you make sure the house is always clean. And you never walk around naked anymore."

The naked comment has my eyes narrowing. "Well, those could just be normal things. They don't necessarily mean I'm in love with him."

Sophia is completely undeterred. "Well, you smile now, too."

My brow furrows. "I smiled before."

"Yes, but it was a sad smile," Sophia replies, widening her big brown eyes on me. "It was a smile that looked like you were pretending."

My heart skips a beat inside my chest. "Sophia, I'm sorry if I ever made you feel that way. I was never pretending with you."

"Maybe a little bit you were," she corrects and crosses her arms on the table to rest her chin in her hands. "It's okay, Mummy. I know why."

"Why?" I ask, genuinely curious to hear what her answer will be.

"Because you didn't love Daddy the way you love Gareth." She shrugs and turns her gaze out the window again, leaving that little truth bomb behind like it's no big deal.

This girl—this incredibly smart, impressive little girl—has been through so much, yet she still sees everything going on around her.

"When did you get so perceptive, Sopapilla?"

She frowns and looks back at me. "What's perceptive?"

I smile. "It's when you notice things that some people don't."

She nods and replies, "Probably when I turned seven."

Her answer is so matter-of-fact, I can't help but giggle and move over to sit beside her so I can hold her the rest of the train ride. She is seven, but she is still my baby, and the smile on my face right now is completely real.

Gareth sends a car to pick me and Sophia up at the train station. A short drive later, we're outside the gate of the Harris family house. Well, mansion is more like it, though it's not old and dilapidated like the Coleridge Estate. It's slightly more modern with giant pillars in the front. My mind reels at the memories Gareth has in this home growing up without a mother, or a father for that matter. Although, it seems like things with his dad have been very good since the wake in Cape Verde, so I'm hopeful their reconciliation is long-term.

Sophia and I walk up the gravel driveway. Just as we reach the front step, the doors burst open. Out comes Booker with his arms wrapped around Poppy, who's holding on to her pregnant belly for dear life. Her cheeks puff out as she exhales and inhales quickly.

"Booker, I forgot my handbag!" she exclaims and moves to turn around.

"Vi, grab Poppy's bag!" Booker yells over his shoulder, then returns Poppy to forward motion. "It's going to be okay, Sunshine. We got you."

"Someone needs to call my parents," Poppy cries as Tanner, Belle, Camden, and Indie hustle out the doors next.

Camden and Tanner seem to be in the middle of some sort of argument, so Belle frantically shouts at Tanner to call Poppy's parents.

"I don't have Poppy's parents' number."

"Then just run over there. Fast!" Belle exclaims. "They only live around the corner for God's sake."

"Wife, we're having a baby. I don't have time to go for a jog right now!"

"Dad! Call Poppy's parents!" Camden shouts back into the house and looks over to Belle. "Dad has the number."

This brings a collective sigh to the two shouting couples as they attempt to make their way toward a vehicle.

Poppy is the first to notice me and Sophia standing here with our jaws dropped. Her eyes fly wide as she plasters on a pained-looking smile. "Sloan, is this your daughter?" she cries out much too loudly as she continues panting against what I can only assume are contractions.

"Yes, this is Sophia," I reluctantly reply, wrapping my arm around her.

"Oh my God, I've been dying to meet her!" she squeals and makes a move toward us instead of the truck that Booker is trying to lift her into.

"I'm sorry but, Poppy, are you in labour?" I ask because surely she can meet Sophia another time.

"Yes, I am!" she bellows out with a crazed sort of laugh. "We can talk after, right?"

"After you have a baby?" I ask, my brow puzzled. Then I realise that rationalising with a woman in labour is not wise. "Yes, Poppy. After is good."

Booker finally wrangles Poppy into the truck and closes the door. He glances over at me apologetically. "I'm so sorry, Sloan. We were all really looking forward to meeting your Little Minnow. Gareth won't stop talking about her."

My attention is diverted from Booker when Tanner and Camden collide into me and Sophia with big, squeezing hugs.

"Is this Little Minnow?" Camden asks, squatting down and giving Sophia's shoulder a playful punch.

"This is Sophia," I reply, my eyes swerving everywhere as everyone rushes all around us. "Are you all going to the hospital?"

"You bet we are!" Camden retorts. "Nice to meet you, kid."

Tanner suddenly drops down and clutches Sophia's arms. He shakes her excitedly while shouting, "Little Minnow, we're having a baby!"

Sophia giggles at the insane look on Tanner's bearded face.

"Tanner!" I glance up to see Vi hustling over to us, but she's gazing down at Sophia. "Sweetie, don't laugh at him. It only encourages him. Just think of him as a naughty puppy that won't stop licking himself."

Sophia giggles again and replies, "Okay."

"Also," Vi says, kneeling down with Rocky in her arms, who has food mushed all over her adorable face. "Little Minnow, I'd like you to meet Rocky. She's very excited to play with you when we're not hurrying off to the hospital, okay?"

Vi looks up at me with a big smile as Hayden comes over and shoots Sophia a wink. The three of them load up into their minivan as Sophia jerks my arm and asks, "Why do they keep calling me Little Minnow, Mum?"

Before I can answer, Belle appears in front of us next. "Because Gareth says you have great footy skills and you're a stellar little minnow out on the pitch. Hiya, Minnow. I'm Belle and that redhead in the glasses is Indie. We're married to those crazy brothers who bothered you a moment ago, but don't be scared. We'll keep a tight lead on them from now on. We have to run to the hospital now, so we'll talk more later, okay?"

Sophia smiles shyly and tucks behind me a bit as Belle jogs up to the car where Indie is sitting in the backseat.

"I want to go with them, Mum," Sophia states, pointing to the cars as they pull away.

Finally, Gareth comes out of the house with his phone attached to his ear. His eyes find mine and a look of genuine surprise flits across his face. "I was just trying to call you."

"We're here," I reply helplessly as the madness begins to settle. Our timing does not seem ideal.

"We're on our way to the hospital," Gareth states, then moves in to ruffle Sophia's hair. "Hiya, Minnow."

"Hiya," Sophia chirps with a pleased smile on her face. I think it's safe to say she likes her new nickname.

I gesture back toward the gate and say, "Should I have that car you sent take us back to the train station, or do you need it?"

Gareth's face furrows in confusion. "Why would you go back to the train station? Did you forget something?"

"No. This just seems like a family thing," I reply, eyeing Vaughn as he walks out of the house and turns to lock the door.

"Sloan"—he moves in close to drop a kiss on my cheek—"you and Minnow are my family. Come on, let's go see my baby brother have a baby."

The butterflies in my belly are unrelenting as Gareth picks Sophia up to carry her back to the car. She squeals with delight and wraps her hands around his neck.

"Minnow!" Vaughn's voice shouts from behind us, and Sophia looks over Gareth's shoulder in response. With a smile, Vaughn says, "Welcome to Harris Sunday dinners!"

She smiles back. Then, like a crazy natural disaster, we follow the loads of people on their way to welcoming another Harris into the world.

"It's bloody twins!" Booker croaks as he bursts through the double doors of the waiting room.

"What?" everyone replies in unison, jumping out of their seats.

Booker runs a hand through his hair, his eyes wide and disbelieving. "I don't know what happened, but somehow the second baby didn't show up on the scans. Now I have two sons!"

"Oh my God!" Vi exclaims, grabbing onto Hayden's arm with an excited death grip. "How is that even possible?"

Everyone's eyes swerve to Belle and Indie—the two doctors in the group—for an answer, but Booker replies, "The doctor said it's more common than people think. It's quite fitting because we were rowing over names and now we get to use both. Oliver and Teddy are amazing. I can't wait for you guys to meet them. Poppy needs a few minutes because she is beside herself."

"I'm sure she is," Vaughn replies with a shake of his head, then pulls Booker into a big hug.

"Oh, and we're engaged," Booker adds as he pulls away with an adorably sheepish expression on his face.

Vi looks like she's going to faint.

"Are you bloody joking?" Camden exclaims, grabbing his brother around the shoulder and mock punching him in the gut.

Booker's face turns red as he replies, "No. I asked her to marry me when she was holding our babies. I had the ring and planned to do it tonight at home, outside our playhouse in the woods, but we never made it there. So I figured, what the hell. A hospital is as good of a place as any."

"Yes, it is!" Vi squeals and jumps into Booker's arms for a hug. "Congratulations! Oliver and Teddy have the best parents!"

"Thanks, Vi," Booker replies, then looks over at Gareth for his usual nod of approval.

Gareth silently obliges, his prideful smile saying so much more than words ever could.

Out of the corner of my eye, I see Sophia chasing Rocky down the empty hallway, their giggles echoing in my ears. As everyone moves in to hug Booker, Gareth's hand suddenly squeezes mine tightly.

I look over at his affectionate expression with tears in my eyes and an enormous smile on my face. I suppose this is what a real family feels like.

I could get used to this.

One Pink Rose

Sloan

"**I**'M GOING WITH YOU, SLOAN," GARETH STATES, HIS EYES HARD and unrelenting on mine as he stands on the opposite side of my kitchen with a dish towel slung over his shoulder.

"Gareth, this is Sophia's grandmother's funeral. She's a Coleridge. And the service will be attended by all of Manchester and London high society. People would definitely recognise you."

"I don't give a toss." He flings the towel into the sink and crosses his muscled arms over his chest.

"We agreed to keep our relationship quiet until after the World Cup. You and your brothers have been front-page news for two weeks straight now."

"None of that matters anymore," he growls and leans back against the counter. "This is different, Sloan. This is real life. I'm not going to let you and Sophia go through this alone."

I inhale deeply and pin Gareth with a look. "I've gone through a hell of a lot worse with Sophia on my own. I can handle it."

"I know you can but I can't!" he exclaims, the veins in his neck protruding angrily. "Don't you understand, Sloan? It will kill me to not be there beside you. For comfort, for friendship, for someone to lean on and look to. I don't *want* you to handle it alone!"

Suddenly, Sophia is standing between us, her arms outstretched like she has to hold us apart. "Gareth is coming, Mummy."

I stare down at her and shake my head. "Sophia, I told you to go up to your room."

"No, I don't want you guys to fight," she retorts.

"We're not fighting," I reply and cut Gareth a look. "We're having a disagreement."

"It doesn't matter. I said Gareth can come and so did Grandmama," Sophia states, turning to face me with her hands on her hips like a tiny little Wonder Woman.

"When did your grandma say that?" I ask, looking down at Sophia, who still has not cried a single tear since I told her the news of Margaret's passing.

"She said it to me the last time I saw her," Sophia answers, a dark expression fleeting across her face as a memory clearly falls down over her.

"What else did she say to you, Sophia?" I ask, kneeling down to look into my daughter's eyes.

Sophia takes a big breath and replies, "We said goodbye. That's all. But, Mummy, please don't be cross at Gareth. I don't want to lose him, too."

I look up at Gareth, whose hard eyes have instantly softened.

He drops down to his knees on the other side of Sophia and gives her hair a ruffle. "I'm not going anywhere, Little Minnow. You're stuck with me for a long, long time."

A sense of anxiety works its way up in my chest. I'm not the only one in this relationship with Gareth. Not by a long shot.

At the church, Sophia sits with Callum and Callie in the front pew. Her brown hair tied back in a low ponytail. Her black dress with a white collar, perfect and pristine, the way Margaret would have liked. I never realised how hard it would be to watch Sophia be a part of the Coleridge family without me. To witness her interacting with her father and his fiancée through an emotional time that I have no place in. I notice that Callum never comforts Sophia. He never embraces her. Sophia simply follows him into the pew and sits down with perfect posture, awaiting her time to give the reading that Margaret asked her to do. Whatever Margaret shared with my daughter when they last saw each other two weeks ago has prepared her for this day better than I could have ever imagined.

Gareth's arm wraps tightly around me as I watch my little girl walk up to the altar, wait as the minister adjusts the microphone to her almost eight-year-old height, and read a passage from the bible with complete grace that she did not get from me.

That is all Margaret.

Through proud tears, I look over at Gareth and mouth a silent thank you. I didn't want him here, but having him here is exactly what I need.

At the cemetery, Sophia chooses to stand under my umbrella with Gareth instead of with her dad and Callie. I watch her quiet reserve slowly begin to crumble as the minister sprinkles dirt over the casket and speaks the final words about Margaret's life.

My little fighter hasn't shed a single tear up until this moment. As soon as one slips out, it's as if the floodgates have been opened. She hides her face in my dress, sniffing loudly and squeezing me around my hips so tightly, I'm sure her arms are exhausted.

Gareth comforts me while I comfort Sophia. When the funeral ends and everyone makes their way back to their cars, the three of us stay behind. Once everyone is gone, Sophia lets go of me and wipes harshly at her tears as she walks over to the burial site.

"What are you doing, Sophia?" I ask.

"I want a flower," she states and points to the spray of roses draped over the casket.

My eyes find Gareth's and he nods his understanding.

"The pink one," Sophia says to Gareth, pointing to the one pink rose that's hidden amongst all the white ones.

Gareth smiles kindly and reaches his long form over to pluck the flower from the casket spray, then kneels down to hand it to Sophia. She instantly presses it to her nose and looks up at me with tear-soaked eyes.

"Grandmama said this one is for me."

Without another word, my perfect little girl turns to walk back toward the limo, passing by a waiting Callum on her way.

I swipe at my own tears as Gareth puts his hand on the small of my back as we turn to follow.

Callum clears his throat as we reach him. "Did you get my email about the meeting next month?"

With a frown, I look over at him and nod. "With Margaret's lawyer? Yes, I got it. I'll be there." I look around, annoyed that he's bringing this up here of all places.

"Good. Don't be late," he tuts, then eyes Gareth for a moment before turning on his heel to join Callie and Sophia in the limo.

"What's that about?" Gareth asks, watching Callum with cautious warning in his eyes.

I shake my head. "Probably Sophia's inheritance. But with Callum, I'm always wary."

Theatre of Dreams

Sloan

O VER THE NEXT FEW WEEKS, LIFE BECOMES A BIT UNUSUAL. Photos of me and Gareth at the funeral appear in several gossip magazines. My website engagement spikes to an all-time high, and my dormant Instagram profile that I set up for my business suddenly gains twenty thousand new subscribers.

I also get a handful of phone calls from potential clients who are searching for custom designs. Freya is busy vetting everyone to establish if they are legitimate. If they are, we may be running a slightly different business in the near future.

I even receive a couple of emails for interview requests which Gareth instructed me to forward to his agent. I suppose this is what dating a Manchester United athlete gets you.

But Gareth takes it all in stride, clearly used to ignoring this sort of attention. He told me that it's the way his father raised them. No social media and no interviews unless thoughtfully coordinated. Vaughn's ideals are also why Gareth doesn't have excess staff members or luxury vehicles and homes like other athletes. The Harris family—dynamic and interesting as they may be—tends to keep a low profile for the most part.

It's kind of a relief. It means that when Gareth's not travelling or training, he's at my house, just being normal despite the current attention we're receiving. We have dinner together with Sophia and Freya. Then Freya and I try to hide our heart eyes as we watch him play with Sophia in the garden nearly every evening. For being a highly-paid, highly-famous athlete, Gareth is very good at the whole domestic, average life thing. It makes me think there's a good chance for some normalcy once he decides to retire someday.

And after the argument Sophia broke up in the kitchen between Gareth and I, it's clear she's getting very attached to him. The notion scares me because I don't want her to become overly dependent on him. There's still so much that can change between us. There's no ring, no commitment. And even that doesn't guarantee anything. I mean, he's still a famous soccer player—modest as he may be. Who knows what our future holds?

I'm riffling through my closet, on the hunt for Sophia's umbrella, when my phone vibrates in my pocket. It's Callum. He's due to pick up Sophia in an hour, so seeing his number gives me a bad feeling.

"Hello?" I answer, my voice wary.

"Sloan, hello. Look, I'm not going to be able to take Sophia this weekend."

"Callum, don't do this," I reply through clenched teeth. "You already cancelled your weekend with her two weeks ago, and she was so disappointed."

"I know, but I'm swamped at the office and Callie has family in town."

"So take Sophia!" I exclaim, my voice high-pitched. "You two are engaged! I'm sure Sophia would love to meet some of her future family."

"Sorry, not this time." Callum's voice is so smooth and business-like, my anger spikes.

"Callum, you can't keep doing this," I grind out. "She just lost her grandmother whom you knew better than anyone. She could use your comfort right now. Please don't cancel on her again. At least take her to lunch or something."

"Sloan, look, I have to go. Tell Sophia I'm sorry."

With that, he hangs up, my phone going silent as I begin to tremble. Releasing a mighty cry, I chuck my phone against the closet wall and cover my face with my hands.

As the tears begin to fall, I'm wrapped up in warm, strong arms. Gareth's scent falls over me as he turns me to face his chest and shushes me while dropping soft kisses in my hair.

"What happened?" he asks, his tone ominous.

"Callum cancelled on Sophia again," I croak, my voice muffled against his chest. "This is going to crush her. I could kill him."

"Not if I get to him first," Gareth retorts, his arms tensing around me.

I pull back and swipe furiously at my tears. "He just makes me crazy because, if this is how our future is going to be with him, I'd rather he disappear forever than disappoint her every other weekend. At least when Callum and I were together, it was easier to conceal these disappointments from her."

Gareth's face tightens at my last remark, his eyes narrowing slightly as he watches me. "Do you want help telling her?"

I jerk my head from side-to-side. "No, she's my daughter. I will tell her."

With a heavy sigh, I move past him to walk out of my closet and go find Sophia. Gareth wraps his hand around my wrist to stop me. His eyes are pleading on mine when I look back and he states, "Sloan, I can help."

My posture straightens. "It's okay. I can handle it. Why don't you go downstairs while I deal with this?"

Sophia sobs in my arms for twenty minutes straight. In those twenty minutes, I think of forty-seven different ways I can murder Callum and hide the body so no one finds out. After she calms down, she asks for some privacy. I decide to take a hot shower, hoping like hell a solution to this mess will come to mind while I do.

When I come out of my bedroom to check on Sophia, I over-hear her mumbling, "I hate my dad."

My heart aches for the pain in her voice, but I slow my steps when I hear Gareth's deep chuckle carry down the hallway in response to her comment.

"Hate is a strong word, Little Minnow."

"I know, but he promised last time he cancelled that we'd go see Rex at Grandmama's lake. I miss Rexy. He must wonder where I've gone."

I tiptoe closer so I can hear Gareth's reply.

"Well, hopefully your mum can take you out there sometime soon. I think there are still some grown-up things of your grand-mother's that need to be sorted first."

Sophia harrumphs. "I still hate him."

I peek around the doorway and nearly die when I see the two of them face-to-face, stretched out on their bellies as Sophia paints Gareth's nails. Gareth's big hand is splayed out on a towel as Sophia sticks her tongue out while trying to keep the polish brush straight.

He watches her for a moment before saying, "You know, my dad used to let me down a lot when I was your age."

Sophia lifts her wide eyes. "Really?"

Gareth nods. "I used to get so mad at him, I broke my own toys just to let off some steam."

She nods thoughtfully and looks back down as she dips the polish brush back into the bottle. "I'd rather paint your nails than break my toys."

Gareth chuckles. "I really do like this colour."

"Me too!" she exclaims as she dabs more on his pinkie finger.

"It's the same red as my team's colour. Perhaps I'll leave the polish on for my game tomorrow."

Sophia giggles and shakes her head in disbelief. "You wouldn't do that."

Gareth narrows his eyes at her. "You're right. But I will leave one painted if it cheers you up."

"It will, it will!" she peals with a giggle that makes my heart soar with joy. She continues painting for a moment before asking, "Do you like your dad better now? He seemed nice at the hospital."

Gareth smiles. "You know what? I do like him better now. I think some men just need a bit more time to grow up than others."

Sophia's brow furrows as she thinks that through. "I'm glad you're all grown-up already, Gareth."

"Me too, Little Minnow. Me too."

Sophia finishes Gareth's nails and smiles big. "I'm all done!"

With a quick roll-over onto his back, Gareth sits up, careful not to bump his nails on anything as he checks out his new manicure. "Tell you what. I'll leave two nails painted for the game tomorrow. One for you and one for your mum so that you guys know I'm thinking about you during my home match."

"That's perfect!" Sophia squeals happily and begins putting the nail polish away.

"Perhaps your mum will even let you come to a match one of these days."

Sophia's eyes fly wide and she turns to look right at me, like she knew I was standing here the whole time. "Can we, Mum? Can we?"

My face heats with embarrassment as Gareth gives me a look for shamelessly eavesdropping. I cross my arms and shrug. "Sure, we can go to a football game."

"Yay! When?" Sophia asks, turning to Gareth, who smiles brightly at her.

"How about tomorrow?" Gareth waggles his fingers at me with a sexy smirk. "I got my nails done special for it."

Old Trafford is insane on game day. With my experience styling loads of athletes and their wives or girlfriends, I knew what to expect for the crowds. Admittedly, though, I've never actually sat and watched a match in the WAGs section like I'm planning to do today. And I certainly never had Sophia in tow like I do now.

Sophia's eyes are wide and flying all over the place as we make our way up to our seats. The music is loud, and the seventy thousand people filing into the park are positively buzzing with excitement. Even a non-soccer-fan like me can't help but get caught up in the energy.

Old Trafford itself has always had an amazing sense of soul and history. You truly do feel like you're a part of something special when you walk through the gates.

The WAGs section has a bit more subdued energy as Sophia and I find our seats. It's full of women who are in no way kitted out in game day gear like Sophia and I. Instead, they are completely dolled up with full hair and makeup, high fashion outfits with killer high heels, and designer purses that cost more than my car payment.

They look fantastic.

I look like the mom who just spent two hundred pounds in the gift shop to buy a couple of jerseys with HARRIS written on the back to make her child happy.

There are a few other moms with children in tow, but the kids are so glued to their handheld devices, they don't even notice the excitement buzzing around them.

I see a couple of my clients and wave to them. They politely wave back, but I can feel them eyeing me speculatively through their giant sunglasses. Then I see a client dressed exactly like me.

"Brandi!" I exclaim, helping Sophia into our row and finding our seats are right next to her. "I didn't know you would be here!"

Brandi smiles and presses her finger over her lips to shush me. "Call me Layla here. I can't let my teammates know I came to Hobo's game in Man U gear." She leans over to give me a hug and offers a wink to Sophia. "Although, I'm certain these WAGs have no idea who I am. Zero interest in women's football, so they couldn't give a toss if I'm here being a traitor."

I laugh at her remark. "Surely you're not a traitor since there are men's and women's leagues. They are hardly competing clubs."

Brandi shakes her head. "You can't use logic when it comes to football fans in England. And definitely not with City and United fans. Besides, there's something really magical about the ol' Theatre of Dreams here."

"Theatre of Dreams?" I ask curiously. "What is that?"

"It's a nickname for Old Trafford. There are several reasons it applies to this organisation. For example, ages ago, some railway workmen came together to play football and created Man U. That's one way. Then, a while back, a plane crashed and killed eight players, but the club went on to reach the finals of the FA Cup that year. That's another. There have been so many times this team has been down a goal or more, then ended up turning it all around. They're called The Comeback Kings. It has a great spirit, this pitch. I'm still a proud City player but, bloody hell, it really is a theatre of dreams. Inspiring, don't you think?"

Brandi looks down and points to Sophia, who's watching her with starry-eyed wonder. "I see it."

"See what?" I ask, gazing down at Sophia.

"She's dreaming already. Aren't you, kid?"

Sophia smiles a shy smile but nods up at Brandi, confirming her thoughts. Suddenly, music begins booming as the Man U players walk out onto the field, each holding the hand of a young child.

Brandi explains that Man U and many other European teams select various local schools, clubs, or youth winners of a tournament to walk out onto the pitch with the players. It sends an overall message that football makes a difference for children. Today, I notice all the children's T-shirts have Kid Kickers scrawled across their chests, and my heart swells with pride to see Gareth's organisation presented like this.

Gareth is holding the hand of the tiniest boy on the pitch. The little squirt is slowing down the entire line as he stares off up at the thousands of people surrounding the field.

Sophia tugs on my arm and whispers in my ear, "I want to walk out with Gareth someday, Mummy."

I smile and wrap my arms around her. "Maybe someday."

My eyes focus in on Gareth's fitted red shirt, white shorts, and black and red socks. There's an intensity in his eyes as he stares out at the crowd, but when he looks down at his tiny escort, his expression morphs to sweet affection. As if drawn to us like a magnet, Gareth straightens and spots me and Sophia in our section.

Sophia squeals, "Gareth sees us, Mummy!" She hoots out a cheer and swirls around to show him the back of her matching jersey that she begged me to buy for both of us.

She tugs on my shirt and, with a shrug, I twirl around and show him the back of mine, too. He laughs and waves back at us. Then he makes a peace sign with his hand and turns it so we can see his two red-painted nails. Sophia's smile could light up a Christmas tree, she's so happy. And that's how she remains for the entire game.

For the next ninety minutes, Sophia, Brandi, and I have a blast watching the game and joining in with the chanting crowds. Sophia and I stuff our faces with chips while Brandi educates us about the game and the rivalry between Chelsea and Man U. This is the second time they've played each other, and Man U apparently walloped them when they first played each other in London a few months back.

The game is a smashing success for the most part, aside from the few minutes during halftime when I overhear some of the WAGs whispering behind us.

"She is a stylist?"

"Is that really how she dressed?"

"She's styled for me before. She's quite good."

"That's the one Gareth Harris attended a funeral with?"

"I wonder which other clients she slept with."

"Better not be my husband."

"I wonder whose child that really is."

Brandi cuts them a scathing look, but I ignore them because Sophia didn't hear their comments and the very last thing I want to do is spoil this day for her by drawing attention to the situation.

Back when I decided to jump all in with Gareth, I knew that I'd be under scrutiny from loads of people. That's one thing marrying into the Coleridge family prepared me for quite well. I don't think I fully considered that Sophia would be under a microscope as well, though.

The thought doesn't sit well with me.

The game is a tense nail-biter, ending in a three-to-one victory for Man U. Gareth had a stellar block on a Chelsea player right at the end, and the two went toe-to-toe with some choice words that I really wished I could hear. It looked bad enough for me to cover Sophia's eyes, but by the time she wrangled my hand off of her face, Gareth was walking away with a haunted expression in his eyes.

Brandi leads us to the gate entrance where the players will walk out after they've cleaned up. I can tell Sophia has fallen even more in love with football than she was before. The spirit of it growing inside of her with everything she sees.

As soon as the stadium doors open, several people rush the gate. I look over their heads to see it's Gareth who's stepped out first. He takes his time, signing programmes, shirts, arms, and papers. Whatever they have, he's signing. He smiles and seems perfectly at ease with the attention.

When he finally reaches us, he ruffles Sophia's hair and says, "That's a great looking kit you have on there, Little Minnow. Want me to sign it?"

"Yes!" she beams excitedly and turns around so he can scrawl his name on the back of her jersey.

Clearly in his own little world, Gareth smiles up at me and asks, "Would you like me to sign yours as well?"

I smile and shake my head at him, murmuring so only he can hear. "You can sign something else later."

He waggles his brows at me, then asks if we'd like to go out to celebrate. Sophia cheers with excitement as Gareth nods to a security officer to let us through the gate. I see photographers snapping photos as we turn to say our goodbyes to Brandi, who's still waiting on Hobo.

We are all smiles as we follow Gareth to his car that's parked in the player lot, but my thoughts are jolted in a different direction the moment Gareth closes Sophia in the backseat.

"I have to tell you something," he says, grabbing my hand and walking me around to the passenger side door.

My eyes lock on his. "What is it?"

He swallows slowly and replies, "I think I remember something from the attack."

Gareth

I drive Sloan and Sophia to a restaurant that I know is kid-friendly and has loads of arcade games that Sophia can play while I talk to Sloan. As soon as we're settled and the waitress has taken our orders, Sloan gives Sophia a nod of approval and she dashes off without hesitation.

Once she's out of earshot, I lean in closely. "Remember when the doctor said that something may trigger my memory of the attack?"

Sloan nods and leans in closely as well, her ruddy lips moist as she pulls in the bottom one and chews on it nervously.

"Well, tonight when I stopped that striker Vince Sinclair from scoring at the end, his teammate said something that sort of clicked things into place."

"What did he say?" she asks, anxiously wringing her hands on the table.

"He said, 'That was a nice shot, Sinny.'" Sloan's brow furrows. "Okaaay…How did that trigger something for you?"

"Because Sinny isn't a nickname I have ever heard Vince Sinclair called before. I don't know if it's new, or if only his close friends use it. But the second I heard it, I remembered hearing that name in my house the night we were attacked."

"Are you serious? Like, was it him? He was there?" she asks, her eyes wide as she processes everything I'm saying.

I shake my head. "I don't *think* so. Vince is stupid, but not that stupid. But I suddenly remember a voice saying, 'Sinny never said anything about a woman.'"

My voice catches in my throat as I tighten my hands into fists on the table. Sloan runs her fingers over mine, silently soothing me as flashes of her being struck and crumpling to the floor flick through my mind.

"God, Gareth. What does this mean? Why would he want to do that to you?"

"I don't know," I admit with a shake of my head. "I should have stopped them. Paid better attention. Looked up before kneeling down beside you."

"You're mad at yourself for checking on me first?" she asks with an incredulous expression on her face. "Gareth, if I wanted a crime-fighter or a vigilante, I certainly wouldn't downgrade to a footballer."

I half smile at her use of footballer and shake my head. "How can you be making jokes when I think I know who was behind the attack on us and just went face-to-face with him on the pitch?"

Sloan runs her hand up and down my forearm. "Because we're

okay. Because you're here, and Sophia is right over there, and we didn't lose anything."

"If I'm right, Sloan—if the police figure out he is connected to the attack—I swear to God, I'll—"

"You'll do nothing, because you're going to go tell the police about this and justice will be served. Then you can go back to playing football and spending time with me and Sophia. You have more than yourself to think about now."

I inhale and exhale heavily, nodding the entire time. "You're right. You're right a lot, you know. It's really frustrating."

She smirks back at me. "If you'd like, I can be wrong about something else so you can punish me later."

"Promise?" I ask with a wicked grin, then we turn our attention to Sophia, who has just commandeered a dance game with a boy who looks like total trouble.

The next day, I call the police station and the detective who was assigned to my case back in December asks me to come in to look at the security footage. They had recommended I not watch it before because it can be quite disturbing for victims of an attack. But with this new information, it seems necessary.

When I arrive, I see he's a portly fellow named Bernie who seems a bit over-worked but appears to be quite sharp.

"Mr. Harris, thank you so much for coming in. I'm told you've had some of your memory return."

"That's right," I reply, stuffing my hands into my joggers.

"Good, good. Perhaps with your new recollection, watching the security footage might help us fill in the rest of the blanks. Come on back."

He leads me into a dark office where a man sits in front of two large computer screens.

"This is Fiero, our computer tech. He's able to enhance images as necessary. Okay, Fiero, take us through. Mr. Harris, you just stop us if you see anything of interest."

Fiero scrolls through the CCTV footage that reveals three men hopping the wrought iron gate that surrounds my property. One with surprising agility appears to find an open window on the second level. Watching him scale the walls of my house like Spiderman is an eerie feeling. An image I'll never be able to forget.

When the footage shifts to interior shots, something substantial sticks out to me. One glaringly obvious item. "I'm sorry, but can you rewind that, please?"

Fiero reverses the image.

"Pause it right there," I state, leaning in closely. "Are you able to enhance the image?"

He nods and clicks a few buttons on the keyboard. The perp's face is covered with a ski mask and a hooded jacket, but his shoes are a pristine bright white. "Can you zoom in on those shoes and enhance it again?"

Fiero does as I ask. When the image becomes clearer, I step back and run my hands through my hair. "I know those trainers."

"Okay," the officer replies slowly, looking closer at the shoes on the man's feet.

"They are the new Adce football trainers that came out a few months back," I explain as the two gentlemen stare at me with confused looks on their faces. "I'm a professional athlete, and I've received early editions of new trainers before. It's generally linked to your sponsors and helps drum up excitement for a new product. I know for a fact that Adce signed Vince Sinclair for an endorsement deal in November. I was offered the same deal and turned them down. I think the man wearing those trainers is somehow connected to Vince Sinclair, who plays for Chelsea."

"How many early editions do these companies usually pass

out?" Bernie asks, pulling a notepad out of his back pocket and begins scribbling away.

"Very limited. Typically only one," I reply, my heart pounding in my chest. "Detective, after what I told you, I know Vince has something to do with this. Whoever is wearing those shoes must have gotten them from Vince as some sort of payment."

Bernie nods and reaches for the phone on the desk. "I'm going to make some calls and see what we can figure out."

"Okay. What do I do until then?"

"Nothing. I don't think you're in any immediate danger. The attack happened months ago and there hasn't been another. So we'll investigate this as quick as possible and get back to you soon."

I nod and Fiero stands to walk me out. "Thank you, Detective."

"Don't thank me until someone is behind bars," he replies and turns his back to me as he gets to work on catching the bastards who did this to me and the woman I love.

More Money, More Problems

Sloan

MARGARET'S LAWYER'S OFFICE IS OLD AND OPULENT. GLOSSY dark wood, old-fashioned drapes, and wood flooring that creaks everywhere I step. There is even a pair of stuffed mallard ducks propped up on the ledge of the fireplace. The entire building makes me feel like I've stepped straight back into the house on Rossmill Lane that I lived in for so many years. The place where I was invisible and unloved.

But I'm not the same person I was when I lived in that house. So much about me has changed. That's exactly why I refused to have Gareth's lawyer come with me today like he adamantly insisted. I'm spreading my wings and learning how to fly on my own at last. I may still be at the mercy of Sophia's father for as long as he's in her life, but that's only ten percent of the time. The other ninety percent, she can be with me.

Somehow, those duckies feel like a joke from Margaret beyond the grave, and I can't help but smile. I suppose that's the beauty of truly enjoying your life. The little things don't bother you like they once did.

Margaret's lawyer, Harry Morrison, is a tall, wiry man with black hair plugs and wearing a suit that costs every bit of five thousand pounds. He spreads out a few papers on his desk and finally looks at me and Callum seated in the wing chairs on the other side of his desk.

"Thank you both for being here today," he huffs in his posh British accent. "I have some business I need to go over with you in regard to the Margaret Coleridge Estate and her will that was left in my care."

Callum smiles knowingly, sitting back in his chair and femininely crossing his legs. "Good to see you again, Harry. Before we get started, can you please tell me why my ex-wife needs to be here for this?"

Harry gives Callum a forced smile. "Well, she is stated in your mother's will as a beneficiary."

"What?" Callum exclaims, nearly spitting when he huffs out an incredulous laugh.

"It's all explained in these letters from Margaret, which she asked me to serve to you today instead of delivering a normal reading of her will."

Harry picks up two sealed envelopes, handing me the one with my name on it and the other to Cal.

Without pause, Callum rips his open and unfolds the paper. "This has to be a joke. Mother wouldn't do this."

With a curious frown, I slowly open mine to see what all the fuss is about.

Dear Sloan,

I have set aside a large trust fund for Sophia, as well as given her the Lake District estate and all the acreage that surrounds it. This home is where I have experienced the utmost joy with her. We have a lot of fond memories there, and I want her to continue enjoying it as much as she'd like.

As I'm sure you are aware, the home and trust fund are worth a large sum of money. Because of Sophia's age, I am listing you as the executor of her estate until she is twenty-five years old. At that time, the trust fund, home, and property will go to her.

This fact will likely not go over well with my son, but I have many reasons for putting you in charge of this. I'm not inclined to inform you of them all, but I will oblige you to some.

I want Sophia's education and dreams to be infinite. That special little girl is full of imagination, hopes, and ideas. I trust that you are best suited to guide her in her quest to follow those dreams, wherever they may lead.

The other significant thing I need you to know is that I've also set aside a lump sum inheritance for you. This is not charity. This is what you are due.

When I first met you in America and my son told me of your unplanned pregnancy together, I was appalled. I thought your modest upbringing meant that you were after my son's wealth and were using this child as a form of entrapment. It is why I asked you to sign that horrible prenuptial agreement before I agreed to let you two marry.

I've now realised that I was wrong—an adjective that does not sit well with me. Therefore, Harry will have you sign some paperwork, then give you a cheque. This is the appropriate amount of money a woman who marries a man like my son should receive in a divorce.

This money will give you authority. It will give you control. It will give you freedom. And please always remember that the woman who holds the purse strings, holds the power.

Sincerely,
Margaret Coleridge

When I look up, the lawyer has a second envelope for me and another for Callum.

Cal rips his open and stands up, nearly kicking his chair over as he does. "This is ludicrous! My mother was not of sound mind when she signed off on this. She couldn't have possibly been!"

"Callum," Harry interrupts, stopping my pacing ex-husband in his tracks. "I assure you, Margaret was of very sound mind."

The veins in Callum's neck protrude angrily. "How could she possibly have these feelings about me? I'm her only son."

I look down and tear open my second envelope. The moment my eyes focus on the number of zeroes, I begin to have my own internal fit. Although, I'm guessing our reactions are for very different reasons.

Harry turns to hand me Sophia's envelope next. A bit thicker since it's a trust and not only a cheque.

I can barely see straight let alone open hers, so Harry takes pity on me and calmly states, "It's even more than yours."

My head is shaking back and forth, but my eyes are trained on Harry. "This has to be a mistake."

"That's what I'm saying!" Callum barks, splaying his hands out on the mahogany desk and leaning over Harry.

Harry's demeanour is completely composed when he replies slowly, "It's not a mistake."

"How much did she get?" Callum asks, moving over to peek at the cheque that's already folded back up inside the envelope. "Sloan, please tell me how much you and Sophia received."

Harry quickly interjects. "Ms. Montgomery, I advise you to not say a word at this time. This is a lot of information you need to digest."

I nod thoughtfully and look up at Callum. A light sheen of sweat has broken out on his forehead, and I can't help but puzzle over how things changed so drastically between him and his mother. It wasn't long ago that they were a united front, intimidating me into split custody. Now, it seems Margaret is on *my* side.

"So, what now?" I ask, my throat constricted as I turn my gaze back to Harry.

Harry opens a large manila file. "I have some paperwork for you to sign and that's it. I can recommend a good financial advisor to you as well, or I will transfer the details over to whomever you'd like.

I do suggest you speak with someone about how to best handle this amount, Ms. Montgomery. It's important."

I swallow slowly, taking in his advice as Callum drops back on the edge of his chair. "So she gets the family fortune and I get the dilapidated house on Rossmill Lane? This isn't right, Harry! The Lake District is a family estate! Sloan's not even a Coleridge. She never took my legal name."

Harry slides a stiff glance to Callum, who looks like he's going to stroke out at any moment. "I'm afraid this is what it is."

I swear I see a twinkle in the lawyer's eyes as he points to all the places I need to sign and hands me the keys to the Lake District estate.

Harry dismisses me, but before I walk out, I turn around and ask, "What about Rex, the dog?"

"Oh! I almost forgot. Mrs. Coleridge bequeathed Rex to Sophia. He is currently living with the groundskeeper in the home on the backside of the property. Rex can stay there, or Sophia can take him with her. It's entirely up to you."

I smile. "Please call and let him know that I am coming to get Rex now."

Harry smiles and nods. "Very well."

"Thank you for your time," I reply.

Without another word, I leave his office, my entire world completely transformed in front of a couple of mallards.

Gareth

When the buzzer sounds off, I hop out of the ice bath. I wrap a towel around myself, hunching over and trying to stop my body's trembling while wiping away the horrifyingly cold liquid dripping off of me. Bloody ice baths are medieval torture. But the older I get, the more I need them. I used to be like the younger players, training for hours a day and going out the same night without a second thought. Not anymore.

Now, I can barely make it to nine o'clock at night before falling asleep. Luckily, the routine at Sloan's house has been an easy one to fall in to since Sophia's around a lot more. Sometimes we go to bed when she does and, bloody hell, it's nice.

My phone lights up on the stretching table beside me, so I hobble my frozen bones over and swipe the screen to answer.

"Gareth, hey! Are you done with training?" Sloan asks.

I've been thinking about her all day because she had a meeting with Margaret's lawyer this afternoon. We got in a pretty big row earlier this week when I wanted her to take my lawyer with her and she refused. I hate that she went alone. I don't trust Callum. Not by a long shot.

"Yes, I'm just cooling down," I reply, forcing my teeth to stop chattering. "Did it go okay?"

"It went better than okay," she replies, her voice high and excited.

I frown curiously as I walk through the hallway from the physical therapy room to the changing room. Most of my teammates have buggered off already, but Hobo and a couple others are still lingering. I reach my cubby and head nod to Hobo, who's sitting a few chairs away, typing on his mobile.

"Where are you? It sounds like you're driving," I ask as I drop down on the chair in front of my dressing area.

"I am," she confirms. "I'm on my way out to the Lake District to pick up Rex. Freya is picking Sophia up from school, so I'm going to bring him home and surprise her!"

A pleased smile spreads across my face. "Rex, the dog, right? That's brilliant! Sophia will be thrilled."

"I know," she replies. "He's apparently been staying at the groundskeeper's house, but I think he belongs at home with us."

"I agree," I reply with an easy smile. "So, is that all? I mean, surely there is more."

"Oh, there's more." Sloan takes a deep breath that sounds nervous.

"Well, I hope you're not going to try to bring a horse back to your place as well because, I have to warn you, I don't think your car has a hitch on the back for a trailer."

Sloan giggles a bit too much and the anticipation for what she's about to say is potent. "Actually, the horses can stay at the lake because it currently belongs to Sophia and, well, me by proxy. Margaret named me the executor of Sophia's inheritance."

"Bloody hell," I reply, my face falling. "Sophia got the entire property? That's quite a shock. I mean, I assumed Sophia would get something, but I'm surprised that Callum isn't in charge of it after how close you said he was to his mother."

"Well, I'm not sure Margaret was as close to Callum at the end because she left me money, too."

"You?"

"Yes, a lot of money. More money than I've ever seen in my entire life."

I run my hand through my hair in confusion. "Why did she leave it to you?"

"Her letter says something about the prenup I signed when Cal and I got married being unfair. But I think a lot of it is because she was upset with how Callum handled joint custody after we got divorced. It's all so weird. I could hardly feel my face when I was signing the papers."

"Right. I imagine this is a lot to digest." I slump back on the chair and puzzle over how this all turned out.

"But, the biggest thing of all is that I'm free!" She giggles happily into the phone, her voice rising in pitch with excitement. "I don't need Freya's rent for the guest house anymore. I don't have to live near Rossmill Lane, or worry about Callum coming after me with lawyers, or work as a stylist even. With this kind of money, the sky is the limit! Hell, I can move back to Chicago if I'd like because I have the means to do so now. If Callum tries to fight me on something, I can really fight back! I feel untouchable, you know?"

"I see," I reply, my voice tight in my throat as my jaw aches from how hard I have it clenched.

"What's wrong? I thought you'd be happy for me!" she peals. "I am finally out from under the thumb of the Coleridge's control. I depend on no one!"

A dark, ominous feeling presses down upon me. Hobo must sense it because he shifts over to the seat beside me with a concerned look on his face.

"Gareth, say something," Sloan adds, her tone pleading.

I swallow down the knot in my throat and say, "I'm happy you're happy."

"Why do you sound weird?"

I clear my throat and look around the nearly empty room, my mobile cracking in my hand as my grip tightens. "I'm fine. There are just a lot of people in here, so I'll talk to you more later, okay?"

"Okaaay," Sloan replies slowly, her tone confused.

I hang up and chuck my mobile across the room. It crashes against the far wall and thumps to the floor.

"Bad service?" Hobo chirps from beside me, shooting a drink of water into his mouth.

I stand up and turn on my heel, yanking my clean T-shirt off the hanger. "Not bad service. I'm just losing it I guess."

"What's going on, Harris? Talk to me," Hobo says, propping himself back inside the cubby next to me and blinking his eyes up at me coyly. "Brandi says it's good for us to talk about our feelings."

I step into a pair of jeans and button them up, cutting Hobo an unamused expression as I fix my shirt. "Sloan sounds like she's going to move back to America."

"What?" Hobo asks, his voice high-pitched and surprised as he leans forward on his chair. "When?"

I exhale heavily and sit down beside him, facing forward with my elbows on my knees and my head hanging low. "I don't know. She didn't exactly say that, but she sounds...different. She got a boatload of money today from her ex-mother-in-law, and I feel like everything is about to change."

I can feel Hobo's eyes on me as he asks, "What kind of strings are attached to this boatload of money you speak of?"

I shrug, my dark mood darkening further. "She didn't say there are strings. Said she signed some papers and that was that. Seemed so simple."

Hobo nudges me in the leg. "My father is British and comes from old money like the Coleridge's. One thing I know about the wealthy British is that they don't do anything without strings. You have seen that with Kid Kickers sponsors, I'm sure. Rich people are always serving some sort of selfish goal. Your brother would like that pun, yes?"

I huff out a small laugh, surprised that there's anything Hobo can say to lighten my mood. "Yes, Camden would like that pun. But what do I do about this? Sloan doesn't seem to want my help. She already refused to have my family lawyer with her today. She thought it would antagonise Callum unnecessarily."

"Perhaps you should have your lawyer look at whatever she signed. Check out her paperwork and such. It can't hurt, no?"

I nod in agreement. "I'll give Santino a call and see what he thinks."

"Super," Hobo replies with a smile. "This will be fine, Gareth. Sloan is not going to move back to America. There is far too much to keep her here."

I look over and shake my head at him. "I'm not entirely sure about that."

Sloan

Gareth is unusually quiet at dinner. I thought he'd have questions about my meeting today, but he doesn't bring it up again. I thought he'd have fun with Sophia and the dog in the backyard, but he's quiet. Solemn. He sits beside me on the patio as we watch Sophia toss a ball for Rex, but his mind is in another place. Maybe all the extra training he's doing for the World Cup is finally catching up to him? I know he's nearing the end of the regular season for Man U and his team isn't finishing out as strongly as he'd like. As the team captain, I've seen how heavily that weighs on him.

But something is off about him.

When I get ready for bed, he finds me inside my closet and reaches around me from behind to hold my body to his. He's silent as his lips touch my shoulder and he kisses a slow path up my neck. When he reaches my cheek, he silently commands me to turn my head so he can have my lips.

I give them to him willingly because I'm hopeful it brings him back to me. His firm hands rub me over top of my clothes, hard and almost painful. He palms my mound and squeezes my breasts so firmly, I cry out into his mouth, the hard caress causing all the blood to rush between my legs.

Without a word, he turns me around and carries me to my bed, pausing to lock the door. He drops me on my back, leaning over to remove my top. Then he hooks the sides of my pyjama bottoms and slides them down with my panties. I quickly move myself up to the top of the bed, my breath heavy in response to the dark look in his eyes.

I lie naked and waiting as he yanks his shirt off over his head and slowly pushes his shorts down so low, all I see are the defined lines of his hipbones and a light smattering of dark hair disappearing into the waistband.

He is all man right now. From his body, to his posture, to the possessive look in his eyes. It's overwhelming.

His eyes lower down to the damp area between my legs. My body involuntarily squirms against the mattress in anticipation for what's to come.

"Touch yourself for me, Sloan," he commands, his voice low and guttural.

My head tilts. "What?"

He licks his lips, not an ounce of teasing on his face. "I want you to touch yourself."

I exhale a breathy sigh while my hand reluctantly moves to my centre. His eyes narrow as I slowly begin to circle my clit. I'm not using any magnificent technique, but watching him watch me is extremely arousing all on its own.

"Do you remember the first time you made me touch myself, Treacle?" he asks, his voice tight.

Our first night together flashes in my mind. My hips lift upward as I ride my hand and moan out, "Yes."

"There's a beauty in this kind of surrender, isn't there? Can you feel it?"

"Yes," I moan out again as Gareth slowly reaches inside his shorts and pulls out his thick, long cock.

He fists himself in front of me, stroking from the base to the tip. His gaze sweeping my body, his forearm flexing with each pump. "But to fully dominate something is beautiful as well. Do you agree?"

"Oh my God, yes," I cry out, my legs squeezing together over my hand in needy frustration.

The bed dips as Gareth crawls up between my legs and stills my hand with his. I watch him curl his fingers tightly around my wrists and move them off to the side. He presses them down into the mattress, leaning over me and whispering against my lips, "What would you do if I took this all away?"

"Took what away?" I pant, feeling the soft head of his erection brush my inner thighs.

"My mouth, my hands, my body, my cock...Me."

He dips his head down to my breasts and latches onto my nipple, sucking it in harsh and sharp. I cry out from the throbbing sensation that shoots straight from my breast and pools between my legs.

"Fuck me, Gareth!" I beg, my voice a mixture of throaty desire and desperation. "Please, please fuck me."

He releases my nipple and bites his lip. There's a possessive expression in his eyes as he looks down at me, like I am exactly how he wants me. Complacent and wanting. Limp and waiting.

His hands cinch tighter around my wrists. "You want me to fuck you, Treacle?"

"Yes!" I exclaim, wrapping my legs around his hips and pulling him to me. "Please, Gareth. I need you to fuck me."

His body stiffens against me, his hands relaxing their grip. "You need me?" he asks, his face unreadable in the dark.

"I need you," I beg, my hands slipping out of his grip and slowly trailing up his arms in tender, loving caresses. "I need you so much."

He inhales deeply and positions himself at my entrance. He holds himself there, waiting for my eyes to connect with his. "You're mine, Sloan. You understand that?"

"Yes," I answer, my body a mess of chaotic stirrings and overwhelming desires.

In one huge thrust, Gareth fills me. Fills me perfectly. Fills me like he was created just for me. Body and soul.

Overstepping

Sloan

Today feels like any normal day. The money that's coming my way still a bit like a dream. A foreign concept that I haven't fully accepted as my own. Right now, my focus is on adjusting to having a dog in the house and keeping him away from the clothes that Freya and I are tailoring for our clients.

After last night, I get the feeling that something has shifted with Gareth. I'm not sure if it's the stress of the World Cup approaching or what, but he still feels off. When he left for training this morning, he didn't wake me like he normally does. He simply slipped out without a word.

Freya, Sophia, and I are busy making dinner when my doorbell buzzes. With excited eyes, Sophia dashes for the door, and I call after her, "Check the camera before you open it!"

I wipe my hands off and head over to see who it is when I hear Sophia exclaim, "It's Daddy!"

She opens the door and wraps her arms around his hips in a tight hug. It's been over two weeks since he has seen her, so it's no surprise that she's having this level of reaction.

Callum's smile seems stiff as he pats Sophia's head awkwardly. "Hello, Sophia."

"Did you come to have dinner with us?" she asks brightly. "Did you come to see Rexy? Mum says we have to keep him in the yard when it's nice out. Come out back, I'll show you!"

She grabs Callum's hand and tries to pull him into the foyer.

"Not right away, Sophia. I need to talk to your mum first." He looks up at me and smiles awkwardly. "Do you have a minute?"

Suddenly, Freya appears in the foyer with us and tuts, "Sophia! I think you and I should take Rex for a walk. Show him around the neighbourhood. What do you say?"

"Yes!" Sophia exclaims, but then her face falls. "Daddy, will you still be here when I get back? Can you stay for dinner?"

Callum looks over at me and plasters on a smile. "I'd love to if it's okay with your mum."

Sophia turns wide, pleading eyes to me. "Mummy Gumdrops, pleeease, can Daddy stay for dinner? Please, please, please!"

Anxiety bubbles in my chest because I know Gareth will be coming over soon, but I don't know how I can possibly say no to her. Fighting back my eye roll, I nod and reply, "Sure."

She squeals with delight, then grabs Freya's hand, yanking her down the hall and out to the backyard to get Rex.

I cut Callum a look. "That was awkward."

"What?" he retorts, straightening his tie.

"You shouldn't have said yes for dinner. This is my time with her."

"Come now, Sloan. We're a family. We should be able to have a meal with each other."

I take a deep breath before replying, "Well, you should be able to stick to our custody agreement and show up for her on the weekends you're allotted. You're really disappointing her every other weekend, Cal."

"That's why I'm here to talk. Can we sit?" he asks, gesturing to the living room.

I roll my eyes and stomp over to the sofa, nerves erupting in my veins over what Callum could want now. I sit down and, instead of

Cal taking the open chair across from me, he takes a seat right next to me. Far too close for comfort.

"Callum, if you're going to try to ask me for more time with Sophia, you should know that I'm prepared to fight."

Callum's eyes narrow as he smooths his blonde coiffed hair back. "I'm not here to fight with you, Sloan. I'm here to tell you I want our family back."

My face contorts into what I can only imagine a Picasso painting would look like. Callum could have told me he is a flying purple cow, and I would have believed that more than I believe this. "You have to be joking," I reply with a laugh. "You're engaged to Callie."

"Not anymore," he replies and scoots in closer to take my hand in his. "I broke it off with her after the funeral. The minute I saw you and that footballer together, I knew I made a horrible mistake."

"Callum," I reply, staring down at his hand wrapped around mine like some sort of evil serpent. "You don't even love me."

"Of course I do, Sloan. You're the mother of my child," he states flippantly like what I said is ludicrous. "I made some mistakes, but I want to be a part of yours and Sophia's lives again."

"But you've cancelled on Sophia two times in a row now. How is that wanting to be a part of her life?"

"I was trying to get my own life together first!" he retorts, his blue eyes fixed on mine. "But I'm different now. If we get back to-gether, you'll see that."

I grit my teeth and stare back at him, willing myself to stay calm. "It's really coincidental that you're saying all of this after our meeting with the lawyer yesterday. What did your letter from Margaret say exactly?"

His face deepens to a crimson colour and he replies, "I was plan-ning to talk to you after the meeting, but you left too quickly."

"Because you were going on and on about the fact that I wasn't a Coleridge!" I exclaim, pulling my hand out of his and sliding away from him.

"That's what I want to change," he replies, shifting closer to me again. "We can be a proper family again. Get remarried. You can take my name, and we'll all be Coleridges together. I'll be better this time around, Sloan. A proper father, the way you've always wanted me to be. I know how hard it was for you to grow up without a father, and I don't want that life for Sophia."

His words pierce through a dark part of my heart that I keep locked away. "Neither do I."

"See? Then we're on the same page. And it will be like old times but better." He reaches out and cups my cheek, the touch foreign and surprising. "You'll still be in complete control of Sophia. I won't stand in your way of that."

I jerk out of his touch, so he drapes his arm on the back of the sofa behind me.

"This is ridiculous, Callum. You don't know me at all. You never have."

"I know it kills you to not have access to Sophia every single day. If we're together again, that all goes away. No more custody agreement. No more part-time motherhood." Callum leans in, an urgency and hopefulness in his eyes I've never seen before. "Don't you want that, Sloan? Don't you want to wake up with Sophia under your roof every day?"

"Of course I do," I reply, my throat closing up over how much I hate this. How much I hate that he still gets to be a part of her life.

"Let me give that to you, darling."

Callum suddenly leans in to kiss me, but I yank back and shake my head in shock.

"What the fucking hell is going on here?" Gareth's deep voice growls. My eyes swerve over to see him standing in the foyer, the door wide open behind him.

Callum is still holding my face, our bodies still touching. Everything about this looks so much worse than it really is. And Gareth is one hundred percent pissed. Like a giant, angry bear ready to attack. He drops his training bag down on the floor and his hands tighten into fists at his sides.

"Gareth, nothing is going on! Callum is crazy." I push back away from him and stand, smoothing my dress down and feeling horrible for how bad it must have looked.

Gareth moves his harsh eyes from Cal to me, and I crumple when I see a flicker of hurt on his face. "You certainly weren't arguing with what he had to say."

"I was just about to!" I retort, crossing my arms over my chest for some pathetic form of protection.

Gareth's stare is unrelenting on me as his jaw muscle ticks angrily beneath the skin. "So you're saying none of what he said is true for you?"

My mouth opens, but no words come out. Everything's locked inside of me in some strange, confused place that I can't fully access.

He nods knowingly. "This actually makes perfect sense, Sloan."

"How?" I exclaim, my voice tight inside my throat.

"Well, you don't need me anymore," he replies flippantly. "You made that perfectly clear yesterday. And if Callum is offering to be a father to Sophia again, then that solves all of your problems. I know how much it kills you when he doesn't show up for her. Getting back together with him means you can protect her."

"Are you crazy?" I shriek, striding around the sofa to stand in front of Gareth. He's tall and looming down over me. A scary mask on his face that I haven't seen before.

"How could you think so little of me?" I retort, my eyes stinging from the way he's looking at me.

"I don't think little of you," he replies through clenched teeth and takes a step closer to me. "I think everything of you. And I know you, Sloan. You will put Sophia first always, and I can't stop you from doing that."

"Sloan, just tell him to leave," Callum interjects, moving over to us and trying to grab my arm. "We were in the middle of something."

"Callum, you go!" I exclaim, turning on my heel and walking straight at him, forcing him backwards toward the wall. "There is nothing here for you. I'm with Gareth, and I want you to leave."

Callum laughs a haughty, bark of a laugh and narrows his eyes at Gareth. "Before you kick me out, perhaps you should ask your footballer why his lawyer is sniffing around our personal affairs."

My brow furrows. I look over at Gareth to see that his hard mask has slipped, revealing guilt. "What?" I manage to croak out.

Callum sneers and adds, "Harry Morrison called me today to tell me that a lawyer from London named Santino inquired about the paperwork you signed yesterday. Said he is the Harris family lawyer and he wants to make sure everything is above board."

"Is that true, Gareth?" I ask, my chest aching from betrayal.

"I was going to tell you," Gareth retorts, moving in closer to me.

I back up. "Tell me that you went behind my back and hired a lawyer to look into my personal business? We already talked about it. I told you I am fine on my own."

"I was trying to do what's best for you," he argues, staring at me with pleading eyes.

Callum chuckles softly from beside us. "See, Sloan? You don't need a man like him. He'll just end up controlling you your whole life. Mentally break you down. He'll probably do the same to Sophia."

Gareth slides harsh eyes to Callum. "Don't talk about my relationship with Sophia."

Cal barks out a laugh and adjusts his cufflinks. "Well, hopefully you're not as overbearing as your father. I heard he's such a monster, your mother killed herself to get away from him."

Gareth lunges at Callum, grabbing him by the lapel and slamming him up against the wall. "You don't know what the fuck you're talking about!"

Callum looks over at me with wide eyes. "You see what this man is like! He's out of control. He better not touch my daughter like this, or so help me God…"

"Shut the fuck up!" Gareth roars, his face centimetres from Callum's. "You are a spineless, worthless, desperate pig of a man. You don't even deserve to be called a man. A man is there for his family, his wife, his daughter. A man shows up when he's supposed to, not just when he needs money! You don't even love Sophia, you fucking bastard."

Suddenly, there's a high-pitched whimper behind me. I turn around and my stomach drops when I see Sophia standing in the open doorway with Rex on a leash. Her wide, teary eyes are on Gareth and Callum. Her chin wobbling, her hands shaking.

She looks over at me, and I drop down on my knees in front of her. "Sophia," I cry, reaching to pull her into my arms.

She pulls away and stares up at Gareth, who quickly releases Callum and lowers himself to one knee beside me. "Sophia, I didn't mean—"

"You're a liar, Gareth!" she cries, her words piercing through the the room like shattered glass. She drops Rex's leash and lunges at Gareth, swinging her tiny fists back and landing them on his chest. "You're not grown-up! You're a liar!"

He turns his face to the side, his eyes wrecked with pain and anguish as he croaks out, "I'm so sorry, Little Minnow."

I reach out to stop her from hitting him, but she yanks her hands away from me and takes off up the stairs with Rex following on her heels, dragging his leash behind him. My eyes connect with Gareth's as we both drag huge breaths into our lungs.

Freya then appears in the doorway, out of breath as she states, "Blimey, Sophia and Rex are too fast for me. We should think about getting an elliptical trainer, Sloan. Or a treadmill. Something! That sewing machine pedal is doing nothing for the circumference of my arse." Her voice stops as she looks around the room and sees us all standing here, frozen in horror. "What have I missed?"

Gareth shakes his head and stands up slowly, grabbing his bag up off the floor. "I don't belong here."

He moves to walk out the door but pauses when I call out, "Gareth."

He shakes his head again, refusing to look back at me. "I don't belong here."

With that, he walks out of my house and out of my life.

25
No Place Like Home

Gareth

SUNDAY NIGHT DINNER. IT'S SUPPOSED TO BE THE ONE DAY A week that brings the Harris family together. The one place that brings us joy and helps us remember why we love being Harrises.

Tonight, it's hell on earth for me.

I'm sitting at the kitchen counter, surrounded by everyone. Dad's holding Rocky. Vi, Hayden, Camden, Indie, Tanner, Belle. Booker and Poppy each with a newborn in their arms. All of them press in around me so close, I can barely breathe.

I tried to stay silent when I first arrived. I wasn't going to tell them about Sloan's inheritance, the fight with Callum, the heartbroken look on Sophia's face, or the unanswered text message I sent to Sloan telling her I am sorry. I tried so bloody hard to keep it all in, keep it safe, keep it silent, keep it protected.

Then they did the Harris Shakedown on me. They got it all out. Every last miserable detail. Now, here I sit, on trial as the lot of them try to figure out my life for me.

"Gareth, tell me exactly what Sophia heard you say again," Vi states, leaning across the kitchen sink and propping her head in her hands.

I groan and cover my face with my hands. "She heard me say

that her father doesn't love her."

"Which is bloody true!" Tanner retorts from the far end of the counter as he stuffs a chocolate into his mouth.

"It might be true, but it's not something a seven-year-old should ever hear no matter how vile the father is," Vi corrects, looking at me with so much sympathy, I want to vomit.

"I didn't mean to say it. I didn't mean to put my hands on him. I just lost it." I bow my head and slice my hands through my hair.

"You were being territorial and protective," Tanner states firmly.

"He was being a Harris," Camden adds.

"It's just like when you went mental on my ex-boyfriend a few years ago," Vi adds another iron in the fire. "You have a temper, Gareth, and you need to get control of it if you're going to be a dad."

"I'm not going to be a dad!" I exclaim, my head pounding inside my skull. "I don't deserve to be a dad," I mumble, shaking my head and seeing the horrified pain in Sophia's eyes all over again.

That look, that expression, that hurt. I put it there. My actions. It was like I was staring in the mirror of my eight-year-old self after one of my father's fits.

I'm a fucking monster.

"Gareth doesn't have a temper nine times out of ten, though!" Booker argues, his voice rising defensively as he bounces his baby in his arms. "It only comes out when necessary, and that Callum bloke was going after Sloan. He had it coming. The arsehole deserved a lot worse. Gareth shouldn't have to apologise for that."

Booker stares back at me with so much blind devotion, it shocks me. This youngest brother of mine is usually soft-spoken and mild-tempered. But he's unapologetic in his statement right now, and I don't feel worthy. Sloan and Sophia aren't my family, and there's nothing I can do to change that now.

Dad remains silent in the background, listening and taking everything in while the rest of our family begin concocting a trip to Manchester for an in-person Harris Shakedown on Sloan and

Sophia. It's a bloody mess. The entire conversation is swirling into madness that I can't stand to sit and listen to anymore.

I mumble something about needing to go to the loo and manage to slip off my stool and out of the kitchen. My body enters into some strange form of autopilot as I bypass the loo and head for the stairs.

I slowly climb each step as my mind drifts off into the past. I pause on the second level and look down the hallway. All four of our childhood rooms positioned two on each side. I can still see Poppy sneaking into Booker's room like she did so often when they were little and thought no one was looking. I can see Tanner and Camden sneaking girls up the stairs. I can see Vi's makeup spread out all over the counter and her screaming at us to stay out of her stuff.

So much of my life has been spent watching over my siblings. Kids who weren't mine. But something about Sophia felt different. She was mine. She felt like mine the second I met her on the pitch at the Kid Kickers camp.

I turn the corner and climb up to the third level of the house. I pause outside the loft bedroom door that we rarely ever went into after Mum died.

I turn the knob that probably hasn't been touched in years and push the door open to reveal the room of haunted memories. The room is completely empty. No bed, no dresser. No photos on the walls. Just light wood flooring, three big windows, and loads of things I'd rather forget. I step inside and instantly recall Mum's bed. Big brass frame, white sheets. An IV cart positioned next to the wall and an oxygen tank nearby. Mum always wore white, silky nightgowns that were so soft, I can still remember the feeling of them. I open the door to the wardrobe where they used to hang. It's empty. Dad burned most of her clothes in the fireplace downstairs shortly after she died. I recall Vi crying because she wanted a jumper of Mum's and he refused.

I couldn't believe how awful of a person he was to not give his only daughter an article of clothing from her only mother.

I hated him so much.

Now, I understand who that man was so many years ago.

He was heartbroken. He was heartbroken because the woman he loved died.

She fucking died.

The past few days, I have felt like my life is over and no one even died. Sloan is fine. Healthy and fine. Rich, and thriving, and independent. She has a daughter who loves her. Money to make all their dreams come true. She's alive.

And I feel like the walls are closing in on me.

I move to the window, then hear a creak behind me. My head snaps to see my father standing in the doorway. His chest is high, like he's holding his breath as he takes in the room before him. He stares closely at every square inch like even a speck of dirt will hold a memory.

His hands tighten on the doorframe as he clears his throat and states in a hoarse voice, "I haven't been up here in years."

I watch him carefully, silently, nervously. He looks haunted but determined as he prepares to walk in. I turn to gaze at the space and reply, "It's not my favourite room of the house, I'll tell you that much."

He forces a tight smile and gingerly takes a step in. "Nor mine."

I slide my hands into my jeans pockets and tip back on my heels. "I was drawn up here for some reason today."

He nods and makes his way over to where I stand, looking out the window as he replies, "Your mother was always good in a crisis."

I exhale heavily. "Is that what my life is now? A crisis?"

Dad turns and leans one shoulder against the wall by the window, the sunlight pouring in and casting shadows over the lines of his face and illuminating the grey scruff on his jaw. "I'm sorry for what's happened with Sloan, Gareth."

"I really messed it up good," I reply, shrugging my shoulders and crossing my arms over my chest. "I didn't trust Sloan to make her own decisions. I broke Sophia's heart and I alienated her father—a man who will always be in their lives no matter what. There's no way I can get back what I've lost."

Dad nods somberly. "It seems you were acting like you had lost already."

My brow furrows at his unexpected response. "Why do you say that?"

"Well, you were assuming the worst from her. You thought she'd move away. You thought she'd take her ex-husband back. It's almost like you were grieving her before she even left you. Similar to what I did when your mother was ill."

His words barrel through me like a punch to the gut. "I wasn't grieving her. I just sensed that she no longer needed me in her life like she did when her marriage first fell apart."

"You were protecting yourself."

"From what?"

"From unimaginable pain. Gareth, I didn't think I'd ever see the day when you'd give your heart to someone. I thought you lost that part of you when your mother died. But when I saw Sloan standing over you in that hospital bed, defending you so fervently, I knew I was wrong. And bloody hell, son, when you woke up and looked at her, I saw how hard you had fallen.

"But you have never been a man who does well sitting idle. You jump in and handle situations. You are proactive, not reactive. But dating a single mother comes with things you can't control. And I think the deeper your feelings grew for Sloan and Sophia, the more afraid you became."

"You're damn right I'm afraid. Sophia deserves a father and, no matter what I do, I'll never be that to her. That's genetics. It's not something I can change."

"Being a father isn't a birthright, Gareth. You should know that better than anyone." He gestures downstairs, his eyes narrowing as he shakes his head. "You have an entire hoard of well-meaning, nosey buggers who love you unconditionally. They won't let you fall. They won't let you break. They will glue you back together and make things whole again no matter how much you try to fall apart. It's not about calling yourself a father. It's about letting them be your family. Sloan and Sophia are your family, Gareth."

A painful knot forms in my throat from his words. Words that I long to be true. "What if I said and did things I can't come back from?"

"Rubbish," he growls and straightens to stare hard into my eyes. "The love of a true family is unconditional. I mean, bloody hell, look at all I've done in my past, yet you still manage to tolerate me."

I can't help but smile at his flippant remark. The ease to which he admits his mistakes now. He is a completely different person than who he was before but, deep down, I know this understanding man was always in there. He just lost sight of that part of himself for a while.

"I more than tolerate you, Dad," I exhale heavily and place a hand on his shoulder. "I love you."

The corners of his mouth turn down as he fights emotions that swell inside of him from the three words I haven't said to him in ages. I pull him in for a long, overdue hug. We hold onto each other, breathing in and out and allowing the natural labels of father and son return to where they belong, even if just for a moment.

Finally, he pulls back and squeezes my shoulders while staring hard into my eyes. "One thing about being a Harris that's both a fault and a virtue is that when we fall, we fall hard. But it's forever, son. That kind of love isn't something that's easy to walk away from."

"Gareth?" Vi's voice interrupts us, her eyes falling nervously around the room as she says, "There's someone here to see you."

She steps back, and my breath catches in my chest when I see Sloan standing in the doorway.

Sloan is here. In London. At my father's house.

My eyes drink in the sight of her, realising it's only been days but I've missed her more than I ever thought possible. She's wearing a long black dress and heels with her hair tied back low on her head. Her eyes are downcast and sad like they were the night she came to my house broken and out of control. The time when she really did need me.

Her gaze lifts to mine, striking me through the heart with her golden, red-rimmed eyes. And that feeling—that overwhelming sense of wanting to both surrender and dominate—is present and potent all around us.

She exhales heavily and her voice is shaky when she asks, "Can we talk?"

Dad clears his throat and claps me on the back before striding out of the room, gently touching Sloan's shoulder as he passes. Sloan tucks her hands behind her back and moves further into the room, her heels clicking on the hard wood as she walks the perimeter.

"Vi said this was your mother's room?" she asks, looking around, the natural setting sunlight illuminating the space in a golden glow.

I nod. "When she was ill, yes."

"A lot of bad memories in here then?"

I shrug. "Some good, too."

Her steps are slow and steady. "Do you feel her presence in here?"

Her question causes an instant knot to form in my throat. "I think I do actually."

Her sad eyes narrow thoughtfully. "What does it feel like?"

I move to the centre of the room, forcing air in and out of my lungs as I turn on my heel to watch her movements. "Like light… Like love."

Sloan's brows lift and she pauses to look out the window as I ask, "What are you doing here, Sloan?"

The corners of her mouth turn up as she peers over her shoulder at me. "I'm Sloan again?"

I shrug my shoulders helplessly. "Who do you want to be?"

She bites her lip for a second before replying, "I want to be many people, Gareth."

She pauses to stare down at her feet, and I hate the sad expression on her face. I'm responsible for it this time. Not Callum, or Margaret, or her custody circumstances. Just me.

"Okay. So, who are you right now? Someone who came all this way to end things with me?"

Her eyes flash up to mine. "Is that what you want?"

"No," I reply instantly. "But I understand if that's what you need."

She nods and bites her lip again. "I'm going to tell you what I need."

I bite down on the inside of my cheek, fighting off the words I want to say in response.

"Callum thought that I needed Sophia under my roof at all times. He thought that would be all I'd need to take him back." She lifts her shoulders and twines her fingers in front of herself. "It turns out he didn't need me. He needed money. I found that out after I spoke to that Santino lawyer of yours."

"You talked to Santino?" I ask, my tone hopeful.

"Yes," she snaps back. "He called me, so I had him look over the papers I signed. Apparently, Margaret had a second trust fund set aside for Sophia that would go to Callum if he ever got back together with me. If he didn't, it goes to Sophia."

"Jesus," I reply, my hands flexing angrily by my sides.

"Yeah," Sloan replies with a small, self-deprecating laugh.

"So, what happened?"

Sloan begins walking again. "I gave Callum the money given to me by Margaret."

My blood pressure spikes. "What? Sloan, you said it was millions."

"I don't care because I don't need it," she states firmly, turning to face me. "What I need comes in a much different sized package." She swallows and walks toward me in the middle of the room, standing only a couple feet away from my face. "Gareth, what I need is to know how you could think I'd subject myself to that dick of a man again?"

My jaw slides back and forth as I look down at the floor. "He is Sophia's father. I think that because you always put her first, you will always have a soft spot for him no matter how awful he is to both of you."

Sloan laughs, her entire body shaking with agitation as she shoves a hand through her hair. "So that's it?" she retorts, her eyes welling with tears. "You think I'm the same emotional wreck of a woman who showed up on your doorstep that night in tears? The one you had to kneel in front of before she crumbled into dust?"

"Sloan…Jesus, no." I step closer to her and her scent washes over me, sweet as always and mixing with the memories of this room. It makes everything inside of me ache. "I think you're incredible. You're the strongest mother I know, and I'm madly in love with you. But I love Sophia now, too, and I would walk through fire before I'd ever hurt her again. So I'll walk away if that is what's best."

Sloan's eyes soften and a single tear slides down her cheek, but she swipes it away before it drops to the floor. "You're right, Gareth. What's best for Sophia does come before everything else. I've always put her first. I had to because she was sick for so long, then recovering even longer. I've always adjusted to other people's needs so much, I had forgotten what it felt like to have any of my own."

She steps in even closer, her face only inches away from me. "But then you happened. And you empowered me to own my feelings. My desires. My fantasies. You let me be who I wanted to be. For the first time in ages, I wasn't pretending anymore. I wasn't playing make-believe like Sophia says I was before. I was being me because of you!"

She grabs hold of my hands, her touch like an ice bath that shocks and zaps all of my senses into overdrive. "Gareth, you have given me my only real moments of pleasure, of happiness, of pain, of crazy, intense passion that I get to feel on my own without having to adapt to someone else. How can you walk away from us so easily?"

My entire body erupts with equal parts joy and pain. "This isn't easy, Sloan. Nothing about this is easy. The majority of my life, I built these cliffs around my heart and never let anyone get in. I never wanted to feel the pain my father felt when he lost my mum. I thought I was doing what was best for you and Sophia. I didn't think you needed me anymore."

"Of course we need you!" she exclaims with a cry. "I want us to be a family!"

With that magic word, I grab her face in my hands and slam my mouth to hers. I part my lips and kiss her with such ferocity, I forget where we are. I forget where we've been and where we're going. I just fall. I jump off that cliff, out of that plane, and I free fall with the delicious words that came from her mouth.

They taste good. Like a promise, and a devotion, and a future.

She tastes like mine.

I pull back, my body tingling with raw, earth-shattering awakening as I stare down at her ruddy lips while dragging deep breaths back into my lungs. "Sloan…Treacle…I love you, and I'm sorry for pulling away. I'm sorry for hurting you and not trusting you. Please dominate me like this anytime you'd like because, as long as you'll have me, I'll be right here."

Sloan laughs and a garbled cry escapes her throat as I wipe the tears away from her cheeks. "Let's just promise to jump out of the plane together, okay?"

My smile is wide, and vast, and happy. Really fucking happy. I press a kiss to her lips and murmur, "Whatever you say, boss."

I wrap her in my arms and kiss her deep, and hard, and soft, and slow. I kiss her the thousand different ways I've kissed her this past year because I'm in. I'm all in now no matter how scary this dive feels.

Sloan and I rejoin the others downstairs. I'm thrilled to see that Sophia has come with her and is in the back garden, kicking around a football with my brothers. Watching them play with her like she's one of their own brings a sense of pride to my chest that is new and different and equally as extraordinary as the day I met Vi's little one.

I ask Sophia if she'll take a walk with me. After some urging from her mother, she agrees.

She's quiet as we walk through the back gate that opens up into the woods behind my dad's house. I explain to Sophia that this wooded park is owned by the city and how we recently got into trouble for helping Booker build a playhouse out here. Then I start rambling about how it is a bit odd for a grown man to want to build a playhouse before he even has kids because, at the time, Booker and Poppy hadn't had their babies yet. But they were best friends when they were Sophia's age, and the house turned out quite cute, so I thought she might like to see it.

I was doing a lot of rambling.

My entire life, I've been a man of few words and kept everything close to the cuff. But the minute I need the forgiveness of a stubborn seven-year-old, I'm suddenly a chatterbox.

Sophia and I find the playhouse that ended up being donated to the park so they wouldn't tear the thing down. It's an adorable topsy-turvy-style cottage with crooked windows and a high peak roof. The truth is, it's some keen craftsmanship that we Harris Brothers wouldn't have had a clue how to build if it wasn't for Hayden, his brother, Theo, and his friend, Brody.

I open the little door and Sophia's eyes are downcast as she steps inside. She immediately sits at the tiny table and looks around the room, taking it all in.

I knock on the tiny doorframe and she glances over at me with a frown.

"May I come in?" I ask, half smiling.

She shrugs, then nods subtly. I have to get down on my hands and knees and turn sideways to fit. There's one other chair opposite Sophia, so I position myself on top of it, wincing when it creaks beneath my large frame.

My knees are up under my chin as I look over at Sophia and ask, "Are you ever going to look at me again?"

She continues frowning and stares down at her hands, her shoulders lifting with another shrug.

"Are you ever going to talk to me again?"

She shrugs yet again and begins picking at the chipped nail polish on her fingers. I awkwardly reach into my pocket and pull out a bottle of nail polish that Vi luckily had in her handbag. I pass it over to Sophia and her eyes flash up to mine.

With a smile, I lay my hand out on the table and drum my fingers expectantly. "I have the World Cup coming up, so I'm going to need a full set."

She smiles a tiny smile and opens the bottle of polish, getting right to work on my nails.

"You know, Sophia, that day you saw me with your dad, I wasn't myself."

"Oh?" she says quietly, still focusing her attention on my fingers.

"No. I was scared."

"Scared of what?" she mumbles as she dips the brush back into the bottle.

"I was scared of losing you and your mum."

She stops what she's doing and hits me with her stunning brown eyes. "Where would you have lost us?"

"Well, not lost physically. I just felt like maybe I wasn't good for you guys. Like maybe you didn't need or want me anymore. It seemed like your dad wanted to be there with you and I was just getting in the way."

She's silent as she continues painting my nails. I think the entire conversation is fruitless until she says, "You do get in the way a lot. You're kind of big." I huff out a small laugh but remain quiet, careful not to derail her line of thinking. "But I like you in the way. I like when you are at our house. It feels cosier with you there, and Mummy is always smiling."

"She is?" I ask, the corners of my mouth lifting at Sophia's observation.

She nods and her face falls. "She didn't smile this week at all. It reminded me of how she was in the old house."

My brow furrows, but before I get a chance to reply, she asks, "Gareth, do you really think my dad doesn't love me?"

"No, Sophia...No." I lean across the table, my tone urgent as I run my hand down her arm in soothing strokes. "You are the most loveable seven-year-old I've ever met in my entire life. There is no way your dad doesn't love you. I just said that because I was angry. I didn't mean it."

She's quiet for a minute as she thinks that through, then dips the brush back in the bottle while softly murmuring, "Sometimes it feels like my dad doesn't love me."

"Hey," I reply, crooking my finger beneath her chin and forcing her to look up at me. She hits me with eyes full of disappointment and sadness, and I know in that second that I will do anything for this little girl for the rest of my life, even if Sloan and I don't work out. "If you'll let me, I will love you enough for one hundred dads."

A tiny smile flits across her face, but she quickly scowls and hits me with a sassy fire in her eyes. "One thousand is more than one hundred."

My brows lift at her challenge. "One hundred thousand is more than one thousand."

"Or more than one million dads!" she exclaims, her posture straight and her smile genuine as she giggles and shakes her head. "That's a lot of love. Just don't squeeze me so tight that I can't breathe. Mummy does that and sometimes I think I might puke."

"You got it," I reply with a twinkle in my eyes. "Can I squeeze you now?"

Her brow furrows as she lifts one finger to hold me off. "Not until your nails are dry."

Birthday Surprise 26

Sloan

GARETH'S HANDS SQUEEZE MY BENT KNEES AS HE SLIDES HIS palms up my thighs until his thumbs tease my centre. "I'm going to kiss you here," he husks and I nod adamantly, my hands stretched out on my bed as I willingly sacrifice myself to this powerful lion in front of me.

He lowers his mouth to my heat—the area of my body that's pulsing with need. His tongue flattens and swipes against my bundle of nerves, and my pelvis jerks in response. He was away for seven days, attending England team training. Now that he's back, I'm like a sex addict getting my first fix. I can hardly control myself.

A low growl vibrates from his chest as he sucks me into his mouth and murmurs against my flesh, "Fuck, Sloan. You taste so good."

I cry out from the delicious pressure and my hips involuntarily buck up into him. His hands squeeze them, his fingers harshly digging in as he holds me down on the mattress to control the pleasure, the rhythm, the drive. I repeatedly call out his name as he licks and teases and eventually plunges a finger deep inside of me, crooking it to hit the G-spot that I want to grind on over, and over, and over.

My orgasm is close. Too close.

I want this to last.

Quickly, I toss a leg over his shoulder and flip us on the bed so he's on his back and his face is between my legs. I smile at his wide, ravenous eyes and grind on him for a beat before shimmying my way down his beautiful, naked body.

"Sloan," Gareth states in a warning tone, clearly not pleased that I took his control away so soon.

With a naughty smile, I wrap my lips around his tip. His grunt of surprise is completely worth the spanking I know is coming my way later. I suck him back into my throat a few times, cupping his balls in my hand before releasing him from my lips with an audible *pop*.

He sits up and pulls me toward him until I'm positioned astride him. I adjust myself and straighten before sinking down onto his wet, hard erection. The resistance is minimal, but the tightness is intense. I swirl my hips on him, stroking myself over his shaft as I take him inside of me so deep that I can feel the fullness in my belly.

Our eyes lock as I press my hands on his chest for balance and rock, and writhe, and move over top of him. Gareth's hands cup my breasts, rubbing and groping and rolling my nipples in his big, meaty paws. He pinches them hard, and I yelp out in pain as a swirl of overstimulation creates a frenzy between us. He slaps the side of my ass and begins pumping his hips up off the bed, thrusting into me hard and fast.

Topping from the bottom. The story of our lives.

Our breaths are loud and our moans are soft as we ride this wave of complete give and take all the way to a riotous climax.

And what a climax it is.

Moments later, we're cleaned up, satiated, and back in my bed.

It's been a little over a month since we made up at his dad's house in London, and things have been good between us since.

More than good.

Gareth's Man U season is complete, but he's been travelling

back and forth to London for England team training in preparation for the World Cup. He comes home to Manchester every chance he gets, though.

Going a week without seeing him was brutal.

Aside from missing Gareth, things have been calmer around here. Steady. Callum is still doing what Callum does best, barely showing up for Sophia on his weekends. Thankfully, Sophia seems to be handling the disappointment well. She has nightly video chats with Gareth that I swear have her smiling in her sleep. It's the cutest thing I've ever seen.

Everything has been nice. Deliciously boring almost.

I'm just beginning to drift off to sleep, happy that Gareth is tucked in behind me again, when his voice cuts into the silence. "I think I'm going to retire from football."

My eyes open. "Are you talking in your sleep?" I ask, turning my head to look back at him.

"No, I'm wide awake," he husks and presses a lazy kiss on my shoulder. "I have one more year with Man U before my contract goes up for renewal. I think I want to retire then."

I turn over to face him, the street light shining in the window, showcasing the deathly serious expression on his face.

"Gareth, be serious," I reply, entwining my legs with his. "You can't retire. You're Gareth Harris. Team captain. Man U star. You're leaving for Russia in two weeks to play for England. What would you do if you retired?"

"Nothing," he replies with a shrug and leans in to kiss the tip of my nose. "My accountant tells me I'm quite wealthy, and I'll have even more money when my Astbury house sells."

His mention of the house where we were attacked brings a frown to my face.

"None of that," he murmurs, pressing his lips to the crinkle forming between my brows. "It was my decision to sell. I told you it has nothing to do with you never wanting to go back there. I just can't shake the image of those people in my home on that security footage."

I rest my hand on his cheek as I think back to how awful that night was and how far we've come. "Well, you're not going to just sit around all day eating toffees. You'll be bored out of your mind."

He inhales deeply and rubs his hand aimlessly up and down my back. "You're right. Doing nothing wouldn't last. The truth is, I am thinking I can be more hands-on with the Kid Kickers program we're opening in London."

My body tenses at his mention of London. I already hate the amount of travelling he has to do for his World Cup training in London. Now he's talking about spending more time there?

I clear my throat and force out an honest reply. "I think you'd be great with Kid Kickers in London."

"You do?" he asks, his voice hopeful. "So you'd consider it?"

I frown up at him in the darkness. "Consider what?"

"Consider moving to London of course," he replies and gives my back a squeeze.

"What?" My eyes fly wide. "You'd want me and Sophia to come?"

"Of course I would," he states instantly. "I wouldn't go without you two. And since Sophia's cancer scans came back clear last week, I don't see what would stop us. I know your work is here, but I also know that you're capable of so much more. London is the fashion capital of England, isn't it? There's loads you can do there, I'm sure."

I bite my lip excitedly at the positively electric twinkle in his eyes. Gareth has been pushing me to make more time for my own designs. Maybe this is the kick I need to take things to the next level.

"Move to London." I repeat the idea out loud to give it full life in my mind. "I'd consider it I suppose. Sophia would hate to leave her friends, but she's young enough to make new ones. And she'd still get to see them when she comes back to visit Callum."

"See? It can work. And all my family lives there, so Sophia can grow up with her cousins."

"Cousins?" I giggle at his term. "I think you're skipping a step there."

"It's all coming and you know it," he retorts and kisses me on the lips with a smile. "We're good, Sloan. You and I are so good."

I exhale heavily and shake my head. This is madness. Complete and total madness. "Do you really want to give up football?"

"Yes!" he exclaims and cups my face in his hand to punctuate his reply. "I grew to love the game because of what it gave my family, but those reasons don't exist anymore."

I bite my lip and watch him curiously. "And what reasons exist for you to retire?"

"Two," he replies, holding up his two Sophia-painted fingernails and trailing them down my bare shoulder. He squeezes the side of my waist and adds, "I hate being away from you and Sophia, and I know my career will never top playing in a World Cup tournament with all of my brothers. The timing seems perfect for me to end on a high, don't you think?"

I inhale deeply and nuzzle my face against his chest, pressing my lips to the heartbeat drumming away beneath the skin. Steady, secure, and strong. Just like Gareth. "I'm with you in whatever you decide," I murmur, unable to wipe the excited smile off my face.

He vibrates with a silent laugh. "You sure you don't want to boss me around again? You were doing so well at it a few minutes ago."

Two weeks later, Sophia's smile is permanent as she stares down at a giant soccer-ball-shaped birthday cake with the entire Harris family pressed in all around her.

It's a beautiful summer night at the weekly Harris Sunday night dinner in London. Except tonight is extra special because Sophia and I were *both* shocked when we walked into Vaughn's backyard and everyone yelled "Surprise!"

The Harris family transformed the backyard into a pink birthday party wonderland for Sophia, complete with balloons, twinkling lights, a bouncy house, and a cotton candy machine, which I'm told is called candy floss in England.

Sophia is a happy little eight-year-old because she didn't know she'd be getting two birthday parties this year. A few days ago, I had a small pool-party at a hotel with a couple of her friends from school. Callum and Callie even managed to show up, which made me wonder if Cal ever even broke up with her in the first place. Not that I care. After the snotty remarks Callie makes to Sophia, I'm not about to warn a girl. Honestly, the two seem perfect for each other. They both showed up in fancy outfits, complained about the heat, and left twenty minutes later. It's clear that nothing will be changing there any time soon.

The candles glow on Sophia's face as the sun begins to dip behind the trees. She struggles to shove her fluffy pink tutu under the picnic table as everyone sings "Happy Birthday" to her at the top of their lungs.

When they finish, Sophia blows out the candles and everyone cheers, with Tanner being the loudest. Sophia side-eyes him hard. She does not find Tanner amusing at all, so he has made it his life's mission to win her over.

"Little Minnow, do you want some of my candy floss to go with your cake?" Tanner asks as he folds himself onto the open seat beside her. He offers over his stick of pink fluff.

I'm seated on the other side of her and can see her roll her eyes. Gareth is standing behind me, and I feel him shaking with silent laughter as he catches her expression, too.

He clears his throat and interjects, "You shouldn't be eating that anyway, Tanner. We fly out for Russia in two days."

Tanner scoffs obnoxiously. "What's the World Cup in

comparison to Little Minnow's eighth birthday?" Tanner nudges Sophia and waggles his brows.

She continues staring at him with complete indifference and a tiny splash of annoyance.

Gareth squeezes my shoulders affectionately and adds, "You're trying too hard with her, Tan. She can smell the desperation."

Tanner drops his cotton candy on the table in a huff. Then he dips his head so he's eye level with Sophia. "Sophia, can you please tell me what it is you don't like about me? I'm bloody dying for your affection! I can't sleep at night! Ask Belle. She'll tell you. Have you not been receiving my letters?"

Belle shakes her head from across the table. "You don't have to answer him, Soph. Keep playing hard to get. It's the best way."

Sophia frowns up at Tanner and with a perfectly serious face, she replies, "Well, maybe when your hair isn't longer than mine, we can talk."

Everyone erupts into a fit of laughter as Sophia looks around with a straight face, clearly not understanding how utterly adorable she is.

"I will cut it for you," Tanner deadpans and slams his hand down on the table. "Wife! Bring me the scissors."

Belle rolls her eyes at her crazy husband and Sophia finally cracks a small grin at him.

Vi begins passing out cake while Booker and Poppy fuss over their twins, Oliver and Teddy. Camden is busy flirting with Indie, and Vaughn watches everyone with a sweet twinkle in his eyes, even as they mercilessly tease each other. Sophia fits right in as she deserts her cake to play with Hayden and Rocky in the grass.

This is the happiest mess of a family I've ever seen. I'm pretty sure my smile is permanent right now. "This is so wonderful, you guys. You really didn't have to do all of this."

Vi slides me a piece of cake. "Well, Gareth did the bulk of it."

My jaw drops and I gaze up at him with wide eyes. "You did?"

He glowers at his sister for a moment, then shrugs. "I wanted tonight to be special."

"Well, it is," I reply, standing up from my seat and wrapping my hands around Gareth's neck. "Thank you. I don't see how it could possibly be any more special."

I feel everyone staring at us with big, dopey grins on their faces, and my brow furrows in confusion. Suddenly, Sophia is at my legs, her big brown eyes watching us with excitement.

"Is it time yet?" she asks, looking at Gareth.

"What do you think, Minnow?" he asks, tweaking his brows at her playfully.

"What are you two up to?" I ask, looking back and forth between them.

Gareth pulls me in and presses his lips to my forehead before twining his fingers with mine. He walks me out onto the grass, under the twinkling lights, and Sophia follows with a mischievous grin on her face.

"Gareth, what are you doing?" I ask, my voice tight and high in my throat.

"I have a special present for Sophia that I want you to see her open," he replies.

Suddenly, Vi is next to us with Rocky in one arm and a giant pink present in the other. Gareth takes the gift from Vi and hands it off to Sophia, who drops down onto her knees and begins tearing at the paper like an animal. Out of the corner of my eye, I see Belle recording with her phone. When I look back down, I see that Sophia has opened the box only to reveal another box.

She pulls out the medium-sized box that's wrapped in matching pink paper and tears into that one next. She giggles and peers up at me when there's a third box inside the second box.

"What is going on?" I exclaim, the suspense killing me.

Gareth's eyes crinkle with amusement as Sophia tears into the final box. When she opens that one, there's a black velvet box inside.

I gasp when I see that Gareth is down on one knee, watching Sophia with so much affection, my heart feels like it's going to explode.

Sophia stands up and holds onto the small velvet box for a moment before handing it over to Gareth. She steps back, but Gareth grabs her hand and pulls her close beside him.

The sight of them in front of me has quiet sobs shaking my entire body. "Gareth," I plead, the suspense shattering my heart completely.

He smiles his perfect, sexy, oh-so wonderful smile and says, "Sloan, when I played football with Sophia in your back garden, she had a lot to say."

Sophia smiles proudly up at me and I sob again. I'm a sobbing, uncontrollable mess.

"I told you about some of the things she said to me, but there were several I kept to myself."

"Is that right?" I croak, my voice wobbling in my throat.

He nudges Sophia with his arm. "What did you ask me, Minnow?"

She looks down and begins shyly playing with her tutu. Gareth whispers some words of encouragement in her ear and she finally peeks up at me. "I asked if he was going to marry you."

"You what?" I exclaim, complete shock and mortification washing over me. "Sophia!"

"Do you want to know what I told her?" Gareth interjects, smiling up at me. "I told her that I hoped to someday, but I wanted to make sure she liked me enough first."

Gareth looks over at Sophia, who looks up at me and chirps in her perfect little British accent, "Mummy, I definitely like him enough to let him marry you."

With a knowing chuckle, Gareth cracks open the box to reveal a beautiful diamond ring. My hands lift to my cheeks as tears fill my eyes, the emotion of the moment completely overwhelming me.

Gareth clears his throat and says, "This was my mother's...I never thought I'd love someone enough to give it to them. But I was wrong, Treacle. I love you more than I ever knew I was capable of loving someone. And I love Sophia more than I thought possible... Enough for more than one million dads even. I love the silly package you two are, and I love the mess you both bring into my life. I know I'm not her father, but I want to spend the rest of my life being her family...and your family, because family isn't just one thing. It's everything. Will you marry me?"

A sob erupts from my throat as I drop down on my knees in front of Gareth and pull Sophia to my side. "Yes!" I laugh and chastely swipe at my cheeks. "Yes, I'll marry you!"

With one arm wrapped around Sophia and my other hand cupping Gareth's cheek, I kiss him. I kiss him and I repeat "yes" against his lips over, and over, and over until I hear Sophia groaning in disgust from beside me.

I pull away giggling through happy tears and watch Gareth put the ring on my finger. I show it to Sophia, who nods happily before cupping her hand to my ear and whispering, "Mummy, you should also know that I asked Gareth for a baby sister."

I cry laughing and hug her to me as Gareth wraps his arms around us. He holds us and loves us completely. It feels good, like how life should feel. And I intend to hold onto this life for Sophia and me with everything I have.

Harris Cup

Gareth

"**A**FTER ALLEGATIONS OF FOUL PLAY BY A CHELSEA PREMIER *League player, the investigation of striker Vince Sinclair's involvement with the break-in and assault at the Gareth Harris Estate in Astbury has come to an end.*"

"Shut that off," I growl at one of my teammates who's playing a newscast on his mobile. "We have a game to focus on. Not that noise."

I toss athletic tape into a cubby in our changing room at the Luzhniki Stadium in Moscow and drop down on a nearby bench. I pop my earbuds in and blast Taylor Swift again, doing my best to ignore the madness that's going on back in England.

Just as we were leaving for Russia, the detective—Bernie—who interviewed me at the police station called to inform me they received a confession in writing from Vince Sinclair. It was some sort of plea bargain Vince had accepted for a lesser charge, which named the two criminals who were in my house.

The entire thing makes my stomach churn.

Apparently, back in November, Vince overheard his coach and Gary Austin making arrangements for the national team to use the Chelsea training grounds for a closed-doors camp—the same camp my brothers and I were invited to train at for the World Cup. Vince got a hold of the list of players and was outraged that he hadn't made the cut. After I showed him up on his home pitch, he was inspired to target me in hopes of ruining Austin's plan to have all four Harris Brothers on the team.

Once word got out that Hobo's house had been broken in to, Vince somehow hired the men responsible for the burglary to do the same at my house with the intention of injuring me. I guess the plan was blown to hell when it was Sloan who walked through the door first.

That's the part that really makes me sick. What would have happened if Sloan wasn't with me? How much worse could it have been? All things considered, walking away with a serious concussion is quite minor compared to what it could have been.

This was apparently the act of a desperate man. The detective told me that Vince has some major gambling debt, and he was relying on a World Cup invite to bring in some new sponsorship opportunities. When he didn't see his name on the list, he went off the deep end.

Vince was fired from Chelsea immediately. He is also facing some serious time in prison, even with the plea bargain. I've tried to separate myself from the situation as much as possible while in Russia, though. I don't need anything distracting me from what we're doing here, which is some really fucking excellent football.

The World Cup tournament is insane. Sixty-four matches in just over thirty days. Twelve different stadiums in eleven cities. There are multiple games happening every day. It's intense.

The group stage was a shaky start for England. But once we made it into the knockout stage games, we really found our stride, which is good for England. Our history in the World Cup hasn't been the most impressive in the last couple of decades. Perhaps Austin's theory of forming good team chemistry over stats has some merit.

The weeks in Russia have passed by as a constant blur of daily training sessions, team bonding activities, and media interviews. My brothers and I are hot ticket items in the press because it's the first time this many players from one family have played on a team together. Hobo keeps trying to add himself in as a fifth Harris Brother, but most reporters continually question his validity of playing for England. It drives him mental and makes the rest of us laugh.

The press have also jumped on the news of my engagement to Sloan. Normally, I hate my life being splashed all over the papers, but I find myself not caring anymore. There was a time when I was reclusive and quiet about so much. My dad's past with Man U, my mother. Now, I find myself opening up to the media in a much more candid way and it feels freeing. I guess finally having good news to share for myself has really changed my perspective.

Dad booked a private jet for the entire month. He has come for every match, along with Vi and various members of our family depending on their schedules, including Sloan and Sophia. They've been fitting right in with everyone like they've always been there. And seeing my mother's ring on Sloan's finger only makes her seem all the more a part of our family.

Unfortunately, I don't get much time with them when they are able to attend a match here. The rule for our squad is that we can only see family members the day after games. But seeing them up in the stands cheering me on is enough to drive my game to an all new level.

Every match we play, I think will be our last. But we continue to come out on top, achieving some of the most incredible comebacks that have been seen at the World Cup in decades.

Now, here I stand in the tunnel alongside all three of my brothers. Twins in the middle, Booker on the end. We're waiting for the all-clear to walk out onto the pitch to warm up for our face-off against France in the World Cup Final.

Tanner grabs hold of Camden's hand.

"Gross. What are you doing?" Camden snaps, yanking his hand away. "Why are your hands sticky?"

Tanner smiles and nods slowly, his beard long and ragged because he hasn't shaved during the entire month of our winning streak. "That's called anticipation, broseph."

"What? Ew…I don't want to know what that means." Camden looks over at me with his nose wrinkled.

I shake my head and smile, reaching down and grabbing Tanner's other hand. "Come on, Cam. Let's do this right."

Booker's hand grabs hold of Camden's free hand, and I see Cam exhale heavily before finally accepting Tanner's.

Feeling our squad pressing in behind us, I shout out, "Three Lions, are you ready?"

"Ready!" they all shout back.

"Three Lions, are you fit?"

"Fit!"

"Three Lions, are you fierce?"

"Fierce!"

"Three Lions, let me hear you roar!"

They holler a loud roar behind me, and over top of their cheers, I shout, "Then let's go out there with our heads held high, our bodies full of endurance, and our hearts ready to challenge! We will not surrender. We will dominate because we are the keepers of this game!"

They chant "Three Lions" over and over behind us as we walk slow and steady out of the tunnel and onto the pitch, where the deafening roar of the crowd surrounds all of our senses and we prepare for the game of our lives.

Before the game begins, I look up into the crowd and find my entire family standing tall in England team shirts. Dad, Vi, Hayden, Rocky, Indie, Belle, and Poppy.

Poppy's parents kept the twins, Oliver and Teddy, back in London as they've been helping her with them while Booker has been away. Especially since they are both much too small to even remotely enjoy the game. And, let's face it, Rocky is too young to understand it as well, but Vi says her obsession has to start somewhere, and what better place than at the World Cup final game.

And what a final game it is.

Not even the light downpour of rain we experience twenty minutes into the match can dampen the energy of our squad on this day. England controls the ball for the majority of the first half. Camden and Tanner volley back and forth like there is a string attached between the two of them. France's defence and keeper have their work cut out for them as the twins take shot after shot, pulling back to Hobo in midfield several times only to come to the net again.

Finally, after a high pass from Tanner to Camden, Cam scoop kicks the ball into the back right corner over the keeper's hands, breaching the scoreboard one-nil.

The second half is when things really get hairy. France readjusted some things during halftime, so Booker and I have our work cut out for us to keep the ball out of the box. We hold firm for the first twenty minutes, but an unstoppable penalty shot brings France back to tie us with fifteen minutes left in the game.

A few minutes later, in a wide and fast breakaway run, Tanner fakes a pass to Camden and chips in a high, floating shot that hits the post flush and drops back into the net. To the crowd's delight, the twins go wild, dancing like complete wankers on either side of the goal post. At one point, Camden reels in Tanner like a fish. It is bloody ridiculous…and brilliant.

We're leading two-to-one with only two minutes left in the game. France is all over our end of the pitch, and I stop two goal attempts before Booker finally scoops one up and boots the game back to the other side.

With less than a minute to go, Tanner takes a hard and fast high shot that bounces off the top pole and back out into the box. As if Camden knew the shot was going to be too high, he's right there in the box and leaps up impossibly high toward the deflection, giving the round leather a header to the far left side of the open net.

The keeper's gloves reach out and graze the side…

"Goal!" shouts Booker from behind me, and the crowd erupts into cheers.

Camden falls to the ground, covering his face in the grass, obviously overwhelming even himself with his luck. It's complete pandemonium in the arena when the ref blows the whistle three times and signals the end of the game.

I turn and lay eyes on Booker, who runs out of the box, straight into my arms. I lift him up off the ground and release him swiftly as we both go tearing down the pitch toward the rest of our team, piling on top of Camden and Tanner. We hug our outside teammates, cheering alongside all of them. By the time the twins are released from the pack, Tanner has Cam tossed over his shoulder. He sees me and Booker and sets Cam down, his face bending with emotion as I pull them all into a giant embrace. The four of us stand in a circle, arms wrapped around each other's necks, heads pressed together, and smiles wide as we take a quiet moment to absorb the exhilarating experience we're sharing together.

The voice over the speaker is screaming, "England has won the World Cup! England has won the World Cup! England is the champion of the world!"

By the time we break apart, Booker is full-on crying, so I pull him under my armpit and ruffle his hair. The coaching staff comes up behind us and we accept hugs from them all the while photographers and camera operators swarm around us.

After embracing nearly every member of the team, I turn around and clap eyes on Sloan and Sophia walking out onto the pitch with my family. I move through the swarm of cameras, ignoring Camden and Indie snogging and Tanner lifting Belle up into his arms. Poppy and Booker are face-to-face, holding each other's cheeks and talking softly to one another.

Dad, Vi, Hayden, and Rocky are crying and hugging everyone, one at a time, but I only have eyes for my fiancée and my number one fan.

Sloan leans down and points me out to Sophia, whose eyes are wide and watery as she takes in the masses of people flocking the field. She turns and finally sees me. Then, the little brown-eyed stunner begins sobbing. Huge, wet tears pour from her eyes as she releases her mother's hand and runs in a dead sprint right for me.

I drop to my knees and catch her, holding her shaking body against me as she becomes completely overwhelmed by everything surrounding us. I can't blame her. The deafening cheers and the tender embraces are enough to make even a grown man cry.

I stand up with Sophia wrapped around my hips and I'm now eye level with Sloan, who's also a teary mess.

And possibly even more gorgeous than she was yesterday.

I cup the back of her head and press my forehead to hers. "I love you." My words are simple because it's all I can think to say right now. The adrenaline of the game consuming all of my good sense.

She holds my face in her hands and kisses me chastely on the lips. "I love you, too. I'm so proud of you."

She laughs and tucks under my arm as we turn toward my family, and Vi all but assaults me with a slightly terrified Rocky in her arms.

"You brothers of mine! You crazy, insane brothers of mine!" she cries, wrapping everyone into a large group hug. "I love you all. And there's one thing that I know for certain: Mum is smiling down at all four of you crazy, wonderful, ridiculous, and incredible Harris Brothers!"

Fond Farewell

Gareth

1 Year Later

THE IMAGE OF SLOAN, SOPHIA, AND OUR NEW SON WALKING OUT onto the Old Trafford pitch is an image I want to remember forever. The fans' cheers are unrelenting as I embrace my family during my final moments on this beautiful pitch.

Milo is only four weeks old, and he's nestled into Sloan as she wraps her free arm around me. He's kitted out in red Man U gear to match his mum and his big sister. Sloan pulls back and has tears in her eyes as I lift Sophia up into my arms and pat the Harris name on her back that belongs to her now as well.

The past year hasn't been easy. Sloan and I were married shortly after the World Cup and were blessed with a pregnancy soon after. We thought our life was going to be full of incredible highlights until my retirement. But once we were married, Callum quit showing up for Sophia entirely. No calls, no emails. Nothing.

We tried our best to protect Sophia from that reality. We gave her excuses for Callum's absence, but after several months, Sophia started to catch on. Then one night, while nuzzled up closely and watching a recording of Camden's match from the night before, Sophia looked up and asked me why I couldn't be her real dad.

I thought she was asking me about the birds and the bees since we had only recently told her about Sloan's pregnancy. I started muttering things about love and our bodies, but she cut me off and asked why she couldn't be a Harris. It was a simple question that inspired me to do something about it.

I discussed my thoughts with Sloan and we quickly put Santino to work to see if this could even be possible. There were a lot of talks with Callum's lawyer. And following the exchange of some hefty funds, Callum voluntarily terminated his rights as a father to Sophia.

Four weeks later, we put pen to paper to make Sophia mine, both in heart and in surname. It was the most special day of my life.

Then Milo was born and I thought that was the most special day of my life.

But staring at them here with me on the Old Trafford pitch with seventy-five thousand fans chanting "Harris" all around us, I think this might be the most special day of my life.

I lower Sophia to the ground and press my lips to the tiny, delicate hand of our boy, Milo, who came two weeks early and had me sprinting into the hospital in my football kit to make it in time for his birth. Sophia was cross for not getting a sister, but to our delighted amusement, she informed us that we can try again next year.

Sounds like a great idea.

The rest of my family joins us on the pitch next, along with my cousin Alice Harris who's visiting from America for the big match. Tonight was a testimonial match put on by Man U strictly to honour my service to the team, so it's entirely a family affair.

Booker has both his one-year-old boys in his arms as Poppy trails behind him with a big smile. Rocky is running circles on the pitch, eating up the crowd's attention. Vi has a large bouquet of white roses in her hands as she's followed closely by Hayden, Camden, Indie, Tanner, and Belle.

I look over at my father to see how he's holding up, amazed that he's standing here at all. He bends down and scoops Rocky up into his arms, his eyes glossing over as he takes in the stadium and smiles with pride.

A microphone is suddenly passed over to me. The crowd instantly dies down, their voices magically muting to prepare for the words I'm about to say. Holding onto Sophia's hand, I clear my throat and attempt to find the words I want to convey on such a special day.

"First, I'd like to thank you all for being here for my farewell to Manchester United and the sport of football."

The crowd erupts into cheers, a faint chanting of "Harris" echoing over at the Stretford End. When they quiet down again, I continue. "Before I say anything else, I'd like to take a minute to honour a family member who isn't here with us today."

I turn to Vi and she nods. She pulls six long-stemmed roses out of the bouquet. Then she hands the remainder back to Hayden and passes a rose out to our three brothers, Dad, and me, and keeps one for herself.

"Our mother was taken from us far too soon, but no one was a bigger Manchester United fan than her. So, Mum, these are for you."

I hand the microphone to Sloan, grab hold of the flower, and gently pull the petals off the stem. I hold my hand out high and slowly sprinkle them down onto the grass. My brothers and Vi move to stand beside me in a long row and do the same.

With shaky legs, Dad walks over to stand beside me and helps Rocky peel one petal off at a time. The two watch the petals sway down to the grass. Out of the corner of my eye, I see the large stadium screen filled with a close-up of the long row of white petals on top of the lush green pitch.

It's an image I want to remember forever.

The crowd quiets for a moment of silence, and I hear Dad sniffling beside me. I wrap my arm around him and we squeeze each other for comfort. He never got his goodbye with this team, so this moment is just as much his as it is mine. I look him in the eyes for a long while and I swear he can hear my thoughts.

We've both truly come a long way with each other in the past year. Becoming a father myself has shed so much light on all that he must have felt when he lost Mum. And in many ways, what Sloan and I have now is what he and my mum never had a chance to be. This moment on this pitch—this experience with our family—belongs to him.

It's his.

It's his and it's ours.

It's our family's moment.

And I'm so proud that he has let go of the pain of the past to be in the present with us. He's not only my father.

He's my kindred spirit.

With a clearing of my throat, I take the mic back from Sloan and state, "Thank you."

My siblings go back to their partners and leave me standing out in the middle of the pitch, staring up at a crowd that has watched me turn into a man on this very grass.

"Tonight I bid a fond farewell to this stadium and the wonderful game of football." I pause, a knot forming in my throat as I fight through the emotions growing inside of me. "I've been playing defence for over a decade, and it's time for me to play some other positions in life."

The crowd cheers loudly, banging their feet on the concrete with encouragement.

"A fan, a friend, a brother, an uncle, a husband...a father." My voice breaks and I sniff hard to fight through my words. "I've proudly called this pitch my home for many years, but it's time for me to put focus on what I cherish most in life...My family."

I look over at Sloan and she hits me with a smile that I am fully prepared to grow old with. A smile that feels true, and sincere, and honest. I'm not one to say I believe in destiny, but the fact that I needed my suit the exact same night everything fell apart in her life feels kismet. We were both free falling in life and became each other's parachutes. We united together and all the pain in our pasts surrendered and allowed us to dominate. Together.

We are so much more than one thing.

We are everything.

She presses her lips to our son and squeezes the hand of our daughter. If I ever doubt leaving this beautiful game of football, all I have to do is look into their eyes. My family.

"My love story with football is special and complete with tragedy, triumph, highs, and lows. But, there comes a point in your life when you have to start thinking with your heart instead of your head. And my heart is calling me home. To my family."

The End

Check out the other Harris Brother books, available now.
Challenge: Camden & Indie
Endurance: Tanner & Belle
Keeper: Booker & Poppy

Or go back to the sister's story before the brothers became the brothers with *That One Moment*: Vi & Hayden

Read on for the full list of all my books and a sneak peek of my social media-viral tire shop rom-com, *Wait With Me*.

Sign up for my newsletter to be notified of the next release date.
www.AmyDawsAuthor.com/news

More Books by Amy Daws

The London Lovers/Lost in London Series:
Becoming Us: Finley's Story Part 1
A Broken Us: Finley's Story Part 2
London Bound: Leslie's Story
Not the One: Reyna's Story
That One Moment: Hayden & Vi's Story
One Wild Night: Julie's Story…coming soon

The Harris Brothers Series:
A spin-off series featuring the football-playing Harris Brothers!
Challenge: Camden's Story
Endurance: Tanner's Story
Keeper: Booker's Story
Surrender & Dominate: Gareth's Duet

Wait With Me: A Standalone

Pointe of Breaking: A College Dance Standalone by Amy Daws &
Sarah J. Pepper

Chasing Hope: A Mother's True Story of Loss, Heartbreak,
and the Miracle of Hope

For all retailer purchase links, visit:
www.amydawsauthor.com

Acknowledgements

Oy to the vey...How do I write acknowledgements for this duet? It's the final Harris Brother and, as soon as I typed The End, I felt... incomplete. Not because I didn't love the end of this story, but because I don't know how I can possibly say goodbye to this family. These crazy brothers were created in the fifth book of my London Lovers Series, That One Moment, and they were just going to be background characters in Vi's book. But as soon as I wrote the first scene with them attempting to climb the fire escape eleven stories into their sister's flat, I fell madly in love with them.

I'd never considered writing sports romance until my readers fell in love with them, too. Next thing I know, I'm rubbing mud on a model for a photoshoot and I have a new sports romance series! What a wild ride this has been! And the emotional journeys for all four of these brothers were so unique for each and every character. I've never had such clear, distinct voices for four men in my books until I wrote this family. What a natural treat that was.

But...I would be remiss to not mention the hordes of people who have supported my journey to the end of the Harris Brothers Series.

First of all, my editor, Stephanie. She has notes upon notes, upon notes that help us remember the quirks of the brothers and their partners. Things like Indie says "peculiar" instead of "weird," and Booker tugs his ear while Camden bites his tongue. She's embraced this family as her own just as much as I have, and I'm so grateful to have her for the entirety of this series.

My special Canadian, Beth. Guh! I have no words for you...Okay, that's a lie. You were that "ungettable" tough blogger whom I chased for a five-star review because I respected your feedback so much and I wanted to make you proud. And I did with That One Moment! But when I was afraid to move into sports romance, you agreed to alpha read for me, and helped give me the confidence I needed! I never realized the type of trust, respect, and friendship that would grow from that request. You push me so hard, and I know this series is what it is because of you.

Jennifer, my brainstorming machine! You consistently saw these characters as real people, and you made coming up with ideas for them a blast. You're a fun creative partner!

Lynsey, my resident British sounding board. You are and will always be my bruv and my Treacle! I love our banter. You are the Camden to my Tanner. Teresa and Gemma, thank you both for your British insights as well! You tolerate my obnoxious American arse so kindly, and for that I am eternally grateful.

Julia, my PA…Girl, I work you to the bone sometimes! Thank you for keeping me on track, yelling at me to get off Facebook, and providing ample story feedback. Couldn't do this all without you.

To my other betas for this duet, Nicole and Franci: Thank you! I needed Gareth to be perfect, and I can't thank you enough for reading and rereading Surrender because I took so damn long to get you Dominate. You are patient saints! And thanks to my magical fast proofer, Lydia, for being more than just a proofer but a shoulder to cry on. Come to think of it, Nana, thank you for letting me cry on your shoulder, too. Helluva lot of crying with this duet, guys!

To my hubby whom I tortured mercilessly with this book. God, it was hard. Gareth had a big story to tell and the stress of that bled into our home life. For that, I am sorry. But I am mostly thankful for you supporting me despite my grizzly bear tendencies!

Lolo, my own six-year-old mini-me. I love you, baby! Thank you for forcing me to take breaks to sing along to The Greatest Showman or go swim in the neighbour's pool. It may have delayed my deadlines, but it was 100% worth it.

And to my angels in the sky…My special six babies who don't get to live here on earth with Lolo: Nothing about your lives is incomplete for me. I'm at complete peace with where you are and where I am, and I thank the Lord for that contentment every day. Not many could go through what I did and be truly at peace; but through this crazy, fulfiling book world of mine, I truly am. I may think of you less…but you are always in my heart.

More about the Author

Amy Daws lives in South Dakota with her husband and miracle daughter, Lorelei. The long-awaited birth of Lorelei is what inspired Amy's first book, *Chasing Hope*, and her passion for writing. Amy's contemporary romance novels are mostly London-based so she can fuel her passion for all things British.

For more of Amy's work, visit: www.amydawsauthor.com or check out the links below.

www.facebook.com/amydawsauthor
www.twitter.com/amydawsauthor
instagram.com/amydawsauthor

Made in United States
Orlando, FL
10 July 2023

34922894R00174